The Bird and the Rose

Bonar Ash

Lutestring Press

Go, said the bird, for the leaves were full of children,
Hidden excitedly, containing laughter.
Go, go, go, said the bird: humankind
Cannot bear very much reality.

Burnt Norton, Four Quartets
T.S. Eliot.

Chapter One

THE EARLY SUN SLANTED AROUND THE CORNER OF THE garage and touched the wall on her left above the Victorian china footbath which held the herb garden. Thyme sprang abundant around its edges, starred thickly with tiny purple flowers; sorrel grew in a dark clump like celery; sage, basil, tarragon and rosemary, her favourite of all, sturdier than the others, its upright branches yew-like in form, sprang upwards, crowned with pale mauve flowers.

She sat slumped on the cold stone back doorstep, her faded woollen dressing gown pulled tightly around her knees. Her crossed arms were pressed into her stomach, her elbows digging into her ribs. She held herself together tightly, aware somewhere at the back of her mind that her feet, bare on the rough, damp cobbles, were uncomfortable with cold but disregarding this, as she disregarded the rising blue slowly overtaking the colourless dawn sky, the passionate commotion of the birds and the white lilac in flower over the tool shed. She was conscious of nothing but the frozen wastes of unfeeling within her and of the sensation she had become used to of being suspended outside of her own body and so impervious to feeling, to pain, to shock.

Memories were slowly returning, painful as warm blood returning to frostbitten limbs. Some vast, winged peril hovered over her head, darkening her with its shadow. Too fearful to lift her eyes and look she sat on, staring at the tool shed door, at the black paint peeling round the latch and the dried-on splatters of mud from the cobbles thrown up by the rain. It had been a wet month, the nights windy and dark with frequent rainstorms, the days mild and friendly with the promise of warmer days to come. The magnolia tree by the front door was in bloom and the orchard was scattered with drifts of daffodils like splashes of sunlight under the apple trees.

She was afraid to move, afraid that if she did she would remember. She would sit there, as still as a mouse, for ever staring at the tool shed door, and never remember, never have to bear it, never know.

HALF A MILE AWAY, Toby lay on his back looking up at the crack in the plaster traversing the length of his bedroom ceiling. The plaster under the lining paper bulged like a swollen vein under a stocking; one day the whole lot would come down on top of him in a cloud of dust and that would be that. He imagined the headlines: cleric asphyxiated under pile of rubble.

He sighed and half-heartedly pushed the duvet aside. He ought to get up but he was still tired; he'd gone to bed late. He glanced up at the ceiling again. He ought to be up there on a ladder sorting it out, not lying down here philosophising about it. He wasn't much of a handyman but he might have to learn how to be; he couldn't afford to pay someone else to do the work and the cottage was his responsibility even though the Church was responsible for major repairs.

His eyes wandered from the ceiling to the window and the patches of blue sky visible through the branches of the chestnut tree growing behind the house. He loved that tree. It rose, massive as a cathedral, its leaves making patterns like chubby-fingered hands against the sky. Today the weather looked good, but when he woke to a wet day he would get up and open the window then dive back into bed and allow himself a few more minutes of lassitude while he listened to the hypnotic rhythm of the rain pattering on its leaves.

The cottage was one of a terrace in the older part of the town, his neighbours mostly young couples in their first home. They painted the walls of their cottages in sugared almond colours, grew lobelias and trailing geraniums in baskets which they hung from chains outside their front doors, and exchanged their wood-slatted gates for wrought iron ones. They covered their front gardens with asphalt and parked their minis there. Some took down their oak front doors and replaced them with glass ones which they then had to cover with wrought iron grilles to prevent people from breaking in.

Toby smiled to himself. He had a weakness for the absurd. He lay thinking about the day ahead: he had several morning visits pencilled in. Carol Podger's leg had been playing her up and Butch was laid up again with bronchitis. He'd been warned about his smoking more than once but argued, convincingly, that his fags were the only things left worth living for. He wouldn't be alive to enjoy them much longer if he didn't pack it in.

Toby's spirits sank. He had to go and see Heather's parents again. She'd come round again last night – late – on the pretext of needing his help, urgently. She didn't know what she'd do if he wouldn't agree to see her and talk to her right now. When he'd spoken to her coldly in an attempt to be off-putting, she'd got upset and cried and it had taken him ages to persuade her to go home.

He had to do something about her. 'Freeze her off,' Tom would have said. 'Your groupies,' he'd called teenagers like her who hung around the church after services and came to Communion for the wrong reasons.

He shifted his legs, searching for a cool place under the duvet which had begun to feel heavy and too warm. He wondered what Rhea would advise him to do about Heather. In different circumstances he would have asked for her advice. He was seriously worried about Rhea. She'd been completely wrapped up in Laurie since he was born and the blow when it came had been devastating. He would have gone round to see her last night if it hadn't been for Heather, another reason he'd felt so annoyed with the girl. Rhea didn't seem to have any relations – parents both dead – or many close friends. And where on earth was Tom? Surely he'd have come back when he heard about Laurie? *If* he'd heard. Nobody seemed to have a clue where he was. He could be in China for all anybody knew.

Toby sighed. If he could only find someone who might befriend Rhea. A woman she could talk to. There was someone he'd thought might be suitable, a small young woman: good-looking, fair hair, nice clothes. In church once or twice. She might be able to help. He ran through his memory bank, trying to put a name to a face.

He couldn't place her. One of the PCC might know. The husband's name had come up at the last PCC meeting ... he'd donated a generous amount of money to the church towards replacing the glass windows in the entrance doors.

4

Richard Carter, that was the name. And the wife was Alice. Toby had seen her talking to Rhea in the market one day last summer, so they had at least met. That was before, of course. Rhea had had Laurie with her. Mrs Carter didn't seem to have children – or had she? Not sure ... but all the same, she might be able to get through to Rhea. He couldn't. He'd tried over and over again ... no good.

He yawned. He was still tired. Early to bed tonight. He'd be yawning his way through his visits which didn't promote good customer relations. He could feel depression settling over him. Jinny Matthews had died yesterday. Cancer. Her husband had been with her and he'd broken down and cried. Two small children. Oh Lord. What a life.

He must pull himself together. He'd be okay once he got going. If you lay in bed too long you were bound to get depressed. One of the few useful pieces of advice his father had given him was that bed was not the place to do your worrying; you couldn't fight your battles lying down; and it was true, you felt so helpless lying flat on your back.

He suddenly saw himself as a beetle ineffectually waving its little black legs in the air, too heavy to turn itself right way up again. His mind strayed from beetles to Kafka's *Metamorphosis* and from there to Dostoevsky's *Crime and Punishment* which he was halfway through. His eyes closed and he began to drift towards sleep again.

He was shocked awake by a spasm of acute physical distress. A feeling of paralysing dread came over him, disorienting because he didn't know where it was coming from. His heart began to pound. He struggled for breath; he felt as though he was suffocating. The hair on the back of his neck prickled. A blackbird sang loudly in the horse chestnut tree.

Then like a photograph coming to life in the developing tray, an image of Rhea formed in his mind. The image was

5

smoky, reminding him of the time when as a boy in India he had watched an eclipse of the sun through glass deliberately smoked to protect his eyes. She was kneeling on the ground, and she was in pain. He sat up, threw off the duvet, swung his legs over the edge of the bed and began to pull off his pyjama jacket.

Chapter Two

RHEA TURNED THE SINK TAP ON AND LOOKED AROUND for her mug. Hers was the Jack Sprat one. On one side of the mug Jack and his wife sat demurely at table, on the other side was the matching nursery rhyme. Laurie's mug had Ride a Cock Horse on it. Rhea kept hers near the tap because she was so thirsty all the time, perhaps because she was never hungry. Water seemed to give her the strength she needed to keep going. But the mug wasn't there.

She bent forward to drink but her hair got in the way so she held it back while she drank with small, difficult gulps. Her throat was swollen and aching. Her legs felt weak, her hands were shaking and her insides felt hollowed out and cold. She reached for the hand towel and dried her face and patted her neck and the front of her dressing gown. The towel smelt musty and stale; she draped it back over the towel rail.

She noticed a plain blue mug half hidden behind the tea caddy. Toby must have put hers away and put the blue one there instead because he thought the nursery rhyme would remind her of Laurie. She felt a moment of irritation which dissipated into nothing.

She went out onto the doorstep and leaned her shoulder against the door frame. The sun was almost fully up now, the light was hardening, daylight was near.

'Mummy cuppa tea? Lonnie cuppa tea too.'

His voice was contented, reasonable. He loved to share, to do whatever she was doing. She wore shoes, he wore shoes. She picked up a fork to weed the flowerbed and he came too. He was companionable.

'Mumma weedin'.'

She stepped down from the back doorstep and crossed the yard and then the terrace. She was in the garden. She saw the sand pit. That was where it had happened. It had been winter. He'd been building a snowman. In the sand pit.

'Laurie?' she called softly. 'Come, darling.'

She stood beside the sand pit and felt suddenly dizzy, as though she had been spinning round and had suddenly stopped. The world jerked and fell away. She put out her hands to stop herself falling. She crouched down, her forehead hitting the wooden surround.

She heard the click of the side gate. That couldn't be Bernie, could it, so early? Laurie adored Bernie. He would rush out with the empties when he heard the whine of the milk float and the wheeze of its brakes, then the cheerful whistling heralding Bernie's arrival.

'Well, fancy you coming out to meet me with all them bottles,' Bernie would say in his deep, slow, interested voice. 'My goodness, you're getting to be a strong lad, aren't you? Soon be helping Bernie with the Sat'day round.' He was quite serious with Laurie; he never winked at Rhea or tried to include her in a conspiracy against

Laurie's weakness and smallness. 'Well,' he would say. 'Must be getting' along now. Bye bye love, see you tomorrow.'

'Bye bye love,' Laurie would echo, waving urgently from the gate. 'Bye bye Bunnie, see you 'morrow!'

'Be careful of the road, Laurie, don't go too near the road. Stay by the gate.'

That was over too, that dread of something happening to him, a nightmare which had never quite left her.

It couldn't be Bernie at the gate, because he never came before twelve and it was very early still. She lifted her head from the wooden surround of the sandpit and saw Toby striding towards her across the terrace.

HE'D MADE it to Rhea's house in under ten minutes. He parked the Honda and walked quickly round the side of the house, through the side gate which Rhea never bolted, unbuckling his helmet as he went. The kitchen door was open. He went cautiously across the cobbled yard to the back garden.

She was crouched beside the sand pit, her dark hair spilling over the wooden surround. He felt a rush of dread which dissolved into relief as she lifted her head, though the look on her face alarmed him. He approached her as cautiously as though she was some wild animal caught in a trap and pulled her gently to her feet. 'Come on. Come inside.'

He put his arm round her and steered her back to the house, noticing, as if through their sheer physicality they held a new significance, the way the sun bronzed the grey cobblestones, the blossom on the lilac tree and a tabby cat which sprang down from the wall on their left and landed motionless on all fours almost at their feet. At the kitchen door they stopped.

'What? What did you say?'

'I asked if I could make you some b-breakfast.' With an effort he mastered his tendency to stammer, always worse when he was stressed. 'I haven't eaten yet myself so I could stay and have something with you.' They had to try to achieve some kind of normality. He supposed that breakfast at half past five in the morning was as good a way as any to start.

She gave the ghost of a smile and pushed open the kitchen door. A Windsor armchair stood against the wall between the door leading into the hall and the archway into the breakfast annexe. He settled her into it, found some tissues in a box on the dresser and put some into her hand. He looked around, rubbing his hands together. Food might help. And a hot drink. He would have known instinctively where to look for a frying pan and a spatula, but in any case he knew Rhea's kitchen well.

RHEA RUBBED her wet cheeks with the tissues which had materialised in her hand. She wasn't sure what had happened or why Toby had come. She felt embarrassed that he should see her like this and half annoyed with him for being there. He couldn't do anything. Nobody could do anything. She watched as he moved around the kitchen collecting eggs and bread and laying down slices of bacon in the frying pan. She looked down and saw Laurie standing by her knee, looking up at her, asking for something – what was it?

'Jus' one more bicky, one more Gari-baldi?' How was it

that he could pronounce some words perfectly, other, simpler words, less well?

He had this habit, whenever he wanted something he didn't think he was allowed, of hunching his shoulders, his head tilted a little to one side and his hands clasped pleadingly in front of him, a note of desperation in his voice. It always made her laugh, it was so ridiculous; it wasn't as though she kept him short of his favourite things; on the contrary she felt guilty sometimes, feeling that she overindulged him, afraid that she did it to compensate for the fact that Tom was absent so he had no father, and that she'd spoil him.

She stretched out her hands to take him onto her knee and found only air. She put her hands over her face and began to rock backwards and forwards. She stood up and clasped her hands together, gasping for breath.

Toby threw down the spatula, went to her and took her locked hands in one of his, holding them tight against his chest while with his other arm around her he rocked her against him, close to tears himself. He felt awed by being in the presence of such passionate grief which seemed to him an almost holy thing.

'Do you want to talk?' he asked her after a while, suddenly conscious that he was holding her close. He let her go and stood away from her.

Rhea looked at him as if she wasn't sure who he was. She shook her head and turned away. 'Oughtn't you to be somewhere?'

He shook his head. 'Phil takes the service this morning. I'm not meant to be anywhere but here. If I cook you some breakfast, will you eat something?'

'I'll try.' She stood looking lost, in the middle of the room.

He prodded slices of streaky bacon with a fork. The delicious aroma of frying bacon began to fill the room. His mouth watered. He must try to get her to talk. Or perhaps it would be kinder to steer her away from the subject.

'Toby?'

He looked round.

She was standing looking down, her forehead puckered in a bewildered frown. She lifted her eyes to meet his. 'Did God take him away because I loved him too much?'

Before he could reply she said quickly, turning away, 'Of course not. How stupid of me – of course not. It's just—'

He stabbed at the bacon with the fork.

She shook her head. 'I suppose it's because I want to know *why* and there's no possible answer. I don't know what to think. I don't know if I even believe in God anymore.'

'You're still in shock.' Toby frowned. In his opinion Laurie's death had nothing to do with God. 'I wouldn't worry about it.'

She came and stood beside him, watching as he prodded the sizzling bacon with the fork. 'I'm glad you're hungry,' she said with faint enthusiasm, after a pause.

'Two of these are for you ... smells good, doesn't it?'

It seemed heartless to be so hungry. But Rhea had turned away and didn't seem to have heard.

SHE STARED through the open door at the leaves of the prunus tree across the yard. The sunlight shone through the leaves, burnishing them blood red. The leaves bobbed and twisted in the light wind against the blue sky. The tree looked alive.

Suddenly she longed to be touching the dancing leaves, to feel their moist, skin-like smoothness against her palms. She pressed her hands down the skirt of her dressing gown, her fingers spread wide. The surface of the cloth felt dry and unyielding, like blotting paper.

She went out through the door and down the side path to the garden. She knelt beside the flowerbed, pushed her hands in among a clump of peonies and held her hands and wrists in the cool shade. She began to finger the smooth, delicately veined leaves, not knowing why this gave her such pleasure and relief. The leaves felt fresh and alive like a child's cool, soft skin.

A crippling pain shot through her. She gave an involuntary scream which she quickly suppressed. She dug her knuckles in below her ribs and gasped for breath, snatching at the tee shirt she had on under her dressing gown, pulling the material away from her chest. She could hardly bear the pain. It died away, leaving her feeling cold and sick.

She walked slowly back to the house. Crossing the grass and the terrace her feet hurt as though she was walking on sharp stones. Her body felt sore all over.

She was surprised to find Toby in the kitchen; she had forgotten he was there.

TOBY SAID HESITANTLY, 'There you are. Food's ready. I've l-laid the table, except for the salt and p-pepper which I couldn't find. Could you—'

He must be mad; what was he doing here? Look at her, she wasn't listening, and she wasn't going to eat anything anyway. He lifted one of the eggs out of the pan and laid it carefully on a plate gleaming with reflected orange light from the hot ring above.

Rhea stood staring at the food. She looked up at him. 'Did you make this for me? I'm so sorry, I don't think—'

'It's okay, I didn't really think you'd want it. Thought it was worth a shot.' He put the plate down on the open grill cover.

'Please, you have it, Toby. I want you to, you must be so hungry. I'll sit with you. It's just – I couldn't eat it myself. You sit down and start. I'll make some coffee.' Suddenly energised, she filled the kettle and switched it on. She reached up to the wall cupboard for a packet of ground coffee, its opening folded over and secured with an elastic band. She prised off the elastic and spooned coffee into the cafetière.

Toby carried the plate through the arch to the annexe and sat down at the table. He picked up his knife and fork. Was there a change? How could he tell? What should he do? He had no idea. She hadn't questioned his being there so early in the morning. Perhaps she hadn't got her sense of time back yet, or perhaps such trivial considerations had ceased to matter. She'd always been such a punctual person; it was one of the things her father had dinned into her, she'd told him: the importance of punctuality.

It had been three months now since Laurie had died. Sometimes being with Rhea felt like being with someone in the early stages of dementia. He dreaded her starting to ask questions again. If she did, he'd have to go through the whole horrible business again and listen all over again to her refusing to believe it.

Some of the time she did seem to understand in an uncommitted kind of way what had happened; it was as though she did know but was involved in a ghastly game of make believe with herself, or as if she had put a part of her brain deliberately into cold storage, refusing to allow it to be reached. Sometimes he found it impossible to believe that sane, intelligent Rhea was behaving in this unnatural way. All he could do was hope that one day something would change, that she would begin to understand what had happened. And that she would find the courage to bear it.

When Laurie died, Toby took two weeks' leave to be with her. He sat with her through the freezing February evenings beside the wood burner, reading or doing the crossword while she sat and gazed into the flames. She couldn't seem to get warm. He didn't try to din the truth into her but treated Laurie's absence as a matter of fact. When she laid a place for Laurie he took away the child-sized knife, fork and spoon and put them back in the drawer. When she got out the button box or the finger paints or the Jack Sprat drinking mug, he put them quietly away again. There was never any argument; she hardly spoke at all; it was like a silent battle of wills between them, or a terrible game.

The friends who called in during the first few days after it had happened were met by incomprehension, almost indifference from Rhea. Some people thought it odd him being in the house and assumed them to be in a relationship, which was annoying, particularly as he would so have loved it to be true.

When his leave was up he tried to persuade her to invite someone to stay but she insisted that she would be perfectly fine alone. When he read emotion in her face as they said goodbye, for a moment he hoped that some clarifying change might be taking place. But no. It was just that it unsettled her to see him go. She had become used to him being there.

After this he dropped in to see her as often as he could, hoping each time that there would be a difference, but each time he was disappointed. As the days passed and winter melted into spring there were moments when she seemed to demonstrate an increased awareness, and he began to worry about how she would cope. He feared for her; he slept badly, he thought of her often and his heart ached.

RHEA PUT Toby's cup of coffee down next to his elbow and sat down across the table from him. She wanted him to eat the food he'd cooked for her; he was always so hungry. For as long as she'd known him she'd been convinced he didn't eat enough. She noticed that he tended to grab whatever was to hand and eat it standing up: bananas, nuts or dried fruit, apples or slices of bread hastily slathered with peanut butter. When he did cook he seemed to have the oddest moral scruples over making the food appetising. She'd wondered sometimes if he'd spent time in a monastery, which might explain his abstemiousness.

This time he had taken trouble for her sake. She watched, feeling vaguely pleased, while he devoured the four rashers of bacon and two eggs and sat sipping his coffee. He was obviously starving but trying not to show it, which for some reason she found touching. She moved to sit sideways, resting her arm along the chair back, her elbow bent, her nose pressed into the soft inside flesh of her arm. The smell of her own flesh was both comforting and terrifying because it reminded her that she was alive.

She said, staring down at the blue checked tablecloth, 'I can't remember – I don't know what they did with him, where he is buried.' She turned her face to the window and closed her eyes against the daylight as though it had suddenly become unbearably bright.

'He isn't b-buried anywhere. He was cremated. His ashes—'

She stood up like someone escaping from a wasp, almost knocking her chair over. Her hands tightened into two fists. She rammed one into her stomach which had convulsed with the shock. 'His *ashes*?'

He flinched. 'It was what you chose, Rhea.'

She must have been out of her mind. What had she been thinking?

He wouldn't look at her. 'Rhea, you know it's only his body—'

She turned her head away so that he wouldn't see the tears welling up, scorching her inflamed eyelids. How could he comprehend the agony of knowing that she would never again hold that small body in her arms again, so warm and soft, so vibrant with life and joy? He didn't understand. How could he?

She dashed the tears away with the back of her hand. 'His body was everything to me! What did I know of his soul?'

She wanted to explain, but dredging the words up felt impossibly difficult, like pulling someone out of a bog. She felt as though she might suddenly find she couldn't talk at all, it took too much effort.

She sat down again and looked at him. 'He was too little for us to tell each other things ... things that might be left now, for me.' Her face hurt with the effort involved in not crying. 'Toby, what if he's calling for me? What if he's frightened and wants me and thinks I've abandoned him?'

· · ·

LOOKING AT HER PALE, shuttered face, Toby searched wretchedly for something to say. The only thing that would help would be the passage of time, but it was no good telling her that.

He leaned forward, his elbows on the table. 'I know that nothing I can say can comfort you. But there will be comfort, whether you believe it or not. One day, I promise you, there will be peace.' Seeing her expression, knowing that every instinct in her was rebelling, he looked at her with a feeling of utter helplessness.

She shook her head and sat looking down at her hands, gripped together in her lap. 'I know you mean it when you say things will get better ... but I can't feel it, it's just words. I'm sorry. There's nothing inside me but misery; it fills every crack of me, it's like a poison.'

He shouldn't have tried to convince her. It hadn't helped.

She turned her face away. Suddenly she put a hand out across the table. Relieved, he stretched his arm out and wove his fingers through hers. They sat for a long time in silence. Gradually Rhea's face relaxed and it dawned on him that simply by holding her hand he was at last being of some comfort to her. This came as a revelation to him.

At half past eight he stirred. 'I have to be at school at nine for assembly. I'm so sorry, but I'm going to have to go.'

Rhea, who had been sitting so still, her head bent, her hand now loose in his, that he'd wondered whether she might not have fallen asleep, turned towards him immediately and slowly withdrew her hand.

'I wish I could stay. Will you be okay?'

She nodded. She seemed exhausted from the effort of talking. She came with him to the back door and stood watching while he pulled on his helmet and gloves. He kissed her cheek, gave the usual blessing and turned away, frustrated. The words must seem so empty and meaningless to her.

SHE WATCHED him walk away down the side passage, turning at the corner of the house to raise his gloved hand in farewell. The expression on his face was so sweet, so tired and sad, that she felt a brief impulse to run after him, to apologise for being ungrateful, for making him sad.

She turned and stood facing the kitchen door.

She was alone.

She shut her eyes and leaned against the door frame. Birds sang tumultuously in the trees bordering the yard. The world tilted and spun remorselessly on, unmoved by her private agony. Earth and air, fire and water: she was the oil-logged bird, the landed fish, the drowning man, the turtle that has wandered too far inland from the sea.

She felt the last vestiges of hope drain away. She couldn't go on. She wanted to be where Laurie was, to be with him.

Chapter Three

Toby walked down the drive to the Honda, parked askew by the gate. His stomach ached with tension. He glanced at his watch: there would only just be time to get home and shave before assembly. He pulled on his helmet and buckled it, settled himself in the saddle and kick-started the bike. The bike sped through the quiet suburbs, past dark gateways in hedges of privet and laurel, past spindly lamp posts like swift grey brush strokes sweeping up from the pavements and pillar boxes bright as red toadstools at street corners. His mind was full of Rhea.

Had he honestly believed that anything he said to her would make the slightest difference? She was still in shock. People in her condition were in no fit state to be talked at, have food forced on them or be criticised for their lack of faith – or for anything else, come to that. Because he *had* felt critical, he'd been dismayed by the sight of her hair, lank and drab with dirt instead of newly washed and glossy, and by the signs of neglect in the kitchen, the unwiped surfaces and greasy sink. He would have thought that Rhea, normally so fastidious, would have clung to the daily routine as a kind of sheet anchor. Showed how much he knew.

He hardly ever thought about his own mother. His memories of her were associated with the feeling of being continually pushed away, of her always being too preoccupied to pay him or his sister Stella much attention. Almost unapproachably good-looking – before she'd met their father she'd been a model for John Galliano – she spent her time either with her head in a romantic novel, so that if you wanted to tell her something you always felt you were interrupting, or in the kitchen where she bottled fruit and made raspberry and strawberry jam from the fruit from their own garden, baked bread and made delicious cakes and scones. Everybody commented on what a wonderful mother she was.

But it wasn't what it looked like; Toby and Stella were forbidden the kitchen while their mother was cooking. She wouldn't be able to concentrate if they were there, she told them firmly; they would chat and get in the way and want to taste things and lick bowls. So the kitchen turned out to be a barrier as unyielding as her locked bedroom door or the romantic novels she loved to bury herself in. Toby's sense of grievance was if anything intensified by the fact that in the kitchen she was ostensibly being a good mother doing good mother stuff.

When she wasn't reading the romantic novels she loved, their mother was so distracted that when he reached his teens Toby began to wonder if she might be taking something.

Stella pooh-poohed this idea and dismissed her behaviour with a shrug. 'She's just doing her Madame Bovary thing, don't worry about it.'

Looking back, Toby thought this a pretty astute diagnosis: his mother had behaved very much like someone in love and yearning for someone she couldn't have; but maybe it hadn't been illicit love she'd longed for – perhaps all she had wanted was freedom.

She died of ovarian cancer when he was thirteen, still too young to have gained any insight into her self-absorbed, unhappy personality. He hung on as long as he could to bitter, regretful memories of the way she had smelt and of being enclosed once or twice in softness and warmth; but these memories were vague and quickly faded; mostly now they were of an almost total stranger.

Their father, a commander in the Navy, had never had much to do with them and after his wife's death he seemed to give up on them completely. They were looked after during the holidays from boarding school by a succession of housekeepers, none of whom were able to put up with his brusqueness and uncertain temper for very long. His death of a heart attack at fifty-four had very little impact on their lives. Stella was working in hospitality management and Toby was halfway through his training for the ministry. Toby's main emotion on being informed of his father's death was a huge sense of relief which generated months of guilt.

Toby and Stella had expected nothing from their father but their mother had been a bitter disappointment, particularly to Toby who hid his hurt so deep that only his sister knew that it was there. The stigma of her rejection stayed with him for years after her death, and he sometimes wondered if it was this that had engendered in him the longing for acceptance and a meaningful role in life that had drawn him so strongly towards ordination. That and the realisation that came to him when he was hanging off a piton halfway up Scafell Pike, that there was a part of him that needed to believe in something unknown and miraculous and that if he didn't allow this part of himself to flourish he wouldn't survive.

Splashing cold water over his face, Toby wondered what Rhea would be doing now, whether she would still be sitting at the kitchen table or would have gone up to dress. Perhaps he should ring her to make sure she was all right? No, he mustn't nag; he had to learn to trust her.

He put the razor back on the shelf, dried his face and went through to the study, his favourite room in the house. He had lined the walls with pine shelves which were laden with his books, thrown a Persian rug from home over the old oak floorboards and set a table by the window, and a chair. His *Imitation of Christ* lay open at the section on the satisfaction of loving God above all things. He picked it up and read:

'*O when will that blessed time come, that time I long for, when your presence satisfies me wholly, and you are to me all in all? Until that gift is given, joy cannot be complete.*'

He closed the book and stood looking out of the window. Maybe you had to be a mystic to feel that this total immersion would complete you, that you needed nothing else. He felt low, which was discouraging. If God satisfied you wholly, surely you would never feel like this.

He took a couple of deep breaths. Depression threatened, but he knew from long experience what would lift his mood: he closed his eyes and started to list in his head all the things he felt grateful for, from the breakfast he'd eaten at Rhea's house to the flower buds on the peach tree outside his widow.

On and on he went, cataloguing everything he could think of to be grateful for until the sorrows of the morning began to dissipate. His spiritual anxiety, his pity for Rhea and his crushing personal grief over Laurie's death lifted like mist slowly rising from an autumn field and dissolved until they were nothing. He felt drained of bad feelings: new born.

He closed his eyes and let peace flow through him. It no longer mattered that he couldn't give Rhea the help she needed. That had to come from God. From Love. In Toby's mind the two were interchangeable. The initiative was not his, but Love's. It was a great weight off his mind.

Along the pavement under the window a little boy came, kicking a stone. Toby could only see his head and shoulders above the low fence but he could tell what he was doing by his bent head, the frown of concentration, the jerky movements of his shoulders and his uneven progress along the perimeter of the fence. He was wearing a yellow jersey; Toby's eye had been caught by the sudden flash of buttery yellow as the boy passed the window. He found himself suddenly transported back to a grey winter's day, this last January it must have been ... it had been after Christmas, certainly, because Rhea had knitted the daffodil yellow jersey Laurie was wearing, for one of his Christmas presents.

Toby and Rhea had taken him down to the coast in Rhea's little Peugeot. Huddled under rugs in the shelter of a breakwater high up the beach, they had watched him, both of them curious to see what his reaction would be to his first sight of the wintery ocean. Laurie had stood on the deserted sweep of shingle in dungarees and wellingtons and the yellow jersey, holding a blue bucket tightly in one hand and staring fixedly, his shoulders a little hunched in surprise, at the wide, grey, surging sea.

Rhea said with an off-handedness which did not deceive Toby, 'Little boys look so sweet from the back, don't they? They have such dear little non-existent behinds. He looks so small against the vastness of that sea and sky! I wonder if he's frightened.'

'I'm sure he isn't. He's spared our adult p-propensity to anticipate disaster.' Toby sometimes sounded severe when he felt that what he was saying was important. 'He's tough, you worry too much about him.' He shook his head. She needed her husband, to take some of the strain.

Rhea glanced at him, her eyes bright. 'Am I being boring?'

'Of course not.' Startled, staring out to the fine yellow line of the horizon, he looked for the right words. 'You – you aren't ever a bore. You know I could n-never find you boring.' It had been on the tip of his tongue, some unguarded admission of his feelings of tenderness and concern for her and Laurie, but the moment passed. 'You are a bit obsessive about him. I suppose it's n-natural to feel like that about a child.'

'They're so completely dependent on you. Grownups can fend for themselves, unless they're ill and then they can at least explain. It's so one-sided, loving a child.'

He had known her only about six months when Tom had walked into her life and within weeks had married her. Toby had been mystified and disturbed by the marriage. At the time he didn't know Rhea very well; she was an erratic churchgoer and showed no interest in the house groups or other peripheral activities of the church. He came across her occasionally in the town and once or twice when out walking in the hills around the town. And then one day Tom was there.

Toby was walking through the marketplace on his way to the vestry when he saw Rhea walking along the pavement with a tall, black-haired man who was looking down at her and holding her hand. Toby was never able to get that moment out of his head. When he remembered it, it seemed to assume some disproportionate significance, the sight of the two of them winding through the crowds, the grey stones of Cooper's Arch and the ancient wall of the Trust House behind them. He saw the people thronging the market stalls, heard the incessant rumble of traffic as the cars came in in single file off the bridge, felt the drizzle and saw the extraordinarily happy expression on Rhea's face as she held Tom's hand and looked up into his face while they walked, slowly, as though it didn't matter where they were going because they were together. It was the togetherness that made such an impression on him, that stung.

He knew he had seen that face somewhere before. He recognised those high cheekbones and deep-set bright eyes, the huge shoulders that diminished his height, making him seem less than his six foot four, and the mass of heavy black hair. The man pulled up Rhea's hand and hugged her arm against his side and looked down into her face, laughing. And Toby recognised Tom with whom he had been at school and whom he had not seen for five years or so, since before he had disappeared somewhere overseas – South America, it was rumoured. His hair was longer, almost down to his shoulders, and in his old, faded jeans and a leather jerkin over a denim shirt he looked like a gypsy, but it was Tom Henderson all right. Toby had particular cause to remember him.

He saw in his mind's eye the ring and the ropes round it caging them in, he, thin, frightened and a good deal smaller than his opponent, his hands inside the swollen gloves feeling as though they didn't belong to him, his stomach dissolving with terror, the yelling of the crowd of boys hemming them in sounding to him like the baying of a pack of hounds, and Tom glaring at him over his dancing hands, his eyes shining his contempt, circling carefully, looking for an opening through which to deliver the fatal blow.

But Toby knew how to box; his father had insisted he be taught from the age of six in the hope that it would toughen his spindly son and make a man of him. Toby knew how to hit Tom so as to hurt him most, and he did this several times, and won.

After it was over and Toby's arm had been hauled high by the referee while his opponent climbed to his feet, Tom muttered in his ear, 'You just wait. I'll get you for this.' But these were only words choked up out of the bitterness of disappointment and defeat. He never touched Toby again; the bullying was over; the nights of crying his heart out with his head under the blankets; the dreaded recreation periods when if a boy was determined to make another's life a misery he could do so without much difficulty since the school was large and supervision negligible at those times. And even though they had subsequently warily become friends, the boxing match having achieved what their headmaster, who was more observant than some of the boys gave him credit for being, had hoped for, Toby's first reaction on seeing Tom again was still, twelve years after the event, a startling frisson of the old remembered fear.

Now, on the beach, watching Rhea gazing at Laurie with her usual concentrated intensity, he knew by the expression on her face that she was thinking about Tom who had left her suddenly and without explanation three months before Laurie was born.

'I've been trying to remember where I met Tom.' Rhea nodded as though in answer to a question. Toby had the strangest impression that she was reading his thoughts. She smiled, remembering. 'It was at a party at a friend's house in Bywater Street. One of those evenings where the alcohol's flowing and people tend to show off rather.' She gave a small eyeroll. 'Doug Driscoll was there – I don't know if you've heard him on the radio – he's a political analyst and a very good writer, actually. He'd written a book about Syria and Tom got into an argument with him.' She picked up a pebble and examined it, her mind obviously elsewhere. 'Which was really stupid because he didn't know half as much about the situation in Syria as Doug did, but he'd had rather a lot to drink. He was incredibly patronising to me – I thought him a misogynistic pig, to be honest.' She threw the pebble away, sat up straighter and linked her hands round her knees. 'He told me later he felt an idiot for having been so patronising, especially as he'd discovered by then that I had a novel out. He gave me a lift home and we sat up all night talking, which kind of changed my mind about him, and in the morning he asked me to marry him. And I said yes.'

It was at times like this, when she talked about people and events Toby could not begin to identify with, that he felt he liked Rhea the least; the self-adulation and pretentiousness of these people seemed to him so unpleasant. But she talked about this side of her life so rarely that it had never been an issue.

Sitting on the beach after her unprecedentedly long speech, he was silent. His mind recoiled from his imagined vision of the party, Tom and Rhea knee to knee, the wine, the argument. He wondered whether what he was feeling was jealousy, and if it was, whether he was jealous of them for having each other, or of Tom for being loved by Rhea.

She said, her attention half on Laurie again, 'Of course, painting was Tom's life, his reason for existing. It was all he really cared about.' She pressed her lips tightly together, looking down the shingle to the sea. The wind parted her fringe, blowing it flat against her forehead.

'You never tried to find him.'

She darted a look at him. 'Goodness, no. He'd have hated that. If he wanted to come back, he would.'

'Would you want—'

'I think he left because of Laurie. Because he couldn't stand the idea of a child in the house.'

'But – his own child?'

'He always thought he'd be no good as a father. His background was a mess; his father used to beat him. His mother had to take Tom away from him.'

'I didn't know. How awful.'

'I think it may have been that. Or perhaps it was just that he didn't want a child just then. I hadn't known him very long, of course ... perhaps I didn't know him as well as I thought I did.'

'Very forceful – personality.'

'And attractive. I did love him, Toby.'

'Might he come back?'

She shook her head. 'I don't think so.' She gave a little shrug. 'Maybe – one day. Anyway, he gave me Laurie.' She moved to kneel upright on the shingle, holding her hair back off her face with both hands, narrowing her eyes to stare at Laurie who was still standing rigid, unmoving, close to the waves. 'I wonder if he's frightened.'

Laurie bent his head back to look at a gull blown in fast by the wind diagonally over the beach, its wings set like a glider, its head turning this way and that, squawking like a child on a helter-skelter.

'No, he isn't, he's waving. Yes! Lovely! Seagull!' She sank down and pulled the rug up over her knees again. She looked away. 'Sometimes it helps to talk about Tom, to convince myself that he existed at all. We were together for such a short time, sometimes it seems like a dream ... but Laurie is so like him, apart from his fair hair. Goodness knows where that came from – both sets of grandparents are dark.'

She smiled at him, and looking at her familiar face and shapely, enchanting mouth Toby felt an intense longing to pull her to him and kiss her and tell her that he loved her, that she was the only woman he'd ever wanted, or ever could. He longed for her, but he hesitated. There was the question of Tom, to whom she was married, after all, even though Tom had now been gone for three years or so and had given no sign that he might return. And he had no idea what Rhea's feelings were. It was obvious that she was fond of him, but did her feelings go any deeper? He didn't want to embarrass her or spoil the relaxed relationship they already had.

He hitched himself up off the elbow on which he'd been leaning with his legs stretched out in front of him and climbed stiffly to his feet. He began brushing the shingle off his jeans. 'Lunch time. I'll get Laurie. He can come with me to get the things out of the car. I've got the key, I think.'

Rhea had scrambled to her feet. She ran down the beach, her feet sinking into the shingle, her arms out to balance herself, her long hair flying. Laurie turned at the sound of her footsteps and began lurching towards her, his arms out, shouting with delight. The wind took his voice and whipped it away. He ran into Rhea's arms and she spun him round and round, his short legs flying out behind him, the bucket clasped behind Rhea's back, his arms tight round her back.

Toby seized his books from the table and left the room. Coming on top of the spiritual elation he had felt a few minutes before, the memory of that awakening into love was shattering. He had put all thoughts of that kind aside when Laurie died and had responded instinctively to the demands Rhea made on his patience, pity and understanding. He'd tried to forget that he had ever been attracted to her, reminding himself that they were friends and that he mustn't presume on their friendship or take advantage of her in any way. He'd thought he had succeeded.

He left the house, closing the door carefully behind him. He was in no mood to face a hundred and fifty restless children, none of them in the least interested in being led in prayer.

Chapter Four

RHEA PUSHED THE BACK DOOR SHUT AND WALKED
through the kitchen, across the hall, up the stairs and along
the landing into the bathroom. She unlocked the medicine
cupboard door and reached for the two boxes of aspirin on
the top shelf. She opened them both and shook the flat foil
containers out onto the green tiled floor. There were twelve,
each holding eight 300 mg. aspirin ... that made ninety-six
pills. That would be enough, surely?

She knelt down and began stripping the foil away from
the pills, easing each one from its tight niche and spilling it
onto the floor. No more need for caution, no need to worry
about Laurie finding them lying around looking like sweets.
She stood up and began pulling other medicine bottles out
of the cupboard, scattering them over the floor. Tom's
sleeping pills which she had always meant to throw away;
Laurie's Calpol from that time he'd been sleepless with
German measles; cough medicine; eyedrops with Poison on
the label; milk of magnesia tablets. She kept the sleeping
pills by her; she would add them to the aspirin mixture, just
to make sure.

'I'm coming, Laurie,' she said aloud as if she could hear him calling her. Her hands trembled, her heart beat thickly. She felt no fear, only impatience that it was taking so long, and the absolute need to see him again.

The white pills fell in little drifts on the green floor like blossoms scattered on a lawn. The strips of foil dropped in shining fragments from her fingers like tinsel from a Christmas tree.

Laurie's face floated into view. She was showing him the tree lit up for the first time. They had spent the morning of Christmas Eve decorating it and had waited impatiently all day for dusk to fall. Now, bathed and in his pyjamas, Laurie had been led by Rhea blindfolded into the sitting room and settled on the sofa.

'Ready, steady – now!' She uncovered his eyes and he gasped and gazed at the tree, at the dark green boughs glittering with frost, the coloured glass balls circling slowly in the heat from the fire, the gleaming rivulets of tinsel and the soft coloured lights like glow worms among the branches. He was too amazed to speak. He turned to her at last, a face softened and receptive with wonder, and in his round eyes two tiny Christmas trees were mirrored so that they seemed to be full of rainbow-coloured stars.

She told him stories about Christmas Eve; that on this one night of the year the animals could talk; how on the morning of Christmas Day, Mary's baby Jesus had been born in a stable in Bethlehem. He listened enthralled, his mouth fallen slightly open, his eyes like round dark caramels, until at last he'd fallen asleep against her side.

The year before he had been too small to take it all in, but this last Christmas Day he had been quite old enough: he had been two years, seven months and four days old.

· · ·

HER KNEES and the small of her back were stiff. How long had she been kneeling there, remembering? Hours? Minutes? She began to gather the white tablets together into one big pile. She stood up and looked on the glass shelf over the basin for the tooth mug; then she remembered: she had taken it downstairs by mistake that morning and left it in the kitchen – she knew just where it was, beside the bread bin. A vague annoyance stirred under the stupefying sense of unreality. She contemplated for a moment cramming the pills into her mouth in handfuls but dismissed the idea almost at once; they would taste foul and she wouldn't be able to swallow them. Or she would be sick, and being sick was to be avoided at all costs. There was nothing in the bathroom that could be used as a mug, short of the mug itself. That was how things come to be invented. If there hadn't been a mug in the kitchen she would have had to invent one. She'd have to go down and get it.

She was so tired. All she wanted to do was lie down and sleep.

When she was halfway down the stairs the doorbell rang. She sank down against the banister rail, her heart thudding. She would wait there and whoever it was would go away.

The ringing went on. It wasn't Toby, he wouldn't ring the bell like that, he'd knock or come round the side. The persistent ringing made her nervous, pulled her back into an awareness of other people. She thought about the pills lying on the bathroom floor. Toby would be upset if she took them but she had to, she had to go to Laurie. Toby would understand, anybody would. She wasn't doing this for herself, it was for Laurie. He was so small, it wasn't right for her to stay here while he was there – for her not to try to go to him, to help him. He'd be crying for her; he wouldn't know where she was.

The doorbell rang on and on. Whoever it was didn't leave, they went on pushing the bell, crazily on and on. She crouched on the stairs, blocking her ears and muttering under her breath, 'Go away! Go away. Please just go away.' But they didn't.

'Who is it?' she said angrily, out loud. She stood up and leaned against the wall, her legs weak. She was shaking all over. She leaned on the banister and shouted again, 'Who is it?'

'It's only me ...' The voice trailed away. At first hesitantly and then with the same resounding, relentless peal the bell rang again.

'Oh, do stop!' Rhea said. She hurled herself down the last few stairs and threw herself at the door.

Mrs Mander, one trembling hand stretched up towards the bell push, recoiled, shocked, as the door opened. Her face looked as though it had been dusted over heavily with flour. Grains of powder flew from her cheeks as she moved her head. Her small, watering eyes stared meanly at Rhea from dark sockets like holes. She stared at Rhea as if she had never seen her before in her life.

Who was this dreadful old woman? Rhea's heart was still thumping from the nerve-wracking jangling of the bell. She didn't recognise her next door neighbour and began to shut the door in her face.

'Oh ... Rhea ...' The old woman was still bewildered but stubborn too now, realising that the door was about to close. 'I just came round to tell you. It's my wireless. It's gone wrong again, and I've only just had it mended. Isn't it shocking?' Her voice rose, quavering, querulous. Her chin trembled and her eyes slid from side to side on a level with Rhea's chest.

Rhea suddenly realised who she was. 'Do you want me to—?'

The crumpled forehead smoothed with relief. 'Could you?' She lifted a bony arm and pushed back her wild grey hair with the side of her hand.

'I'll come, I'll come.' Rhea began to close the door. 'Only I must change; I haven't got my proper clothes on. I'll come in a minute.' She was nearly crying with the irritation of it, this invasion just when she had at last decided what she wanted to do.

Already her neighbour had turned away with a new purposefulness, shuffling with short, uncertain steps down the drive. She staggered and involuntarily Rhea rushed forward and took her arm, quite prepared to be swatted off like a fly: Mrs Mander didn't always welcome assistance, it depended on her mood.

The pressure of the clinging, unexpectedly weighty hand on her arm forced Rhea into an awareness of the old woman swaying and tottering by her side. She felt an infinitesimal shift inside her. The core of ice, the angry lump of pain and rage began to soften.

She was permitted to support Mrs Mander as far as the gate.

'You ought to get your husband to do something about these loose stones.' Mrs Mander picked her way delicately over the neatly laid path. 'Somebody'll break their neck one of these days. It's a disgrace.'

Rhea looked sideways at the raddled old face. 'I haven't got a husband.'

'What, mislaid him, have you?' Mrs Mander gave a

raucous chuckle and dug Rhea in the ribs with a pointed elbow. ''Course you got a husband. I've seen him.'

'That was a long time ago.'

'I left my stick behind.' Mrs Mander's tart tone altered in a flash to pathos. 'I turned the wireless on for the news and not a sound came out – not a sound.' She stood still and looked piteously up at Rhea. 'Isn't it dreadful? It's an antique, you know.'

Rhea stood and gazed down at her, feeling a sense of surrender and of giving in to the inevitable. 'I'll be round in a minute.'

Back inside the house she stood in the hall with her hands over her ears, trembling and taking deep breaths. What a farce, what an unbelievable imposition, going on like that as if nothing had happened. Didn't she know about Laurie? You'd think even she would realise Rhea needed to be left alone, not be bothered with her silly old wireless. Who cared about her wireless – who cared?

But she remembered how exultant Laurie had always been at the prospect of a visit to Mrs Mander whom he'd loved, completely disregarding her terrifying appearance and endless complaints. And Rhea remembered how Mrs Mander had changed when she saw him, her face lighting up and even her voice seeming to alter, to become lighter and higher and more cheerful as she told him about the little boys she had looked after when she was Miss Cox, in her working days before she had married George Mander; about the two titled families whose offspring she had raised strictly but kindly, with a firm hand and a belief in discipline for the sake of the child.

Tiny Miss Cox, pretty then, and sprightly, if you could believe the photos in her dusty old albums; with light brown, curly hair and taking a size three in shoes. Now she was old and bent and miserable but when she spoke to Laurie, always using her special voice and bending down so as to be nearer his height, Rhea recaptured a hint of the youthful Miss Cox in the sparkling eyes, the doting kindliness with which she smiled on him and told him what a fine young man he was and what a credit to his mother.

Remembering Mrs Mander's interactions with Laurie, Rhea felt almost cheerful as she climbed the stairs and washed her face, climbed into her jeans and rummaged through a drawer for a jersey. But the cheerfulness didn't last, it had been a kind of mirage and already she felt it draining away; anguish rose like a tide of nausea inside her. But when she went into the bathroom to wash and found the medicine bottles scattered and the pills in a heap on the floor she looked at them in astonishment, hardly recognising them.

Suddenly galvanised into activity she scooped up the pills as though they were cake crumbs and dropped them into the lavatory pan. She threw in Tom's sleeping pills and pressed the flush. She squirted the eye lotion out of its little plastic bottle into the basin and washed it away.

When it had all gone she stood looking at the basin with a feeling of astonishment. It was like a miracle: Mrs Mander had saved her. It scared her to remember how convinced she had been of wanting to die, to follow him; it had seemed at the time the logical thing to do. But now with the spell broken she could see that it didn't make sense, it was too simple a solution for such a complicated problem; it wouldn't work. She might die and find herself nowhere near him.

She felt very far away from him at this moment, as though he had never existed, as if she had imagined the whole thing. Had none of this happened? Would she find him playing in his room or downstairs in the kitchen raiding the sultana jar, or in the sitting-room watching *CBeebies* astride the rocking stool? She half turned towards the door and the illusion fell away and she knew he wasn't there.

She went back into the bathroom and sat down on the edge of the bath. She dreaded the returning of despair, but she feared even more the delusions hovering over her, threatening her with their promise of peace. Laurie's cloak-shaped towel was draped over the heated towel rail: it was white, edged with yellow gingham, with a little pixie cap attachment at one corner. It was still dented with his shape. She picked it up, fingering its softness and warmth, then, her heart beating hard, she buried her face in it, breathing in its clean smell, yearning for some hint of him.

She looked fearfully round at the bath itself. Three yellow plastic ducks, a rubber penguin with the inside hollowed out for soap – only the soap had long since been used up – and a little blue boat in which sat a little man with *Coastguard* written in red letters round his white, peaked cap. Laurie had played with the little boat, splashed it, sunk it and rescued it over and over, dozens and dozens of times. The little man's face beamed happily at her. He reminded her ludicrously of Laurie. He had a curving smile like the smile on the Happy Face biscuits she remembered from her own childhood. Sometimes Laurie would turn the little man upside down and say, 'Now he got a sad face,' and back again: 'Now he happy again!'

She could see him sitting in the water on the blue rubber slip mat, chattering under his breath as he commanded, positioned and manoeuvred his battalion of plastic debris like an admiral bullying his fleet.

'Time to come out now,' she would say kindly at the last possible moment from her seat on the linen basket.

He would look up, his hair in flat, damp curls against his forehead, his bright eyes vague and his preoccupied face flushed with some deep, private excitement. 'Not jus' yet. Soon.'

'Aren't we going to have a story? I'm longing to tell you a story when you're in bed.'

He would scramble to his feet, discarding his toys with the cheerful disloyalty that always cost her a pang. 'I'm gonna tell *you* a story.'

He usually tried to postpone falling asleep. 'Have a little play now,' he would say when his story was finished. This would have partly been read by Rhea and partly recited by heart by him. Now he was wriggling upright onto his elbows under the bedclothes.

'No more play now,' she would say firmly. 'More play in the morning. It's late now, time for you to sleep. Listen! The birds are going to sleep too.'

'Are you goin' to sleep?'

'Yes. Soon.'

'All right all right,' he would sometimes say then, in a disgruntled voice which made Rhea want to laugh.

'We'll say our prayers.'

Laurie brightened and slapped his palms together briskly. 'Jesus first.'

'Dear Jesus, thank you for our happy day. Thank you for the sunshine and the flowers and the rain which made our spinach grow. Thank you for our food and for our cosy beds. Thank you for Mummy and thank you for Laurie. Keep us safe until the morning.'

'Amen,' shouted Laurie. 'Now God.'

'Our Father, which art in Heaven, hallowed be Thy name ...'

The pain seeped up from somewhere deeper than the

40

source of tears; she hardly recognised it as grief, this feeling; it was like a wound deep in her being, at her very heart's core. It felt as though she was crawling through each endless moment like an insect struggling across a vast, ploughed field; and she had only just begun. The field stretched ahead without boundaries, infinitely daunting, to cross it an impossible task, to get to the other side of grief. It could not be done; she would never feel any different from this moment, she would never recover.

LATER, when it was dark, she lay face down on the carpet outside Laurie's room, her fingers just touching the door. She couldn't go in but neither could she leave. She knew exactly what was inside: his animals ranged along the windowsill, his boxes of toys, the giant plastic ice cream cartons in which were stored his Lego, farm animals, dominoes, crayons, puzzles. She visualised the pull-along cart full of bricks, the jack in the box, the pink stuffed snake she had bought him in a moment of foolishness.

After it happened she sat for hours on his bed staring at the posters on the wall – Spring in the Countryside, Autumn in the Countryside – which he had loved. Staring at his little blue plastic telephone, at his mushroom money box with the key missing, at his dinky cars, his shelves of books, his musical box – and none of it had meant anything. She had felt nothing. And now she couldn't bring herself even to open the door.

She dreaded most of all the evocative smell that waited for her inside the room. The little-child smell, clean and powdery. And there were so many booby traps to remind her of his babyhood. She had never been able to bear throwing anything away. There were nappy pins still in the drawer, zinc and castor oil cream, and the samples she'd been given at the hospital of baby soap and nappy rash ointment. There was his bone rattle and one abandoned rusk hardened into stone and the exquisite pair of bootees Alice had brought back for him from Spain, white, embroidered with little pink and blue rosettes, too beautiful to wear.

If she could just bring herself to peep around the door, to open it a crack so that she could see the corner of the shelf with the hammer pegs on it and the edge of the curtain. It would be a start. She strained to remember which animal sat on the left of the windowsill. It might be Panda; that wouldn't be so bad ... it might be Lion, or Mouse, or Koala. As long as it wasn't Sammy, his teddy bear. Laurie had slept with Sammy every night since his first birthday, had held long conversations with him as they lay face to face on their sides under the duvet. Sammy knew more about Laurie than she did.

But it wouldn't be Sammy. Sammy was in Laurie's bed behind the angle of the door, propped up on the pillow where Laurie himself had left him.

She pressed her face down into the dusty carpet, her knuckles hard against the door. Waves of panic broke through her; her curled hands grew cold and clammy with fear and nausea.

My little boy, my darling ... come to me.

But the empty bed, the lion, donkey, panda, koala, mouse and duckling ranged along the windowsill; the dinky cars on the radiator shelf, the tinkly ball, the small blue painted rocking chair – the very silence mocked her. He is not here, it said. He has gone.

Chapter Five

WHEN SHE WOKE SHE WAS LYING ON HER SIDE STARING at a pile of pillows heaped near her nose. She still slept in the old Italian four poster she and Tom had bought at an antiques fair in Lewes in the first week of their marriage. They had gone to try for some sketches Tom had his eye on, and there had been the bed.

After securing the paintings at a low cost – they were by a little-known artist and nobody else had shown much interest – Tom began to bid for the bed, Rhea by his side, tense, almost hopping with desire, and in a few minutes it was theirs. They had to wait a week for it to be delivered and when it arrived in pieces and had been lugged upstairs and reassembled with some difficulty by Tom, Rhea, excited by the image in her mind of delicate soft flounces billowing against the smooth, purple-brown sheen of the wood, began to swathe it in white spotted muslin. She spent hours making the draperies and when it was done Tom laughed and said it was pretty but dreadfully virginal, that she was surprisingly virginal altogether, considering her books, hadn't they better do something about it?

He took her there and then, pinning her down like a starfish on the ancient mattress over which she had thrown a pale blue satin quilt to show off the bed to him. He was passionate, lustful, painstaking, excited by the newness of their surroundings and wanting to arouse in her an avidity to match his own. At first she resisted, accusing him inside her head of not taking time to appreciate the aesthetic beauty of the bed – nonsensical thoughts – she was not ready, not in the mood. But he kissed her breasts, rammed her head roughly down over the side of the bed, kneaded his hands fiercely into her stomach and lightly down her loins, and in a moment she was frantic, ready, crying out to him the appeal he loved to hear and responded to with a kind of triumph. He knew how to rouse her, she told him often, often, when exhausted, spent, rueful – and he told her for a fact that she never made love willingly.

She used to ask herself if this was true. She often wanted him but she didn't volunteer herself. Pride and shame held her back. She had no idea where it came from. Fear too that she might disappoint him or that her own desire might ebb. She didn't trust herself. If he made the first move then these anxieties were removed. She told herself that she was selfish. You're a congenital prude, Tom said, laughing because he knew he could always overcome her.

She stared at the outline of Tom's pillows against the window light. She remembered that she had woken late in the night on the floor outside Laurie's room, shivering with cold, and had dragged herself to bed. She had not changed into her night things; she was still in them from the morning before when she had gone upstairs to change and had forgotten. That was after the old lady had called.

Oh my God. Mrs Mander. She'd forgotten all about her, she'd forgotten to go and see to her wireless.

She threw back the duvet and got out of bed. She must go now, at once, before she got around to thinking, before the panic got hold of her again. But she had to wash her hair first; it was stiff with dirt and smelt. She couldn't remember when she had last washed it or washed herself. Perhaps she smelt too. She couldn't remember so many things. She remembered going into the bathroom but had she washed? She'd better have a bath.

Because it wasn't possible to bathe with all Laurie's toys around her she took them off the edge of the bath one by one, wrapped them in his towel and put the little bundle on the floor outside his bedroom. She did this feverishly and fast, not letting herself think of anything at all.

She had a quick, thorough bath and washed her hair. She wrapped her hair in a towel, turban fashion, and dried herself. She heard Tom's voice saying, 'You've got legs like a games mistress, strong and sexy, muscles in all the right places.' She had a good figure, slim and taut, with a narrow waist and full breasts. She'd always felt so full of health, so well. Tom had adored her body, which had no blemishes. No swollen veins or stretch marks, no extra fat anywhere, but not too thin either, with a gentle roundness, a tapering line from hip to ankle and shoulder to wrist that was a joy he said, to his artist's eye. She had sat for him frequently without clothes, a little abashed at first but soon relaxed, careless and liberated.

'You see?' Tom had laughed at her as she skipped about naked, making coffee for them both during a break in the sitting. 'See how you respond to tuition? If you ask me it's a good thing I happened along.'

Toby had stumbled in on them once. Rhea was

modelling for Tom in the kitchen. He had seated her on an old wooden chair by the open range, placing her feet on the fender at the base of the stove. He'd draped a towel round her middle and bent her forward, her body turned slightly towards him, her arms raised and her hands holding her hair up off her neck; an excruciating position to hold, especially since Tom refused to let her rest her elbows on anything. The focus of the composition was to be the firelight playing on her naked neck and breasts. He called it *Girl with a Stove.*

When the knocking came on the back door she moved instinctively to lower her arms but Tom said, 'Don't move your arms, whatever you do,' and went on painting.

Toby put his head round the door, said, 'Oh, sorry,' and withdrew.

'Come in, Toby,' Tom shouted. 'We'll have none of your prudishness in here if you don't mind. Come in, for fuck's sake, sit down and wait a moment while I finish.'

'Come on, Tom, there's no need to be rude.' Rhea's voice was muffled by her arms and looped up fronds of hair 'Poor Toby is embarrassed. So am I. Let him go. Better still, let me get dressed. Much better idea, my back is breaking.'

'Not yet,' Tom said between his teeth, his eyes on the painting and on Rhea.

During the long silence that followed she heard the scrape of a chair being pulled out at the other end of the room, a match struck as Toby lit his pipe and the grate of his heels on the quarry tiles as he stretched out his long legs in front of him. She could see him in her mind's eye, crossing his feet, settling down and leaning his head against the back of the chair, relaxing as he smoked. Knowing his tendency to be almost pathologically self-denying, his pipe smoking was in Rhea's opinion the most unlikely of all his habits. He smoked with an air of conscious relaxation as if he thought it would be good for him, as other people did yoga or meditation.

'Do you have to sit with your back to her like that?' Tom said absently, ten minutes later. He was almost finished. 'Does the sight of her offend you?'

'Of course not. But I might offend her.'

'Oh, she won't mind. You don't, do you, Rhea?' Then, without waiting for an answer, 'Anyway, she's got a beautiful body, beautiful. I could paint her for ever and never grow tired of her. She's so strong – so fluid, like water.' He rambled on. He was always cheerful if things had gone well.

Rhea said suddenly, 'I want to stop now, Tom.'

'Okay, okay. I've finished for now, anyway.'

She leaned back and let go her hair which fell warm and soft and heavy around her shoulders. She stood up, releasing the towel which fell away from her hips and left her naked. She felt angry without quite realising why. 'You wouldn't mind who saw me like this, would you?'

Tom looked surprised.

She picked up the towel, wrapped it round herself and walked past him, past Toby who glanced at her without expression, and out of the room, slamming the door.

'I wouldn't say that.' Tom seemed hardly to have heard what she'd said. 'I'm pleased with this. It's good. *Girl with a Stove.*'

RHEA BANGED on Mrs Mander's front door and called out softly, so as not to startle her, 'Hello, Mrs Mander? It's me, Rhea.'

The chain rattled, the door opened as suddenly as though Mrs Mander had been standing there in the tiny square hall all night waiting for her knock, and she stepped inside. Mrs Mander hobbled eagerly ahead into the small dining room to the left of the hall. She didn't seem aware that a whole night had passed since she'd rung Rhea's front door bell.

'In here, dear.' Her voice quavered but after a brief pause persisted, resentful, demanding. 'My radio's broken, and all my clocks have gone wrong too ... that one isn't working ... look, dear, they've all gone wrong.' She gestured hopelessly towards the mantelpiece and let her hand fall at her side, turning to look at Rhea with an expression of bitterest pessimism.

The hands on the heavy mahogany clock in the centre of the mantelpiece had stopped at a quarter to three. Rhea said bracingly, afraid that the old lady might start to weep and anxious to forestall her, 'Let's have a look at your radio first.'

She crouched beside the old fashioned radiogram in the heart of which a green light glowed. 'It's lighting up, anyway, so it can't be anything too serious. Let's see ...'

'Of course it's serious,' Mrs Mander protested shrilly. 'It isn't working! Look – it doesn't work, there isn't a sound.' Desperately anxious to show, to convince, she edged her way at alarming speed round the heavy oak table standing square and ugly in the middle of the room.

'Here we are.'

'... morning story comes from Birmingham,' said the radio. 'John Aylesford reads his own story, *Surprise Ending*.'

Rhea smiled. 'There you are. It's working.'

'Well!' Mrs Mander seemed completely amazed. 'However – whatever did you do? How did you do that?'

'It was switched to gramophone instead of sound so the radio wouldn't work. It's that switch there, see? It has to be left over that way, not there, or there. If you leave it where it is it'll be all right.' She had no hope that these instructions would be remembered.

'But I never use the gramophone.' Mrs Mander shook her head. Her voice trembled. 'Never touch it. Do you think someone turned it over? But who would do a thing like that?' She looked fearfully over her shoulder at the front door then gazed at Rhea in bewilderment, her lips quivering.

'Perhaps you switched it over by mistake, thinking it was the volume control.'

'Oh, I never touch that switch. No, *I* haven't touched it. I wonder who it could have been ... who ...?'

'Well, it's all fixed now. If you leave it like that it should be all right. Shall we have a look at the clock now?'

'It isn't working ... look.'

She was easy to distract, that was something. And she'd remembered about the clock. Rhea lifted it down from the mantelpiece. 'It may need winding. Have you got the key?'

'It's in there. In the back there's a little hole, and the key's in the hole. Here, let me have a look ... isn't it there?' Alarm braced the frail voice. 'Who could have taken it? Whoever would do such a thing?'

'Perhaps it's up here on the mantelpiece.' This was catching, she was beginning to feel slightly rattled herself. 'I'll have a look.'

'It won't be up there. I should have seen it if it was lying up there. I had a letter I wanted you to read, now where did I put it?' Distracted again, she became more cheerful. 'Can you see an air letter there, dear? My eyes are so bad. Is there a blue letter tucked behind the clock there? Or perhaps it's on the windowsill. I've got so many papers all over the place. Now, where can it be?'

'I'll put the clock back till the key turns up. An air letter?'

'You've found it?' Mrs Mander spun round, her face lit up. 'Oh! I thought you said you'd found it. Oh dear, what a shame. Wherever can it be?'

'There's a note up here about a chiropodist appointment on Friday May 10th. Oh dear, that's today. Did you know about this? It says ten o'clock. Um – that's in twenty minutes.'

'Chiropodist appointment? *I* haven't got a chiropodist appointment. What's that about, who put that note up there?'

'There's someone at the door. I'll see who it is. Are you expecting somebody?'

'*I'm* not expecting anybody. Perhaps they'll know who ... I've lost the letter I wanted you to read. Now, wherever can it be?' Bowing deeply, she shuffled through drifts of paper piled like autumn leaves along the low windowsills.

On the doorstep stood Nurse Paul, the district nurse. She was plain, her body thick set, her legs short and squat, but glorious red-gold hair adorned her head like a crown. She came in every day and sometimes twice, to make sure her patient had survived another night and to check that she had taken her pills.

'Hello, dear.' She beamed at the sight of Rhea. 'Is she ready then?'

'No, she isn't.' Rhea held out the appointment card. 'She doesn't remember. I've just told her about it but she doesn't believe me.'

'Oh God, I wonder if she forgot to take her pills this morning. Did you take your pills this morning, dear?' she bellowed, striding in and enfolding Mrs Mander within one powerful arm.

'My pills? *I* don't know.'

Nurse Paul raised her eyes skyward. 'I'll have to tell the doc. I don't think she's to be trusted – are you, dear? We'll have to get you one of those boxes with the days of the week on them, won't we? I thought the day would come,' she said to Rhea. 'Now, dear, are you ready to come with me now? I'm taking you to see the chiropodist – up at the day centre, do you remember? Some hopes. He's going to look at your feet.' She gave a great bellow of amusement. 'Come on.' She threw an arm round her and gave her a squeeze. The flesh bulged round the short blue sleeves. All of Nurse Paul's clothes tended to look too tight. 'Are you coming with me, then?'

Rhea gave Nurse Paul the appointment card. 'Shall I get your coat, Mrs Mander?'

Mrs Mander looked at her, then at Nurse Paul. 'You're taking me to the centre?' She seemed completely bemused by the speed and turn of events.

'Yes, dear, that's right, to have your feet seen to. Only we'll have to get a move on, dear, or we'll be late.' Nurse Paul nodded vigorously and released her.

'All right, then.' She began to shuffle towards the door. 'I'll need my stick. And my keys. I haven't got my handbag.' She turned and stretched out her hand gropingly towards the table. 'Is that it there?'

'This?' Rhea picked it up. 'It's a nice one, isn't it? Shall I check your keys are inside?'

'Could you, dear?'

Rhea opened the brown leather bag. A large bunch of keys, a black spectacle case, a handkerchief, a wallet stuffed with ten-pound notes. Hastily she closed the bag. 'They're there.'

When Mrs Mander was safely installed in the front seat

of Nurse Paul's blue council minivan Rhea said quietly across the rooftop to Nurse Paul, 'She really shouldn't carry so much cash around with her, it isn't safe. Anybody could take advantage of her. Somebody ought to be responsible for her. Hasn't she got any relations?'

'Oh, I know, dear, it's awful, she'll be robbed one of these days. Still, what can we do about it? She goes down to the bank and takes it out, then she forgets she's got it. Nobody can stop her if she wants to get her hands on her own money, can they? Still, it's a shame.' She climbed in behind the wheel and shouted across her passenger, her voice deadened by the glass, 'Well, here's loving and leaving you. Must be off now, or we'll be ever so late.'

Rhea walked up her own front path. She stood in the sun in the front garden, staring unseeing at the dead flowers on the forsythia bush by the gate. She thought about Mrs Mander, about her husband George who had died last year, about Brendan their son, in Canada. She thought hard about them all, trying to feel pity, trying to subdue the hard beating of her heart and the panic she could feel again rising like a fever in her blood.

'Hello.'

Rhea turned round.

Alice was standing by the gate. 'Can I come in? Are you busy?'

Rhea looked at her in great surprise. Alice didn't usually drop in, she phoned first. There she stood as if nothing had happened, as if everything was normal. 'No ... not at all.' She smiled. 'I'll make us some coffee.'

In the kitchen she switched the kettle on and set out mugs. She opened the fridge door. 'Oh dear. No milk.'

'That's okay. I take mine black. Shall we sit outside? It's such a fab day.'

It was. Rhea hadn't noticed. She made the coffee and they took their mugs outside and sat side by side on the terrace steps, Rhea wondering why Alice had come. Alice picked at her fingernails and brushed invisible specks off her immaculate blue jeans. She looked as pretty as ever but there were shadows under her blue eyes.

'I thought I might go to church tomorrow.' She set her mug down by her feet. 'I think it would be good for me. Dick was cross when I told him I was thinking of going; he can't bear that sort of thing.'

'What sort of thing?'

'Oh, you know. A lot of nonsense, he calls it. Richard Whatsit is his hero.'

'Dawkins?'

'That's the one. Dick thinks he's wonderful. Talks a lot of sense, he says. Still, I'm gonna go.' She said casually after a pause, 'You know that curate? Do you still see as much of him as you used to? What's his name? Tobias?'

That was why she'd come.

Alice snorted, turning her face up to the sun. 'Wherever did his mother dream that one up?'

Rhea could have told her, but she stayed silent. Toby's mother had been sitting in the theatre watching *Tobias and the Angel* when her waters broke, Toby had told her. They had managed to get her to the hospital in time for the actual delivery, but attributing his early arrival to the emotion engendered in her by the play and deeply thankful for having the whole thing over and done so quickly, she had named him Tobias. She had vacillated for some time, Toby had told Rhea, between Tobias and Raphael.

'Can you imagine what my life would have been like, and me a priest, if she'd come down the other way?'

Rhea shifted her feet on the paving stones. 'Tobias

means God is good. It's coming back into fashion, I think. It suits him, don't you think?'

Alice said nothing. She ground a dead leaf, left over from autumn, into the stone with her trainer.

Rhea cast about for something to say. 'How are the children?'

'Oh, all right.' Alice sighed. 'They've gone for a walk with Minna. She's quite good with them. She's been with us four whole months now and she hasn't even hinted at wanting to go. The last one only stayed three weeks, and the one before that, that French creature who never stopped eating, d'you remember her? Bright red hair. Danielle, that was her name. She only stayed five weeks. It's Dick. He will try and flirt with them. He treats them like sex-starved slaves.' She picked up her mug and sipped.

'How is he? Dick?'

'Oh ... Dick's never at home. He's probably got a woman somewhere; I wouldn't be surprised. He's got the flat, you see. He only comes home at weekends, and not always then.'

'Oh dear, poor Alice.' Rhea rubbed her eyes with the heels of her hands.

'Oh, I'm used to it, darling. I stopped crying over Dick years ago. What's the use? He doesn't like me, and that's that.'

Rhea dropped her hands. 'You don't mean that.'

'I do.'

Rhea frowned. 'But he married you, he must like you. You've been married how long?'

'Six years.' She sipped her coffee. 'He used to, 'course he did. He left his first wife to marry me, did I ever tell you? I was his secretary. Good one, too, though I say it myself.' She sighed. 'I was the light of his life for a while. It's the children that are the problem. He's quite fond of them really, but only when they're being good little cardboard cut outs, you know? The minute they start behaving like actual human beings he goes round the twist in about five minutes.' She shook her head, sipped again. 'Having children was the worst mistake we ever made. He might still love me if it wasn't for them.' She stopped suddenly. 'Oh God. Oh, how awful. I'm so tactless. Tactless me.' Her words resounded in the crestfallen silence.

'It's all right, it's got nothing to do with anything, don't worry about it.' Rhea picked up her mug and held it, warming her hands. But her heart had started to beat faster.

'I wish I hadn't been away at the time. You had nobody. Poor Rhea.'

'I had Toby. He's been marvellous. Honestly, it's all right.' She looked away with careful composure. Please Alice, she thought, don't say any more. Now she had at last discovered how to cry an unending supply of water seemed to lurk perilously near the surface, ready to spill over at the slightest hint of sympathy.

'I can't imagine what it would be like to lose one of the children.' Complacently, Alice examined the nails on her left hand. 'I just can't imagine it. Of course, it would be terribly, terribly sad.'

Rhea recoiled, astounded, mortified. She stared down the garden at next door's tabby cat stalking across the lawn.

'Rosemary starts school in September.' Alice's voice was gloomy. 'I'm starting Danny at play group at the same time so at least I'll have a bit of time to myself then. Mind you, Minna's very good with them – they adore her. Danny calls her Mummy sometimes, isn't that a hoot?'

'Don't you mind?'

Alice nibbled a rag nail and considered. 'No. Why

should I? Sometimes I don't feel a bit like their mother, to tell you the truth. Dick certainly doesn't behave like their father. He never sees them if he can avoid it. He leaves coming home till he thinks they'll be in bed.' She shifted her feet. 'He says children are the woman's department. I don't know why he expects me to find them so engrossing. Looking after whining kids was the last thing I had in mind when I married him. Of course, that was a different world. I can't think why I stay with Dick,' she went on after a pause. 'If I had money of my own I'd definitely leave him. The children are the problem.'

'Perhaps Dick really is preoccupied with work. He may be worried about the business.'

'He is a bit, but he could come home if he wanted to, it wouldn't make any difference. He does most of it on the phone anyway. I know, I was his secretary, don't forget. Anyway, that's not what's worrying me.' Her eyes slid to Rhea, then away again. 'It's the sex. He never wants to, he pretends he's tired. That can't have anything to do with the business, can it?'

To Rhea's irritation and surprise Alice suddenly burst into tears. She cried neatly and quietly into a small lace-edged handkerchief from which Rhea caught a whiff of some delicious scent.

Rhea, extremely surprised by the hanky, hankies being associated in her mind with maiden aunts or grandmothers, tried to feel sorry for her. 'Oh dear. Look, oughtn't you to talk to somebody about all this, get some help to sort things out? Relate, or something. Don't they—'

'I'm talking to you.' Alice blew her nose.

'Yes. Yes – but I can't – I don't know what you ought to do.'

'I don't want to *do* anything. I just wanted to tell somebody. It gets a bit nerve wracking, bottling it up the whole time.'

'Of course. Of course it does.'

'Sometimes I wish I could talk to Toby … he has such a sweet face, so understanding and kind.'

'What, about sex?'

Alice heaved a breath and tucked her hanky back in the sleeve of her tee shirt. Her tears had dried as quickly as they had come. 'Well, about everything. I'm sure it would be a help. Do you think I could talk to him?' She slid a glance at Rhea.

Toby was a grown-up; he could look after himself. 'You could always try. You know him to speak to, don't you? He's busy, of course. He has all kinds of committees and things in the evenings.'

'He finds time to come here.'

'We're friends. He went to school with Tom.'

'I don't see what that's got to do with anything. Dick's known Jeremy Ashcroft for years but it doesn't stop him playing footsie with me under the table when they come to dinner. He bruised my leg quite badly last time.' She snorted. 'He's a sexy brute, that Ashcroft. His wife is too. They're probably at it like rabbits. It doesn't seem to stop him wanting to have a go at me though.'

Rhea tried to remember what sex was like. 'Well anyway, Toby never tries anything like that with me if that's what you're thinking. It wouldn't occur to him.'

'Hmmn.' Alice's expression said that she didn't believe her.

Rhea suppressed a rush of anger. 'Toby is not interested in me in any way other than as a friend and Tom's wife. You mustn't start imagining things. He isn't the sort of man who's out for himself. He's a good man.'

'Yeah yeah.'

'No, Alice.'

They sat for a while in silence. Rhea drained her mug and stood up. She made up her mind. 'Come to tea on Tuesday. Toby often drops in on Tuesdays. You can meet him properly and you won't have to waste any more time speculating about him and making fantasies.'

Standing in the hall when Alice had gone, Rhea reflected that just now with Alice she had felt a surge of real anger. How encouraging; perhaps this meant that the numbness inside her might eventually thaw. Her mind felt illuminated, as though a light had been switched on inside her head. Alice's needling had done her good.

Footsteps crunched on the gravel, approaching the front door. She went to open it. Alice had left something and come back for it. She was always leaving things – umbrellas, handbags, gloves.

Toby stood with his hand raised to ring the bell. Behind him the garden was full of bird song, the sunlight gentle on the small front lawn. Rhea heard and felt all the beauty of the visible world from which she had been cut off, as if she'd been sleepwalking and had suddenly woken up.

'Toby.' Already the elation was receding. She tried to hold onto it. 'Come in.' She stared at him, willing the happiness not to fade.

'I've been seeing someone down the road and thought I'd pop in. I can't stop for more than a few minutes, I'm afraid.' He frowned. 'What's happened?'

'I don't know.' She put both her hands in his.

Toby looked down at her. She stood looking up at him, her hands enclosed in his, her eyes radiant, alive. It was almost like seeing the old Rhea. He had hesitated to come, feeling that he mustn't see her so often, that for his own sake as much as hers he ought to keep away.

The sight of her animated face was like an unhoped-for miracle, and at the same time he felt unworthily disappointed that this change had not come about through him: she could evidently get on without him; perhaps better without him; it was like a sign. From now on he wouldn't visit so often. But he was cheered by her expression which was full of tenderness and affection.

'It's great you're feeling brighter. Did something happen?'

She shook her head. 'I can't explain. I felt a moment of hope. Simple as that.' She gave a dismissive shake of her head. End of subject then. 'Will you come to tea on Tuesday? Alice wants to meet you.'

'Alice? Alice Carter, d'you mean? Funny, I was thinking about her just recently. She's been away, hasn't she? Greece or somewhere.'

'She's only been back a week or two. Will you come?'

'Don't see why not.' Her fingers felt so small and soft in his hands. He glanced over his shoulder through the open door, longing to stay. 'Sorry, Rhea, I can't stop I'm afraid. Flying visit.'

'Of course.' She made a little relinquishing movement of her fingers and let go of his hands. 'Go on. I'll see you soon.'

SHE STOOD and watched as he strode off down the path. He turned at the gate and lifted a hand in farewell. Already the light in her mind was fading, the darkness coming down. She wondered fleetingly whom he had been visiting and where he'd left his bike, and slowly closed the door. The sound of the Yale bolt sliding home seemed to trigger something inside her head and the healing illumination, already waning, snapped off as suddenly as it had come.

That night she had the first of a series of nightmares that began to torment her, making her afraid to fall asleep. She and Laurie were on the South Coast somewhere, playing and laughing together on the downs at the top of steep chalk cliffs. Below the cliffs the sea surged and broke over jagged black rocks. There was an atmosphere of love and happiness in the dream. They played the wheel game, a game they'd often played in life, Rhea holding Laurie by his hands and spinning him round at arms' length until his legs were horizontal and she was whirling on the spot under their combined impetus, spinning, spinning, both of them laughing and breathless, Laurie squealing with delight.

But in the dream at the height of the spin she let go his hands and he flew out over the cliff and down, his scream of betrayal and terror echoing in her ears, his legs and arms jerking in an instinctive effort to save himself, and she saw her own face suddenly devilish, her laughter demonic.

She woke to the sound of her own frightened breathing to a reality scarcely less horrifying than the dream. She threw back the duvet, hurried to the open window and leaned on the sill, her body shaking, her heart throbbing with terror, looking out onto the four o'clock quiet of the street.

A slender streetlamp cast a misty aureole against the young cedar of Lebanon nestling in the skirts of a giant pine, one of a range of tall pines and beeches fringing the garden on the other side of the road. The lamplight illuminated the cedar's straight, pink-mottled trunk and the lowest layer of boughs, narrow, horizontal slabs of paler green. The ancient trees behind, outlined against the greying sky, stood immobile in the windless darkness like drooping skirted dancers, huge and old, their gnarled arms gracefully spread, poised as though waiting for some expected music to begin, to dance.

She pulled on her dressing gown and ran down to the kitchen to fetch the radio. She came back upstairs with it, turned it to Classic FM, put it on the floor and leaned against the windowsill listening to the slow movement from Mahler's Fifth symphony, her heart thudding, willing the panic to subside.

Gradually the nightmare receded and her pulse slowed. The sky lightened and still she stayed leaning against the windowsill, comforted by the music, listening on and on: Mozart, Beethoven, Vivaldi ... and finally, Strauss' *Blue Danube* waltz.

A dawn wind rose and the branches of the cedar began to sway as though in time to the music. *See, Laurie?* her heart said. *Look at the tree ... it's dancing.*

Chapter Six

ALICE KNOCKED ON THE DOOR AT HALF PAST NINE ON Sunday morning. 'Well, I went,' she said, following Rhea into the kitchen. 'Didn't think much of it, either. Dead depressing, that awful hush and the vicar shouting away at the altar and all the people completely baffled.'

'How do you know they were baffled?' Rhea couldn't help being amused. 'You can't expect to take to it at once. Have you never been to Communion before?'

'I've only been to *church* twice before, not counting christenings. And lots of weddings, of course.'

'Perhaps Evensong would be an easier way to start.'

'I've tried Evensong. I liked that, it felt kind of sexy with the gloom and the lights and all. And I've been to that morning thing, Matins or whatever it's called. But Communion, no thanks. Still, I saw Toby, gorgeous as ever. He is gorgeous, isn't he?' She plonked herself down on a chair and watched as Rhea took the kettle to the sink. 'Who's the girl with the black hair and those two noisy kids? Dunno why she doesn't put them in the kids' crèche thingy.'

'Ann Broucher. She does, usually. There was probably a reason.'

'They were quite disruptive, actually.'

Rhea hid a smile. 'Ann's nice, she's very involved, she organises the flower rota and coffee after the Family Service.'

'Oh. One of those.'

'Someone has to do it.' The kettle boiled. She spooned in coffee and filled the cafetière.

'She and Toby seem to have quite a lot to say to each other. Do you think she's pretty? She's quite old, I suppose?'

'Early thirties, I should think. Wouldn't you like something to eat, Alice? Are you sure you only want coffee?'

'That's fine, thanks. I said I'd be back by half nine and it's that now. Dick's home this weekend. I had something I wanted to ask you. Will you come to dinner, darling, one day next week?'

'Dinner? Oh, Alice ... I don't think so. Not now – not so soon. It's kind of you—' Her stomach clenched. She took down two mugs and fished a teaspoon out of the drawer.

'It won't be formal. Just supper really. Dick and I would love you to come. It would do you good, you must get out sometimes, you can't stay here brooding for ever, you need to get back your interest in life. Anyway, then I can ask Toby.'

'Oh, Alice!'

'I'm desperate to have him over. I must.'

'You hardly know him. You haven't even met him properly yet.'

'Yes, I have. We've spoken at least twice. Anyway, Dick knows him. And I'm meeting him on Tuesday, aren't I? Do say you'll come. Please. Just a few friends, nothing big.

You'll like them, I promise, and it will do you good to get out.'

Just a few friends? So not just her and Toby. Even worse. She couldn't possibly go, she would have to make conversation, and they would ask about Laurie. She couldn't. 'You can ask him to dinner by himself, you don't need me there.' She carried the mugs through to the table in the annexe and pulled out a chair.

'Dick might get suspicious. You must come, then I can tell Dick I'm asking Toby for you.'

'Oh, Alice, do you have to be so devious?'

'Please, darling. Please come. Love you for ever. You must, you have to, I can't manage it unless you do.'

She was impossible. 'Alice, I would hate it, I would behave badly, I don't feel up to meeting strangers yet, you must see that, surely. I don't want to have to talk to people.'

'You're talking to me, aren't you? I need you to come. You must. Please, Rhea. Don't be mean.'

Rhea closed her eyes. 'You are the end.' She sighed. 'Oh, all *right*. I'll come. Under protest, mark you.'

'That's marvellous!' Alice got up, went through to the kitchen and leaned against the dresser, holding her mug and hunching up her shoulders with excitement. She dug down into the bread bin. 'Darling Rhea. I knew you would!'

Rhea got up and trailed after her. 'It isn't marvellous at all.'

'It will be good for you. My good deed for the day. You're running out of bread.' Alice closed the bread bin and chewed enthusiastically. She hugged herself. 'I'm all excited now!'

'I knew you were hungry. You should have said.' Rhea stood leaning against the sink, looking out of the window. She would have to go to the shops tomorrow, that was the last loaf out of the freezer. She dreaded the thought of public places, the ghoulish curiosity of strangers, the genuine distress of those who had known Laurie. Kind Emma at the baker's, for instance. Laurie had always since he could walk been the money giver and change receiver. Emma had loved him. She'd be bound to say something.

So many people had written and she hadn't read any of the letters or cards. She'd come across a pile of them unopened in her desk when she'd been looking for her chequebook yesterday. Perhaps Emma had written; she might expect thanks or give advice.

The front door slammed. Alice had gone again. Had she been rude? She slumped down in the Windsor chair and stared at Alice's mug still sitting beside the bread bin. She must wash up. She was so dreadfully tired. She leaned her head back against the wall, her neck at an uncomfortable angle, and fell asleep.

SOMEONE WAS KNOCKING FURIOUSLY on the front door. The bell rang, strident, and again came the thunderous knocking, as though someone was using a stick or a shoe to make as much row as possible. Bang bang bang. Again, the bell rang.

She opened her eyes. Sunshine was slanting in through the open kitchen door and pooling on the hall floor. She had slept with her head at an awkward angle; her neck hurt when she moved. Half awake, she staggered along the hall to open the door. She waited for the next tyrannical onslaught to subside then opened the door.

'Thank goodness.' Mrs Mander fell forward as the door opened and put out a hand to clutch Rhea's arm for support. Her back was bent over even further this morning and her hands must have been shaking when she put on her makeup: her mouth was a smudge of crimson between dollops of white powder adorning each cheek. She clung to Rhea's arm, trembling and tearful. 'I can't remember what I wanted you for.' Her voice quavered, her eyes cast up and down the road for inspiration. 'It's my wireless.' She frowned with the effort of remembering. 'It isn't working.'

Rhea held the angular, weightless arm tightly as they moved at a snail's pace to the square house next door. The arm felt as thin and insubstantial as a chicken bone inside the coat sleeve, beneath the layers of cardigan and blouse. Mrs Mander put her other hand into the hedge every so often for additional support.

'You should have brought your stick,' Rhea remonstrated gently.

In the musty dining room Mrs Mander clutched the table edge with surprising strength and gestured with her free hand in the direction of the radiogram. 'See? It isn't working. Not a peep out of it.'

Rhea transferred the switch from gramophone to sound. 'There you are. It's up to its tricks again.'

Amazement dawned in the crumpled face, morphed into misery. 'I've lost my bag. All my money. Chequebook, keys – everything.'

'I'll help you look for it. Try not to worry. Hadn't you better sit down, Mrs Mander? You're shaking so.'

'Call me Mavis.' Obediently she sat, her eyes on Rhea.

'You sit there on the sofa and I'll make you a cup of tea, then we'll look for your bag. When did you have it last?' she called through from the kitchen, filling the kettle at the sink. She looked down at the worn lino, at the ancient gas stove and the ascot water heater over the sink. George Mander might have been well off, but he was surely mean; he could at least have given his wife a fridge and some central heating. How on earth did she keep warm in the winter?

'I had it when I got back with Nurse. I know I did because I would have needed my keys to get in and they were in my bag. I came in here and took my coat off ... and Nurse came in and chatted for a while and then she went off and I sat here until I came to find you.' She hesitated, struck by an idea. 'Do you think Nurse—'

'No.' Rhea set down a tray with milk in a jug, a cup and saucer, sugar and a spoon. Mrs Mander looked at her with sly excitement in her sunken eyes. Rhea went back into the kitchen to make the tea.

When she returned with the pot Mrs Mander had sunk into a mournful reverie, her chin resting on her chest.

'Have you enough food for today, Mavis? There's nothing much in the larder. I noticed when I was looking for the tea. You haven't much bread left.'

'I don't like getting too much at a time, it goes stale so quick. What I like is those soft rolls you buy in a cellophane bag. I like those, they're easy on the teeth. I don't get in much food as a rule, I get a good meal up at the centre so I don't need to keep much food in the house.'

'The centre's closed on a Sunday, isn't it?' She put a cup of tea on the table level with Mrs Mander's nose.

'Oh no, it's never closed. We get a good meal there every day. That's where I go to get my feet seen to, you know.'

Rhea knew perfectly well that the centre was closed on Sunday. She would have to bring her some food.

'Is it Sunday tomorrow?'

'It's Sunday today.'

'Today? No, it's not. My sister's coming from Ashtead on Sunday. We're going out to have lunch with Mr Perry.' She picked up her cup with a hand that shook.

'Who's Mr Perry?'

'He's one of the partners in George's firm. He's been good to me, he has, since George died. Comes here sometimes and takes me out to tea in Richmond Park or for a drive in the country.' Cautiously she sipped her tea.

'How lovely! How is your sister?'

'Oh, shocking. She's got those things in her eyes, you know, what do you call 'em ... she's got to have an operation.'

'Cataracts?'

'That's it. Can't see to read or anything. But she's got her family to look after her, they live near and she sees her daughter every day. That's my niece Irene, she's a nice girl, she is, not like some I could mention.' Her teacup clattered in the saucer.

'Some?'

'George's family. Vultures they are. They can't be bothered with me, oh no. They only came to visit when George was alive because they wanted to borrow money. They ring me up, you know.'

'Do they?'

Mrs Mander lowered her voice mysteriously. 'They ask for money.' Her voice hardened. 'But I won't give them a penny. Not a penny. Brendan's the same.' She lifted her cup again.

'Is he?' Rhea remembered Brendan; she'd met him on his last visit over from Canada when his father was in hospital at death's door. She hadn't liked him much. 'How awful for you. That reminds me, I must look for your bag.'

'What d'you want with my bag?'

'You lost it. You wanted me to look for it.'

'I never did. I haven't lost my bag.'

'Well, where is it then?' Rhea snapped, her patience deserting her.

'It's here.' She poked around herself on the sofa. 'It was here a moment ago. 'Tisn't here now. Did I lose it?'

She turned eyes heavy with the complexity of the mystery onto Rhea, who relented. 'You told me you had.'

'Well, I never. What shall I do?'

'Don't worry, we'll find it. Now where do you think it might be? Are there any special places you've been where you might have laid it down?'

'Nurse Paul,' she said at the door half an hour later, 'she's lost her bag and everything in it. We've searched high and low and it's nowhere. She's so muddled, she keeps contradicting herself, and she has no food in, she thinks the centre is open today and it isn't, is it, on a Sunday?'

'Now now, calm down, dear.' Bulky and vigorous, Nurse Paul filled the tiny hall. Under the dark cap her gold hair gleamed. 'Hello, dear,' she shouted up the stairs. 'It's only Nurse.' She grinned at Rhea. 'It'll turn up. It always does. Have you tried the suitcase on top of her wardrobe?'

'Of course not,' Rhea said indignantly.

'Ah well, that's where it'll be then. She's started doing all these funny things, see. It's come on rather quickly actually.' She plunged into the dining room.

Rhea pursued her. 'What has?'

'Senile dementia, that's what she's got, I'm afraid.' She dumped her attaché case down on a chair.

'But she's so lucid most of the time.'

Nurse Paul nodded, glancing professionally around. 'Yes, but it's getting worse. Now where is she, for goodness' sake? I wonder if she's forgotten to take her pills. Mrs Mander, dear!' she bellowed suddenly. 'What are you up to now?'

'I'm up here,' came the disconsolate reply, rather

muffled. 'I can't get the door of the airing cupboard open. It's locked itself and the key isn't here.'

Nurse Paul raised her eyes skywards and lumbered out. 'For goodness' sake,' Rhea heard her muttering as she jogged up the steep stairs, 'what did you want to get into the airing cupboard for anyway? Oh! Thank heaven for small mercies.'

The voices mingled, Nurse Paul's sonorous and soothing as a monastery bell, Mrs Mander's plaintive as a child's. Their footsteps creaked overhead, moving from the landing to Mrs Mander's bedroom overhead. Rhea sat down on an upright chair by the table and put her elbows on the table among the tea things, comforted by the companionable noises which washed over her soothingly like the distant sound of waves. She wanted people to be there but not their voices, demanding, nerve-wracking with the ever-present threat of a direct appeal.

Thumps and bangs as if heavy objects were being dropped on the floor came from above. Weighty footsteps vibrated on the stairs and Nurse Paul came in, her hair awry under her cap. She looked harassed. 'Goodness knows what she's done with that bloody bag this time. Look dear, she's going out with her friend Mrs Whatshername at twelve and her sister's coming over to go out with them too. Reason I came today was to get her ready in case she'd forgotten. You pop off now, I'll do the washing up. I expect you've had enough, eh?' She stood leaning on one muscular arm on the table, surveying Rhea with kindly dispassion. 'I'll tidy her up and see to her. You go off home now.'

'What about her keys?' Rhea stood up and feeling suddenly lost, started to collect the tea things onto the tray.

'She's got a spare in that drawer there. She's forgotten, needless to say, but it's there if it's needed. You leave the tea things, dear, I'll do them. Thanks for making the tea, it's nice for her if you can pop in every so often; she does get low sometimes, especially at weekends.'

She ushered Rhea to the door and stood watching as she walked down the path. At the gate Rhea turned to wave goodbye but the front door was already clicking shut and Rhea, feeling snubbed, thought that Nurse Paul had seemed awfully anxious to see her go.

Chapter Seven

Setting the tea things out on a tray in the kitchen, Rhea watched through the window as Toby uncurled into the deck chair she'd put out for him on the terrace. He swept back his hair with both hands, leaned his head back and closed his eyes.

When she went out to join him he was fast asleep. She sat down beside him on the top step of the flight of stone steps that led down to the lawn. Laurie would have been waking now from his afternoon nap. He would be sitting on the stairs still clutching Sammy against his vest, his hair standing out in a halo round his head, flat at the back where he had lain on it, his eyes large and round, his expression solemn, groggy with sleep but trustful, echoing everything she said slowly and huskily as they planned the afternoon ahead.

'After we've had our lunch, shall we go and feed the ducks?'

'Feed the ducks.' Pleased look.

'We might see some pigeons too.'

'Pigeons too.' Even better.

'And hear the lovely church bells!'

'Lovely church bells.' He roused himself suddenly. 'And duckies say hullo a Lonnie.'

'But dinner first.'

'Dinner first.' Then the slow grin, the hunching of his thin shoulders with pleasure and anticipation. 'After dinner sweets, too.'

'After dinner. Dinner first.'

'No sweets now.'

'Dinner first. Gorgeous dinner. Come and see.'

Then hand in hand the slow plodding down the stairs, pausing to sniff the roses on the chest in the hall, to point at the porcelain dove on the windowsill, to bang the gong.

A flutter of wings brought her back to the present. A blue tit had flown down from the cherry tree and alighted on an old bread roll which she'd hurled out onto the lawn that morning. The tiny bird swung, balanced capably like a sailor on a rocking boat, working at the bread with tiny, forceful pecks, turning its little panda face incessantly left and right, right and left and over its shoulder. How did they manage to stay so lively with all that worry on their minds?

'How peaceful it is here. I'll go to sleep if I'm not careful.' Toby's quiet voice seemed to grow out of the stones of the terrace behind her. He yawned suddenly. 'Sorry. It's been a bit of an afternoon. Had an interview with an enormous Polish gentleman who seems to think it's okay for him to thrash his wife insensible twice a day. Alcoholic, apparently. He doesn't understand a word of English and was paralytic during the interview so you can imagine how far we got. He's coming to see me tomorrow when he's sobered up.'

'What does his wife think about it?'

'I don't know, I didn't see her. Not much, I shouldn't think.'

'I know somebody Polish who might be able to help. He's the gardener at Dick and Alice's. Theirs is that lovely Georgian house at the end of the avenue, Hammond House. His English is good.'

'How well do you know him? Do you think he'd be willing to help with this gentleman? His name's Hulski, by the way.'

'Don't see why not. He's quite friendly. He was lovely to Laurie, he made up stories for him about the stone lions on the gateposts. His name's Tad. Shall I go up and ask him now?'

'Oughtn't we to ask Dick first?' He leaned back again and closed his eyes.

'He's bound to have some free time; they don't own him. Perhaps you're right, though, I'll give Alice a ring.'

'I could wander up there if you like.'

'Alice is coming to tea; we can ask her then. No,' as Toby opened his eyes and started to sit up, 'you wait here, you look so comfortable it seems a shame to move you.' She stood up. 'I'll walk up and meet her and if Tad's around we'll ask him and report back to you.' She touched him lightly on the shoulder. 'You relax, we won't be long.'

Walking up the Avenue she realised with a small shock that something felt different: she wasn't dreading the meeting with Tad even though she hardly knew him. If the subject of Laurie came up she was almost sure she'd be able to manage not to get upset. Almost. The threat of disintegration through having to talk about Laurie skated over the surface of her imagination like a dancer on thin ice over deep water, not quite breaking through. As long as the ice held, all would be well.

Half an hour later she was back, having failed either to encounter Alice or to locate Tad. Alice's white MG was parked behind Toby's motorbike in the drive.

Rhea walked round the side of the house onto the terrace. Alice was perched up on the old garden table, the laden tea tray on the table beside her, chatting to Toby who was lying back in the deck chair with his eyes closed, presumably listening.

Rhea went to join them. 'Hi, Alice! Oh, Toby, you made tea. Well done!'

Toby said, his eyes still closed, 'Alice made it, actually. Hello Rhea. Any luck?'

'I hope you don't mind, darling. The poor man was parched and we didn't know how long you'd be.'

Rhea noticed a cup and saucer on the ground beside Toby's chair. 'No, that's brilliant. Thank you. I walked up to meet you, Alice, I forgot you might come in the car. Afraid not, Toby, Tad was nowhere to be seen.'

'I've been out shopping.' Alice looked sexy and young in tight pink jeans and a sleeveless pink silk top. Silver bangles chinked as she lifted an arm to push back a strand of hair from her face which was turned up to the thin spring sunlight. She had discarded a pair of gold sandals and swung small, pale feet with pink toenails. Even the soles of her feet were as soft and white as a child's. 'I was just telling Toby about salsa classes.'

'Have you been trying to persuade him to go?' Rhea poured herself a cup of tea from the big, rose-covered teapot, added milk and sat down on the step. 'Oh, you didn't bring the biscuits. I'll get them. I suppose you've introduced yourselves. I assumed you had.' She pushed herself to her feet, suddenly weary. 'Toby knows Dick, didn't you say, Toby?'

'I've met him once or twice.'

Alice rolled her eyes. 'Scattering largesse, I suppose. That would be just like Dick. He's keen on his public image. Wants to be loved, you know, like most dictators.'

Toby's eyebrows went up, though his eyes remained closed. 'That's a bit harsh.'

Alice scowled. 'You don't know Dick. He's not a very nice man. Unfortunately, I found out too late. I was infatuated I suppose. Ah well.'

Rhea went into the house to fetch the biscuits. Poor Toby, he was supposed to be off duty but perhaps a priest never was.

She came back with the plate of Island Bakery ginger and chocolate biscuits she'd set out before leaving the house. Someone had thoughtfully moved her cup and saucer from the terrace to the table, presumably to prevent it from being trodden on. 'Have a biscuit, Toby. Take two. Alice?'

'Not for me, darling, got to watch the figure.' Alice straightened her back so that her small breasts pressed provocatively against her thin top and crossed her feet gracefully at the ankles.

She was posing for Toby, Rhea realised, feeling sorry for her. It was a little obvious. Still, she did look nice. And slim. Rhea smiled at her. 'I don't think you need to worry too much, Alice.' She moved the tea tray down onto the terrace and sat down on the steps. She linked her hands around her knees and looked at Alice's swinging feet. It was hard to believe she had been that carefree once.

Allice leaned back on her hands and squinted up at the sun. 'I'll never get a tan at this rate. Only been home from Greece a week or so and even that pathetic glow has vanished. I just freckle, it really is the absolute end. Wish I'd brought a hat now.'

'You can't possibly need a hat in May. Anyway, I love your freckles. You've got such lovely creamy skin.' Rhea made a small grimace. She oughtn't to flatter her, Alice was vain enough already.

'D'you really think so?' Alice held up her arm and admired it, turning it this way and that. She put up her other arm and extended her fingers, her head on one side, making her hands into birds flying. 'My mother had very white hands. It is quite attractive, I suppose.'

Rhea turned her head and saw Toby watching her.

He quickly withdrew his gaze. Some tea slopped from the cup he was holding onto the terrace stones. He looked down at the dark stain beside his chair.

Rhea sipped her tea. 'Have you asked Alice about Tad? I couldn't find him up at the house.'

Alice lowered her arms. 'It's Tad's afternoon off. Of course, you can borrow him, any time. Dick won't know, he's never at home.'

Toby looked dubious. 'I'd rather it was all above board. I'll make an appointment with him in his time off.'

Alice shrugged. 'I'm sure he'll be thrilled to help. Go on about the woman who pinches everyone's washing, Toby, it's riveting.'

'It's common knowledge,' Toby said, darting a look at Rhea. 'It was in the Surrey Comet.'

She hoped she hadn't looked disapproving. 'Of course.'

'I haven't told Alice anything she couldn't pick up on the Kingston grapevine.'

'How disappointing.' Alice put her head on one side. 'Toby's been regaling me with hilarious anecdotes of parish life, Rhea. Kingston sounds a positive den of iniquity! I'd no idea so much drama went on behind those decorous front doors.'

Toby passed his cup across for more tea and said, 'I only told her about Beryl.'

Rhea filled his cup and handed it back. He didn't have to justify himself to her. 'More tea, Alice?'

Alice made a play of draining her cup then jumped down from the table and knelt beside Rhea. The pink jeans strained around her slim thighs. She looked so pretty, all fair and shining as she smiled up at Toby while Rhea poured her tea. 'You will come to dinner with me, won't you?' she coaxed. She was kneeling almost at his feet.

Rhea couldn't help noticing Alice's round breasts pushing against the clingy soft top and her smooth round arms. She felt relieved that at least now her own hair was clean.

Toby drank his tea in one go, put his cup down beside his chair and lay back. He closed his eyes again.

'Rhea's coming,' Alice went on, her head on one side. 'My friends would absolutely love you. I've been trying to persuade him,' she told Rhea.

'You make him sound like some kind of sideshow.'

Alice laughed and picked up her cup and saucer. 'Well, let's face it, darling, he's a bit different from the other men I know. It makes a pleasant change not to be leered at.'

'You needn't worry. Toby never leers.'

Toby's eyebrows went up although his eyes remained closed. 'I *am* here.'

Alice twisted round to look at Rhea. 'You will come, won't you, darlings?'

Rhea shook her head. 'I've changed my mind. I can't possibly. I'm sorry.'

'Oh, *Rhea.*' Alice stood up, holding her cup and saucer. 'You said you would. You promised.'

'I didn't exactly promise.' Rhea looked at Toby for help.

He had opened his eyes again but he was looking at her speculatively. He gave a small shrug. 'It might do you good.'

Alice frowned. 'Why do you need doing good to? You always look the picture of health to me.'

Rhea swallowed a mouthful of tea through the lump in her throat. She couldn't believe Alice; had she honestly forgotten? She looked down the lawn at the flowering currant, in full bloom.

'Oh hell.' Alice screwed up her face. 'I forgot. I'm sorry, darling. Sorry sorry. I'm such a scatterbrain.'

Rhea put her cup down. 'The thing is, I don't think I can face that kind of evening just yet. I'm sorry. I think Toby might have to come by himself.'

'You don't mean that, do you, Rhea?' Alice stepped back to the table, holding her teacup steady so as not to spill the tea. Her bottom was round as an apple and she was so slim that from the back she looked hardly grown up. 'Toby's right, it would do you good to get out. You couldn't possibly mind coming to Dick and I, would you, Rhea? Not if Toby comes too.' She paused by the table and smiled down at him again. 'You haven't said you'll come yet.'

Rhea sighed. *Dick and me.*

Toby, his face set, put his cup and saucer on the ground beside his chair. 'It's very kind of you, Alice.'

He was annoyed with Alice for forgetting about Laurie. He mustn't be; Alice hadn't known Laurie, not really, why should she remember?

Rhea sipped her tea. She didn't want to go to this dinner party in the least. Perhaps she could say she was going then make an excuse nearer the time. Oh dear ... no, that wouldn't be honourable. But she had to shut Alice up, make her stop.

She put her cup down. 'When would you like us to come?'

Alice's face lit up. 'Really?' She put her cup and saucer on the table and jumped up to perch on it again. 'Oh, that's great. Friday? Come about eight.'

'I'll have to see about a—' Rhea stopped and bent her head, her eyes clouding with shock. She'd been going to say, a babysitter. 'Friday is fine.'

Toby, his expression fierce, threw her a glance. He leafed through his diary. 'It's okay for me too, Friday's my day off.'

The sun had gone behind a cloud and a small wind had arisen. Toby glanced at Alice's thin top. 'Aren't you cold?'

'Well, perhaps just a little.'

Rhea said, 'Would you like a jersey? I can get you one of mine.'

'I'm fine, honestly.' Alice crossed her arms and rubbed her hands briskly up and down her goose-fleshed arms. The short silence that followed seemed to Rhea to be full of Alice's unsuitable nakedness. Toby leaned down and put his cup on the ground.

Rhea gave a bird-like cry of alarm and scrambled to her feet. 'The cake! I bought you a cake! Oh Toby, and you're always so hungry!'

Toby caught her hand and held her back. 'I don't want anything more. Perhaps for Alice but—'

'Nothing for me, thanks.'

Toby gripped Rhea's hand as if unwilling to let it go.

Alice frowned down into her teacup. 'There. Finished.' She held her cup out to Rhea. Rhea detached herself from Toby and took it from her.

Toby looked at his watch. He swung his legs round and

put his feet on the ground. 'I'll have to go in a minute. What are we going to do about your friend Tad?'

Alice looked surprised. 'Are you friends, Rhea? He's our gardener.'

Rhea sat down again. She wound her arms around her bent knees. 'Could we have his phone number do you think, Alice? Toby can ring him and find out when it will suit him to come and referee.'

Toby looked at her and smiled. 'Translate,' he corrected her.

He looked so relieved. It was because she had held herself together. She had managed.

Alice looked from Rhea to Toby. 'I can bring him over if it would help. The au pair can always look after the children.'

Toby looked at her in surprise. 'You have children?'

'Two. Danny and Rose.'

'Take your word for it,' Toby said, rubbing his hands over his face.

'I beg your pardon?'

He dropped his hands and looked at her as though surprised by her tone. 'Sorry, what I meant was, I've seen you about quite a bit but you're always on your own. Most of the mothers—'

'Most of the mothers what?'

'I was only going to say that most mothers are more or less glued to their offspring, but you never seem to have yours with you. Don't you like them?'

Rhea watched the thunderclouds gather in Alice's face. 'Toby! Don't be so rude! It's none of your business how Alice chooses to look after her children.' She put out a hand. 'Don't mind Toby, Alice. He only teases people if he likes them.'

She waited in vain for Toby to reinforce this remark.

'Oh, does he?' Alice burst out in a voice like glass breaking. 'Well actually I do mind rather, as a matter of fact.' She jumped down from the table and fished around with her feet for her sandals, her head down, one hand on the table to balance herself. 'It's nobody else's business how often I leave my children with Minna, that's what she's there for. What do you know about it?' she said in Toby's general direction. 'You just – you don't know the first thing about it. You try looking after two whining kids day after day all by yourself, see how you like it.' She began walking away across the terrace. She broke into a run.

Rhea got up and set off after her. 'Alice! Wait!'

Toby said behind her, 'Perhaps they wouldn't whine if you spent more time with them.'

'Alice.' Rhea caught up with her around the corner of the house, out of Toby's sight. 'Do stop. Wait. Don't go off like that, you can't drive when you're upset, it isn't safe.'

Alice pulled away from her restraining hand. 'Leave me alone. What do you care? You don't care what happens to me. Nobody does. He thinks I'm a bad mother and don't care about Danny and Rose. Of *course* I care about them. It's just I'm so miserable and the only thing that cheers me up is to get out of the house and go around the shops or something. They'd be bored sick. He doesn't understand.'

'Of course he doesn't. He shouldn't have said that, he'll be really sorry, honestly, he'll feel bad about it, I know he will. Come back now and I know he'll apologise.'

'He wouldn't mean it, whatever you say, you're just trying to make me feel better. I know what it looks like to someone like him, surrounded by do-gooders all day. He thinks I'm selfish and useless. Just because we're well off. I

82

can't help being married to Dick. I wish I wasn't, I'd do anything not to be – anything. I'd be better off dead.'

'You don't mean that. For goodness' sake Alice, come back.' She watched as Alice disappeared around the corner of the house.

Toby came up behind her. 'Well, bang goes Friday night.'

'Yes, that was really clever. Congratulations. What on earth got into you?'

'All I said was—'

'I was there. I heard. Honestly, Toby. Alice is fragile at the moment, she's miserable, she's going through a bad patch. Just because she doesn't show it.'

'She's a spoilt little madam.'

'I'm amazed at you. You're supposed to care about people, you can't just rubbish someone because they're rich. It's stupid. I thought better of you. Why are you punishing her?'

'I'm not punishing her. Don't be so melodramatic.'

'It's so unlike you.'

'Perhaps you don't know me very well.'

'Perhaps I don't.'

He glanced down at her face and said nothing. They walked in silence back to the terrace. 'I was about to b-beg her pardon for upsetting her.' He picked up the tea tray. 'She didn't give me a chance. She was off like a hare.'

'You hurt her feelings. You shouldn't criticise people without knowing anything about them.'

'Oh, she'll be all right.' They listened as Alice's car started up in the drive. 'Lucky she's parked behind me. That could have been embarrassing.'

'You're not a bit sorry, are you?'

'Nope. All that preening and prancing. I don't think

she's half as upset as she's pretending to be. Or thinks she is. Or something. I'm sorry I upset your tea party.'

'What about Tad?'

'Oh bother.'

'Too right.'

'That is a bind.'

'You are in a funny mood, I must say,' Rhea said, cheering up. 'You remind me of Tom. He used to do that sort of thing all the time. You're usually so careful about not treading on people's toes.' Too careful, she had sometimes thought, exhausted by his unchanging good manners.

'Perhaps it's just that we're getting to know each other better.'

They turned towards the house. Rhea glanced at him. 'You're wrong about Alice, you know. She is a bit vain but she's kind hearted and she's fun. I like her.'

'She's certainly very good to look at. Like a little Dresden shepherdess, all complacency and femininity and guile.'

'Guile?'

'It was childish of me.' Toby put the tea tray down on the kitchen table. 'Tell you what I'll do, I'll call on her on my way home and apologise. Will that do? It might save the Tad situation.'

'Now who's being devious?'

'It was rather unfair to attack her like that. She annoyed me, I suppose.'

'Her marriage is going through a bad patch. And at least she does leave them with Minna, whom they like.' She looked away and said with an effort, 'Some mothers go off and leave their children on their own all day long, as you know very well.'

'Not mothers with her advantages and only because

they haven't any choice, mostly. I'm not condoning it but it's different, that's all.'

'So it *is* her money you're so annoyed about. That's what this is about.'

'No, of course not.' He nudged her with his shoulder. 'Pity there isn't a hedge. I could shove you into it.'

Rhea started to move the tea things to the draining board. 'You're in a very strange mood today. First you attack a girl you hardly know on my terrace, then you're threatening to shove your best friend into a hedge.'

They moved to the kitchen door and stood facing each other.

He looked down at her. 'Don't be provocative,' he said seriously at last. 'It doesn't suit you.'

'I'm not being provocative.'

'Yes, you are.'

She blushed and looked away.

'I'll see myself out.'

'Okay.'

'Can you rest? You look tired. Sleeping badly?'

'I'm fine, honestly.' She looked away.

He turned away. 'Thanks for the tea.'

When he had gone, she realised that he hadn't said God bless you, as he usually did. Unexpectedly, she felt deprived.

Toby walked swiftly up the path to the church for Evensong, his emotions in turmoil. What on earth had got into him? He felt thrown by the strength of his feelings for Rhea. Was this the reason he'd been so unkind to Alice? Because he *had* been unkind, he'd behaved in a way that was completely out of character. He hoped. Maybe he was wrong about himself, after all.

The fact was that while he'd been relaxing on Rhea's terrace it had struck him that contrary to everything he'd thought he believed, he wanted to marry and have children, and that the person he wanted to do these things with was Rhea.

There was no rule that said that an Anglican priest couldn't marry, but he'd always believed that marriage wasn't God's will for him. How could he serve God with his whole heart if his life was bound up with a woman, someone whom it would be his duty and delight to love and cherish? His love and reverence for her would be a distraction from his true goal which was a total dedication to God. If it was wrong to want these things, he'd better turn his back on them before they took hold of his imagination and it became too difficult to turn away.

He wasn't a saint. He was young and strong and a man. Who was he trying to impress? His father? (Who, he seemed to need reminding, was dead.) Oh, Lord! Why couldn't it be straightforward? Why must there always be all this anxiety and uncertainty getting in the way?

How could it be wrong to love a woman and want to share her life? How could some aspects of material existence be good and others sinful? What was he so afraid of losing? His eternal soul?

He reached the vestry door. He wished he could see his way more clearly. Sometimes he imagined his body as a prison against whose bars his spirit fluttered, longing to escape. But maybe he was wrong. Maybe his body wasn't a prison at all but a key capable of delivering him from himself.

It didn't help that Rhea didn't seem to need God the

way he did. She was kind and sensitive, but in her, he sensed, the divine flame burned low. Or was that unfair? Perhaps she just never talked about what was important to her spiritually. And after all, most of the time he had known her Laurie had been her main preoccupation, which was natural and right. Perhaps he wasn't doing her justice. Perhaps he really didn't know her very well.

He opened the door to the vestments cupboard. He'd never felt more in need of advice and help. He'd better bite the bullet. He would go and see Robert, his spiritual advisor. But first he had to go and apologise to Alice. No question. At least he could be certain about that.

Chapter Eight

IT DAWNED ON RHEA GRADUALLY THAT THE BANGING
sound reverberating through her dream was someone
pounding on the front door, and the sound of flowing
water, translated into the heavy seas in which in her
dream her little boat was perilously rocking, was rain
pouring in rivulets down the roof and overflowing from
the gutters.

Half awake, she plunged down the stairs, pulling her
dressing gown on as she went, and wrenched open the door.
She never bothered to lock it now she was alone in the
house. On the doorstep Mavis stood, holding in one quivering hand a china plate on which a small lamb chop sat in a
pool of congealed, greyish fat. Rhea put her hand over her
stomach. The plate wobbled perilously.

Mavis trembled and shook from head to foot. Her eyes,
fixed on Rhea, were radiant with manic self-righteousness.
'Just look at what they've sent me from the hospital. What a
disgraceful thing to give anybody ... don't you think it's
shameful? They expect me to eat it, you know.'

'Who do? Who gave it to you?' Rhea leaned against the

door post, her eyes fixed in fascination on the chop which looked at least a week old.

'The nurses.' Mavis appeared irritated by Rhea's slowness to catch on. 'They brought it to me from the hospital. Don't you call that a cheek?'

'Which hospital?'

'It's an absolute disgrace. I just wanted you to see it. Don't you think Mr Henderson ought to see it too? If I could just step inside and show it to him—'

'He isn't here.' Rhea looked into the crumpled, humourless face, at the vexed, lightless eyes holding only the vision of self and suffering. 'How about I take you home now?' she said gently. 'Have you had any breakfast?'

'This is my breakfast, supposed to be, only I don't know how they expect me to eat it. Fancy giving me a thing like this.' She turned away as if disappointed by Rhea's unsatisfactory reaction and hobbled down the path in the rain, sweeping the damp air aside with small swimming movements of her free hand like a duck's webbed foot as she strove to keep her balance.

Rhea ran after her. 'Let me take the plate.'

But Mavis, her eyes blank and uncomprehending, held on tight. For a moment or two they struggled, then Rhea let go more suddenly than she intended and Mavis whirled off-balance towards the gate. Rhea rushed after her and seized her as she sank into the hedge, catching the plate deftly with her other hand. Lucky the chop was welded so firmly to the plate; Mavis would have lost it long ago had it been fresh.

A large young man in a dark blue uniform was standing on the pavement outside the gate watching this performance with interest. The rain made dark spots on his blue shirt and formed a mist over his curly brown hair. A police car was parked outside Mrs Mander's house.

'Morning, Miss.'

Mavis, being helped out of the hedge by Rhea, muttered something about the disgraceful state of the National Health Service. Rhea guided her through the gate.

'Is this lady a Mrs Mander?' The policeman walked beside them as they progressed towards Mavis' front door, Rhea supporting her across the uneven pavement.

Rhea glanced up at him. 'Yes. You wouldn't happen to have the time, would you?'

The officer looked at his watch. 'It's five thirty-five.'

'Oh glory.' She glanced up at the sky. Mercifully the rain seemed to have stopped.

'We had a call half an hour ago from this lady.'

'Really? Did you call the police, Mavis?'

Mrs Mander stood stock still. 'Did I what? Call a police-man? Why would I want to do that?'

'That is the question.'

'What was it about?' Mavis yelled at the policeman who glanced uneasily at the sleeping houses to the right and left of them.

'About some tools gone missing? Look, could we go inside for a few moments? I think we might be causing a bit of a disturbance.'

It was nice of him to put it like that. 'Mavis, your tools have been missing for months. I know you lost your hand-bag, but didn't Nurse Paul say it had turned up again?'

'Lost all the money out of it though. About a hundred pound it was.'

'You really shouldn't walk about with large amounts of money in your handbag, madam. That's asking for trouble, that is.'

'Who asked your opinion? Who are you, anyway?'

'I am an officer of the law, madam.'

'Hoity-toity.'

Alarmed by the sour expression on his face Rhea tried to indicate to the policeman without actually tapping her head that Mavis was having one of her off days.

The officer frowned. 'We have to answer every call, however unlikely they may seem. Do you happen to know where the tools went missing from, miss?'

'The garage, I think. You were quite upset about it at the time, Mavis, weren't you?'

Mavis muttered something unintelligible. 'He took most of the silver too, you know. My own son. Took it all back to Canada with him. Wanted the piano too, but I wouldn't let him.' She detached herself determinedly from Rhea's grasp and forged ahead up her own front path, her thin beige legs groping uncertainly over the uneven crazy paving.

The young man pursed his lips. 'All on her own then, is she?'

Rhea nodded.

'Well off, is she?'

Rhea shrugged. 'She seems to leave an awful lot of cash lying around. It's rather worrying, actually.'

He shook his head sadly. 'A lot of unscrupulous people about, take advantage of an old lady living on her own. It would be helpful, miss, if you could keep an eye open for any unusual characters hanging about, callers, you know, anything suspicious. You can give us a ring any time. Where did she lose her bag then?'

'In the house, I think. She hides things and then forgets where she's put them. She's probably hidden the money somewhere too. Nurse Paul says she's always doing it.'

'Nurse Paul, that's the district nurse, is it?'

Rhea nodded. 'She comes in every day.'

Mavis wiped her feet pointedly on the door mat. The

front door stood wide open. She swung round suddenly as Rhea and the policeman reached the front step. 'Have you shown him the food?' Then as Rhea shook her head she turned with anticipatory fervour to the policeman. 'Bloomin' disgrace I call it.'

'What is?'

Mavis' eyes lit up. She turned eagerly back to Rhea. 'Here, where's that plate? There – look! Just you look at that!' She started to shake again.

Rhea hoped it was excitement. She didn't look well.

'What is it?' The policeman looked down at the large, unwieldy plate Rhea had been carrying all the while.

Mavis thrust the plate under his nose. 'That's supposed to be my breakfast, that is. All the way from the hospital. How would you like to be told that was good enough for you, eh? How would you like that?'

'I shouldn't like it at all.' He shook his head, amused.

'Don't you think it had better go in the dustbin now?' Rhea suggested. 'You can't possibly eat it, can you?'

'No! Oh no!' Mavis clutched the plate flat against her chest, chop side down. Rhea closed her eyes. 'You can't put it away yet. I haven't shown it to the Jenkins, or Mrs Peel, or Lucie Atwell—'

'Lucie Atwell?' demanded the policeman sharply. He had two little girls with a bookcase in their bedroom kept well stocked by a nostalgic grandmother.

'You know – Mabel. Up the road there.'

'Mabel Lucie Atwell,' the policeman repeated. Disillusion spread across his face.

'I was going to take it up there now.' Mavis started off down the step again, the plate pressed firmly against her chest.

'Look.' Rhea put out her hand and caught her sleeve.

'Don't go now. Isn't someone coming to see you today? Your sister or Mr Perry or someone?'

'My sister lives in Ashtead,' Mavis told the policeman, stopping halfway down the path. 'She's coming to see me and we're going to have lunch with Mr Perry.'

'That's nice.' He glanced at Rhea, who shrugged.

'Yes, it is. Come in and have a cup of tea.' Mavis turned and headed for the house again.

'That's very kind of you, madam, but I think I ought to be getting back to the station, if there's nothing I can do for you.'

'Who called you out? Has somebody had burglars? I caught a burglar once.' She turned to Rhea, her face glowing with pleasure. 'I've got a certificate to prove it.'

'Goodness, have you really?'

''Course I have. Don't you believe me? I don't tell untruths, you know, not like some people. What do you think of that, then?' She looked up at the policeman, a roguish twinkle in her eye.

'That's very good. Not many people can say they've caught a burglar. As a matter of fact I haven't caught one yet. Mind you, I'm pretty new to the force.'

'Well, what about that!' She beamed at Rhea. 'He's a policeman and he's never caught a burglar and I have! I'm not a policeman.'

'No,' he agreed.

'Never thought it was quite my line really. Well—' She shuffled into the hall, suddenly tired. 'Bye bye son, thanks for looking in.'

'Ta-ta then. Take care now. Cheerio.'

Rhea walked with him to the gate. 'I'm sorry you were bothered.'

'Be keeping an eye on her, will you?'

'I'll stay till the nurse comes as her mind is wandering so. She should be here about eight.'

'Quite an entertaining old lady, isn't she?'

'She certainly perked up today. I haven't seen her so cheerful for a long time.'

'One for the lads, is she?' He smoothed his face into gravity again. 'You're quite sure about the tools, are you, miss? Only I'm supposed to investigate the call, see.'

'Well, it can't have been recently that they went, if they went at all. She told me the same story right back in the autumn. It's quite possible her son did take them.'

'With her permission?'

Rhea shrugged. 'Maybe. I'll check with Nurse Paul and let you know if anything really has gone recently but I'm afraid she accuses everybody of all sorts of things – even me. It depends on the mood she's in.'

'It's a real shame. Sad to see the mess some people end up in. Well, I'd best be getting along now. Thanks very much, miss.'

'Goodbye,' Rhea said.

While the kettle was boiling for Mavis' tea she watched him through the front window sitting in his car talking into a transmitter for several minutes. After a last glance at the house he drove away.

'Would you like some Weetabix?' Rhea called through from the kitchen.

Mavis was sitting huddled on the sofa as though exhausted. The plate with the chop on it was in the kitchen on the draining board. Rhea had decided to leave it to Nurse Paul to deal with since Mavis became worked up at the slightest suggestion of being parted from it. Perhaps they should frame it and hang it on the wall.

'What time is it? Is it dinner time? I ought to be getting down to the centre, I don't want to be late.'

'It's not time yet, Mavis. It's only six o'clock.'

'What, in the morning? Six in the evening, you mean. Have I had my tea?'

'It's morning. It's quite early, not even breakfast time, really.'

'Goodness gracious! The shops won't be open then. They won't be shut, either, not all day. That's nice. I like to think the shops are open. It's somewhere to go when I feel like a bit of company.'

'Have your cup of tea.' Rhea carried it through. 'Nurse Paul will be along soon. Would you like me to read to you?'

'You stay with me. I get lonely by myself. Did I tell you about the time I looked after the little Andrews boys, Sir John that is now, and his brother Philip? Lovely little boys they were, proper little gentlemen, beautiful fair hair and blue eyes. Your little fellow reminds me of them sometimes, in his ways, you know, although of course his eyes are brown. I was with them for six years, got to love them like my own. The light string over my bed isn't working, Rhea, do you think you could have a look at it for me? There's a bit of string tied to the switch, Nurse Paul did it for me so I wouldn't have to keep getting out of bed to turn the light off, but she didn't make a very good job of it, it keeps slipping off. Now, where was I?'

'I'll ring an electrician later, they'll rig up one of those extension things. But I'll go and have a quick look anyway.'

'Morning all, Nurse here! The rain's stopped and it's going to be a smashing day. How long have you been here, dear? Did you have a good night, Mrs Mander? Has she been a nuisance?' Nurse Paul asked Rhea in the kitchen, hardly bothering to lower her voice as she filled a tumbler at the sink for Mavis' pills.

'No, of course not.' Rhea lowered her voice, not wanting Mavis to hear. 'She called the police.'

'The *police?*' Nurse Paul frowned. 'Whatever for?'

'She thought some tools had gone missing. You know, the ones she lost ages ago. I'm sure Brendan must have taken them. She's very confused this morning. I explained to him that she'd just got muddled. Oh – and she's got a chop.'

'Not that sodding chop again, I thought I'd thrown it out. I wonder if she got it out of the dustbin again, I wouldn't put it past her. If it's the same one it must be green by now.'

'Almost. She simply refuses to be parted from it.'

'Well, I don't want to be parted from yesterday's liver and bacon but I don't have much choice in the matter. Life must go on,' she yelled, handing Mavis the tumbler and two large pink pills.

'What's that you say, dear?'

'Oh, never mind, dear, never mind. Can't be repeating everything three times over, can I?' She blundered back into the kitchen.

Rhea frowned. 'Is something the matter, Nurse Paul? You seem a bit upset.'

'Upset? Oh God, dear, no, never mind me. Everybody has their problems, don't they? Nothing for you to go worrying your head about.' She gave Rhea a look of penetrating concern. 'How's things with you, anyway? Pretty bloody awful I should think. I know. I've been there. Oh well, life goes on.'

'You look tired.'

'Had a bit on my mind lately. Been busy on the circuit and Mrs M. is getting a bit much, too, poor old dear. We'll have to find her somewhere to go if she doesn't improve. We just haven't the time to be looking after people in her condition, it just isn't practical.'

'Find somewhere?'

'A home, dear, a home. She can afford the best, let her have it. There's one or two quite good places round here where she'll be well looked after. She wouldn't get lonely like she does now, and she wouldn't have to worry about getting food in or keeping warm, that sort of thing. It really would be the best thing for her.'

'But her little home.' Rhea balled her hands into fists. 'All her things. She'd hate leaving them, she'd be miserable. She's independent, she's proud, she hates being pushed around.'

'You think of something else then,' Nurse Paul snapped. 'Honest to goodness, it's the only answer. Her son isn't going to come and carry her off to Canada on a white charger, is he? Not bloomin' likely. Feel like looking after her yourself, do you? 'Course you don't. You're a writer, aren't you? You wouldn't get a minute's peace. Look, love, take a tip from me, don't try to take the world's sorrows on your shoulders, it doesn't work and you destroy yourself in the process. I used to think I could save the world, now I know better. You take my tip, keep well out of it. You can't solve her problems, nobody can. You leave it to us, we'll sort her out and in a week or two you'll have forgotten all about her.'

'Nurse,' Mavis called petulantly. 'Nurse!'

Nurse Paul rolled her eyes. 'See? Oh, before you go, can I ask you a favour? Could I leave her pills with you? Only I can't leave them with her, see, Dr Wood doesn't think she's to be trusted, she's been acting so peculiar lately. He's coming to see her later when he's on his rounds and he wants to have a look at her pills. If he could call in on you it would save me coming back from the centre or him having to chase round after me if I'm not back there, if you follow me. Would you mind?'

'Not at all. Where are they?'

Nurse Paul pressed two small bottles into her hand, looking almost fearfully over her shoulder. 'Best not to let her see. She gets that suspicious. She's got a bit of a persecution complex if you ask me.'

Rhea wandered home and was still standing aimlessly in the hall when half an hour later Nurse Paul knocked loudly on the front door. She was breathing heavily, her face flushed. 'I'm just off now. Thought I'd let you know her bag turned up, since you've been worried about it. I found it in her bedroom. She'd done it all up in a parcel, believe it or not, and addressed it to Miss Mabel Lucie Atwell, Petersham. Isn't it a marvel?'

'Gosh, lucky she hadn't posted it. She seems to have her on the brain.'

'She's got one of her verses tacked up on the back of the bathroom door, it could be preying on her mind. I'll whip it down quietly when she isn't looking. We don't want her tipping right over the edge, do we?' She gave her usual breathy snort of laughter, but her eyes kept their look of anxiety and the lines across her forehead and indented between cheeks and nose seemed today more deeply engrained, making the faintly simian look more pronounced.

She turned to go, pulling off her cap and smoothing the glistening coil of her hair with her other hand.

'Was the money still in it?'

Nurse Paul half turned, frowning. 'No, that's the devil of it, the bloomin' thing was completely empty. God knows what she's done with it, flushed it down the loo, I expect. Oh well, must be going, no peace for the wicked.' She gave a sudden unconvincing bellow of laughter.

She was worried about something, it was obvious. Rhea closed the door, wondering how old she was and whether she had a boyfriend. It couldn't be that much fun, looking after people who the moment your back was turned, forgot all about you.

ALICE TURNED up at the door. Rhea was asleep again in the Windsor chair and woke with a start when the bell rang. She opened the door. 'Alice, hello. I've done something stupid.'

'Hi Rhea, nice to see you too.'

'Sorry. Sorry.' Rhea gave a huge yawn.

'Well, pardon me. Am I boring you? Can I come in or do I have to stand out here on the doorstep all day?'

'Sorry. No – of course, come in.'

Alice stepped over the threshold. 'What, darling, what have you done?'

'I said I'd pick up Tad and take him over to Toby's and now I've told Nurse Paul I'll stay here till the doctor comes to see Mavis next door, so I can give him her pills.'

'You've double booked. I do it all the time.' She looked closely at Rhea. 'Are you all right?'

'Fine. I was asleep, that's all. I wondered if you might be able to go and pick up Tad and take him to Toby. Or you could stay here and wait for the doctor if you're still too cross with Toby to go near him. Would you have time—' She stopped. It might not be tactful to assume that Alice had unlimited time because Minna would be looking after the children.

'I was going to offer to pick up Tad anyway. I've got one or two things to say to that pompous curate of yours. Mind you, he did apologise very nicely yesterday.' She swaggered into the kitchen. 'I didn't half make him grovel.'

'Oh, he apologised! Jolly good.' Rhea followed her, rubbing her face with both hands.

Alice pulled out a chair and sat down. 'Nobody speaks to me like that and gets away with it. I'm going to charm him until he begs for mercy. He's not going to know if he's standing on his head or his heels. You just wait.'

'Who, Toby?'

'You needn't sound so surprised. He's a man, isn't he? The trouble with you, Rhea, is you haven't got eyes in your head. There is a man crying out for a woman to love.'

'D'you think?'

'Yes, I do.'

'But you're married!'

'What's that got to do with anything?'

Rhea went to the sink and filled the kettle. 'Maybe nothing as far as you're concerned, but Toby isn't like that, he's got principles.'

'All the more fun, I like a challenge.' Alice opened her shoulder bag and found a lipstick and a compact.

Rhea spooned coffee into the cafetière.

Alice's eyes shone butterfly blue. She snapped open the compact and started to smear on lipstick. 'I know I can make him mad for me. Just you wait.' She blotted her lips on a tissue and put everything back in her bag. She put the bag on the table.

Rhea reached up and unhooked two mugs from the dresser. 'But what will you do with him then?'

'I'll worry about that when it happens.' She got up and began to walk agitatedly about the room. 'He's the most beautiful man I've ever seen. Don't you think he's beautiful? That lovely, exciting face!'

Rhea stood waiting for the kettle to boil. She thought about Toby's face. She saw his eyes, a clear, light grey, deep set under a high forehead; a straight nose and a mouth well shaped and firm; his face saved from effeminacy by the hungry-looking hollows under the cheekbones and by the expression in his eyes which was often a little wary and reserved. She remembered the way his reserve would vanish and his eyes light up, his self-consciousness forgotten, when his sympathy or interest were aroused. Yes, it was a lovely face, powerful and voluptuous, she realised, seeing him through Alice's eyes.

Had she missed something? Apparently she hadn't really seen him, so had she not been listening to him either? She wondered if what she was feeling was jealousy. But she'd known him long before all this trouble, and as far as she could remember she hadn't loved him then. But perhaps there hadn't been room in her heart for anyone but Laurie.

Alice said, 'I've never felt like this about anyone before. If I can't have him I'll die.'

The kettle boiled. Rhea waited a moment or two then filled the cafetière. 'I don't want him to get hurt.'

'You're just cross because you can't have him yourself.'

'That's pathetic.' She carried the cafetière over to the table in the annexe.

Alice followed her, pulled out a chair and sat down. 'Well, what's the problem then?'

'Alice, you're *married*. He sees you as Dick's wife, not a free person, unattached. It makes a difference, however attractive he might find you. Don't you see?' Rhea went to fetch the mugs.

'I'll explain to him about Dick.' Alice dismissed her husband as though he was an irrelevance. 'I'm sure I can make him understand. And by a person unattached I suppose you mean yourself?'

'For God's sake, Alice!' Rhea banged the mugs down. 'All I'm trying to say is that you should think about Toby's feelings too, not just yours. He's a priest. Think what it would do to him if he were to go against his principles like that; he might even lose his job. He isn't an ordinary man, he's special and sensitive and he really cares about these things, about being true to himself and loving God. He isn't like other people.'

'You sound as though you're in love with him yourself.'

'Anyway, I don't think he's the kind of man who has affairs. He just isn't like that.'

'You mean he hasn't with you. That doesn't mean anything. Perhaps he just doesn't fancy you. I mean, I know you're friends.'

Rhea poured their coffee. 'I don't know whether he fancies me or not. I've never thought about it.'

'Oh darling, I'm sorry. It's just I'm so jealous of you, you see so much of him all the time, you have so many opportunities and I hardly ever see him. And you don't even want him.'

How did she know? Rhea might want him very badly indeed. Unnerved by Alice's onslaught she couldn't have said just now what her feelings were about Toby or anything else. 'Well, you've got another opportunity this morning.'

'And I'm going to make the most of it.'

'Oh, Alice. You're just bored.'

It seemed as though the moment Alice had gone the doorbell rang again. Rhea, who had settled down in the Windsor chair and fallen asleep again, woke with a start and leapt to her feet. She opened the door and blinked at the stranger standing on the doorstep. He was tall and strong looking and he was carrying a black bag. He also seemed to be in an extremely bad temper.

'Your doorbell doesn't work. I haven't got all day to stand out here. I've got patients to see to.'

'It works fine.' Rhea suppressed a yawn. 'I was asleep.'

'Why don't you sleep at the proper time. It's half past twelve. Still, at least you're dressed.'

'You're Mavis' doctor.'

'I'm Dr. Wood and I've come for Mrs Mander's pills, if you can be bothered to find them for me. Please don't take all day about it, I really am in a bit of a hurry.'

'If you're going to be so rude, you can stuff your pills.' Rhea closed the door.

The doorbell rang again. She counted to ten and opened the door. The doctor was standing there with his eyes closed. 'Please. I really am very sorry. I had no sleep last night and I am very, very tired.'

'Well, that makes two of us then. Here are her pills. Goodbye.' She closed the door. 'And I hope I never have to see you again.' After a moment she heard his footsteps retreating and the sound of a car starting up. 'And I hope you heard that,' she said childishly into the silence.

DEPRESSED by her conversation with Alice and annoyed with herself for losing her temper with Dr Wood, Rhea was delighted to see Toby when he arrived at her door later in in the afternoon. He'd called in to give her a run down on the morning's efforts with Tad and Mr Hulski, the inebriated Pole. The sun had come out and now, having refused tea, Toby was sitting on the terrace on the garden bench, his long legs stretched out in front of him and his arms folded across his chest.

'Tad and Hulski couldn't stand each other; they practically came to blows. The person who managed to avert complete disaster and bloodshed was good old Mrs Hulski who is a tower of strength both physically and mentally and more than a match for either of them. It turns out – wait for it – she actually enjoys being thrashed and encourages her husband to beat her up. He drinks afterwards because he feels guilty about doing it. I think he quite enjoys it at the time.'

'Glory. Good old S&M in the heart of suburbia.' Rhea sat down beside him. 'Whatever next!'

'All this from Tad with enormous relish, embroidery and gesticulation. And copious expressions of disgust, of course.'

'So Mr Hulski drinks because he hits her and not the other way round, how fascinating.'

'It's weird. It imposes a big moral problem for him. His feeling of degradation and guilt is so aggravated that I think he's going to need years of counselling to sort him out. He's practically an alcoholic already.'

'Perhaps she ought to have psychotherapy. Or is it something you're born with?'

'Haven't a clue. She had a pretty weird childhood from what Tad managed to discover. Anyway, they've agreed to go off on Monday to see a counsellor, which is a step forward I suppose. Let's just hope he doesn't kill her over the weekend.'

'At least they've agreed to do something about it.'

'They're not a bit embarrassed about it. Once they started talking it was almost impossible to stop them.'

'Lucky to get a counsellor so soon.' Rhea watched his face. 'What did Alice do while all this was going on? Did she sit in on it?'

'No, she sat in my kitchen and did her nails, toes as well, while she waited. She has a handy little case with bottles and brushes and nail files in it, like a do it yourself break in kit. She was very good and quiet and took Tad home afterwards. She said she was going to look in here.'

'Perhaps I didn't hear the bell.'

Toby's face had been particularly bland and cheerful when recounting Alice's part in the affair. He looked innocent and a little secretive. But when he asked Rhea how she was his face changed and became serious and inward-looking. Her heart sank; was she always going to have this effect on him now, making him look so solemn and so sad? Alice seemed to be good for him.

But all the same when prompted she couldn't resist the temptation to talk about Laurie.

'I keep seeing his beaming little face and that ridiculous mop of – I miss him so much.'

Today she couldn't disguise her misery. She sat looking down at the paving stones, her hands clasped between her knees. 'I'm sorry to be such dismal company. I just can't seem to accept what happened as God's will. It seems blasphemous to me.'

There was something arresting about the silence that followed this remark, as if she was hearing in the distance something shatter and break.

Toby stood up and began walking about, pushing at some fallen cherry blossoms with the toe of his sneaker. He bent to pick up some of the wilting flowers and held them in his cupped hand. 'Come on Rhea, you can do better than that.'

She was immensely surprised by the irritation in his voice. She had spoken almost without thinking. She felt an answering spurt of anger. 'I'm sorry.'

Toby turned back to the bench and stood looking down at her. He dropped the flowers and put his hands in his pockets. He seemed to tower over her, his annoyance with her making him seem a stranger, giving him a kind of power.

She didn't like people to be annoyed with her. 'What have I said?' She realised at once what it was.

'I wish you didn't feel you had to placate me with these trite intellectual red herrings, like throwing bits of Christian to the lions. You don't. You don't have to talk at all if you d-don't want to. I come here as your friend, Rhea, not as some kind of spiritual or moral advisor. Look at me.'

She looked up at him, tied by the unusual force of his will.

'I do have legs under my cassock, you know. I'm a human being just like you. I'm not even particularly clever. Your brains are probably in much better c-condition than mine are, with your writing and whatnot. No, please don't interrupt. You don't honestly want me to sit down and argue the philosophical problem of pain and suffering with you, do you?'

Her face grew hot.

He squatted down and said more gently, taking her hands in his, 'Why don't you just say, "I'm heartbroken, I'm completely overwhelmed by grief"? Do you think I won't understand, that I expect you to work it all out like a good little Christian and get over it in a few weeks as if nothing has happened?'

She wondered if he was going to start accusing her of vanity and egocentricity.

'Please don't feel you have to put on a b-brave face with me. You expect far too much of yourself and not nearly enough of other people.' He gave her hands a little shake. 'I do understand, you know. I love you to bits, Rhea.'

She was startled but not surprised. She knew he loved her. She would have been much more surprised if he'd said he didn't love her. Not as a lover, of course. It was the love of comrades, of close friends.

'It hurts when you put up these barriers,' he said more calmly. His eyes had become evasive. He searched her face for some kind of response, and she thought she glimpsed disappointment in his face as he stood up and began to walk about, his hands deep in his pockets, his head bent. He stopped in front of her again. 'You're a human being, not a saint. God doesn't expect you to give up your beloved child without any kind of struggle. He gave you the gift of love, so you're having to suffer now.' He stood looking down at her. 'Rhea, let's get one thing clear. God did not ask for, or cause, Laurie's death. There are all kinds of reasons why we suffer.' After a pause he said, 'You know this already.'

Rhea looked at the fallen cherry blossom lying in clusters on the terrace. The night had been windy. Spring has come, she reminded herself. In the twilight world she was inhabiting there were no seasons, no day or night.

She said, as though checking items off a list, 'I can't ever have Laurie back. I've lost him as surely as if I'd had my arm pulled off. I won't ever experience the love he felt for me or the warmth of him, or see his face again.' She looked up. 'There's no doubt about it, he's gone.' She shook her head. 'You have no idea how horrible that is.'

He put his hand out in an involuntary gesture of

comfort, then put it back in his pocket again. 'We're all going to die. You'll die too, just like Laurie. Then you'll see him again.'

'But *how?*' She shook her head and looked up at him. 'How will I recognise him?'

'I don't know! I only know you have to trust in Providence. You have to.'

She stood up and walked a little way off, bent down and scooped up a handful of blossoms. She touched the pink flowers already browning round their edges, with small, gentle strokes. It would be so much easier to go off her head ... perhaps then she'd be able to appreciate simple things again and learn to love these lovely things as she used to. She might be able to feel happy again, if she were mad.

She turned and saw Toby's anxious eyes resting on her. He was standing by the bench. She saw the worry and tension in his face before he had time to smooth the anxiety away. She wondered whether, engrossed in her thoughts, she might have let something slip by. Perhaps he had spoken and she hadn't heard?

She went to him impulsively and put her arms round him. 'You're so kind, Toby. You're the kindest man I ever knew.' She laid her cheek against the rough, heathery sweater, her longing for physical touch suddenly overwhelming.

She felt his arms come around her, his cheek against her hair. She was surprised by the warmth emanating from him, the living heat; she'd forgotten how it felt to be held close to another human being. She buried her nose in his sweater and breathed in the smell of the wool and the faint scent of soap and aftershave and Toby. She relaxed against him as he held her cautiously but strongly, and was infinitely comforted, and the flowers fell unnoticed from her hands.

Chapter Nine

Whyever did I agree to go tonight? Rhea asked herself wearily. Do I really have to spend the evening watching Alice flirt with Toby, taking bets with myself over whether he'll give in or not? Because she wasn't nearly as confident as she'd pretended to be that he'd be able to resist the onslaughts of a determined Alice once her mind was truly made up.

She dragged her evening dress out of the wardrobe. She'd been making her bed and remembering Laurie's gay trampolining on the springing mattress, his tunnellings under the duvet and the routine switching on of her bedside lamp in the early mornings. She'd been remembering the bee game, the bird in a nest game, a hundred other silly little things. Silly, silly, she told herself in despair, remembering his ecstatic abandon as he landed on his back and bounced, his little strong legs flying out, his blissful expression.

Everywhere, he was everywhere, and the house was so quiet without him, so pointlessly tidy and dull. She would never, ever get used to it and it was a double whammy because she would never write another word as long as she lived. The thought of the emotional effort required for putting pen to paper literally nauseated her.

She had hung the sea green dress on a hanger outside the wardrobe and now she stood holding the soft material in her hands and looking at the dress. The faint aroma of scent clinging to it evoked memories of other evenings, dances and parties with Tom and Tom's friends in another life it seemed, such a long time ago. But there was no accompanying sensual awakening, no remembered thrill.

She couldn't go to this dinner party; she couldn't do all the necessary gilding and garnishing. She rushed to the mirror over the wash basin and looked at her reflection and what she saw almost made her laugh. She certainly couldn't go like this with blotches all over her face and black rings under her eyes. She looked as if she'd walked into a door.

She sat on the edge of her bed and pressed her palms against her hot forehead, trying to put the various aspects of the problem into some kind of order. If she didn't put makeup on then everyone would look at her and she'd ruin the evening for them all; she would be the spectre at the feast. She couldn't face putting makeup on. So she couldn't go. Sorted.

If only it was midsummer ... her face would be tanned so nobody would notice. Perhaps she ought to ring Alice and ask her to give her a rain check on dinner party invitations till August.

She wandered upstairs and walked about her bedroom, twisting her fingers together and feeling absolved. If she didn't turn up Toby wouldn't know she wasn't coming until too late; Alice wouldn't mind because she'd only asked Rhea so she could ask him. What a relief, what an escape! Why hadn't she thought of this before?

But when Alice walked into the house at lunch time on

the way home from the hairdresser and accosted her in the hall as she came lethargically down the stairs, Alice said sharply, 'Good grief, Rhea, you are coming, aren't you? You aren't going to let me down?' She looked at Rhea more closely. 'You haven't been asleep again, have you? Did you know your front door wasn't shut properly?'

'Alice – I—'

Alice, clearly aghast, put her hands over her ears. 'No! I won't listen! You're coming and that's that. You've got to come, I shall simply never forgive you if you don't, my numbers will be all wrong.'

'But just look at me.'

'Well ...' Alice put her head on one side and scrutinised her face. 'That's nothing a bit of cold water and some makeup won't sort out.'

'That's the problem.' Rhea leaned on the banister rail and felt that she could never make Alice understand. 'I can't face doing all that, spreading all that muck on my face.' It would be like daubing a corpse with lipstick, was what she felt like saying. Even if that was what they did do.

Alice hurled her shoulder bag onto the chair by the front door. 'I've never heard such a load of old rubbish in my life.' She stared at Rhea as though trying to make up her mind whether to hit her or burst into tears herself. 'How can you be so selfish? Come on.' She pulled off her jacket. 'I've got a bit of time to spare. Up you go. You're doing it now, the whole works. Bath, hair wash, makeup. I'm not leaving till you're done.' She began pushing Rhea back up the stairs. 'Come on, I haven't got all day.'

Later, Alice dumped Rhea in front of the medicine cabinet, her hair wrapped in a towel turban style, with strict instructions to get on with it. Perfectly relaxed now that she'd got what she wanted, Alice sat gracefully on the edge of the bath, her fawn trousered legs crossed at the knee, a chiffon bandeau holding her hair back from her forehead. She had had a chignon hairpiece put into her hair and her own short curls clustered round her ears and forehead in little waves and ringlets. She looked even more alluring than usual, which was saying something, Rhea thought, sighing and looking at herself in the mirror.

Forgive me, darling, she said into the deep internal silence echoing with the sound of his voice, his footsteps, his laughter. Forgive me for putting this stupid stuff on my face as if I seem to care two pins about what I look like. Because I don't, it's all pretend, it's for other people's sake. I haven't forgotten the fun you had with this lipstick, the one I'm holding in my hand, and this green eyeshadow, your gentle 'Mumma, look!' and your adorable face turned up all smudged with pink and green – and I wasn't cross, was I? I hugged and kissed you and we laughed at your reflection in the glass and you said, 'Beautiful face!' with such awe and delight ... and I wondered if after all you might turn out to be a painter, like Tom.

You always loved to mess about with finger paints. Do you remember the time you took off your sandals and made patterns of feet in the semolina we spilt all over the kitchen floor? And I haven't forgotten how every morning you came running to me here and tugged at my jeans demanding, 'Powdah, Mumma,' and how you screwed your eyes up tight and waited for me to dab my powder puff onto your ridiculous little nose ... You know what I told you, that when things hurt we have to be brave and not make too much fuss? Well, whenever I'm not upset, it's not because I've forgotten you but because I'm having to be brave.

Alice eyed her sternly. 'Rhea, why are you crying? You'll ruin your makeup.'

'I'm not, am I? Sorry. Lucky I haven't got as far as mascara then.'

'Yes, get on with it. Eyebrows?'

'Doing them now. Talk to me, Alice. Tell me what you're wearing tonight. Anything. Just talk.' She looked at Alice's reflection in the mirror. She'd gone to an awful lot of trouble for a small dinner party at home.

'You'll like Martin.' Alice spread her hands and admired her pink nail varnish. 'He's awfully dishy, and he's nice too. He's got a mistress but that won't go on for ever, rumour has it that things aren't too healthy in that department at the moment. She's coming tonight too. Martin's a doctor.'

'Who's Martin?' Rhea looked at her face critically in the mirror. Alice's complete lack of empathy was in its own way consoling.

'What? Rhea, what's the point of me talking if you aren't even going to bother to listen?'

'Sorry. What's his surname?'

'Wood. He's one of the GPs at the health centre.'

'Oh, him. I've met him. Briefly. He seemed rather bad-tempered. He came to pick up Mavis' pills.'

'He's not bad-tempered. It must have been something you did.'

'I only saw him for about five seconds.' Rhea snapped the lid of the makeup box shut. 'Five seconds was quite enough. There, that's done. Thanks, Alice.'

Alice sat up. 'Not bad. You need a bit more blusher. Here, let me do it. Gimme that Maybelline stuff ... that's better. Goody goody. Now you won't let me down ... *promise.*'

'Okay. I promise.' She sat down beside Alice on the side of the bath, suddenly weary.

She walked down to the front door to see Alice off.

Alice paused with her hand on the door handle. 'Go and dry your hair. Eight o'clock. Don't forget. Don't bother to see me out, you go and get started, I still don't trust you. I must fly, there are still a thousand things to be done. Minna won't have done anything; she's got no initiative, that girl. I'm having all pink tonight, roses, candles and napkins all matching. Rather fun! See you later then.'

'Eight o'clock.'

Rhea waved Alice goodbye then trudged back up the stairs and went into the bathroom. She looked around for Laurie's little boat. She remembered she'd put it in the bundle with his bath toys which was still on the floor outside his bedroom door.

"Dance to your daddy, my little laddy,
Dance to your daddy, my little man."

The gay little tune leapt into her head like small feet tapping, dancing over the bathroom floor.

"You shall have a fishy in a little dishy,
You shall have a fishy when the boat comes in."

She sat in a frozen, mouse-like stillness. Pain coursed through her. She waited, her breathing quick and shallow, for it to pass. She got up and went into her room as though in response to some invitation or command, convinced that something or someone was waiting for her there, but when she opened the door there was nothing. Nothing but the fleeting sense of something having been there that she dismissed immediately as an illusion, the product of her desperate desire to see him again.

IN THE EVENING, worried about being late, she was ready much too early. She paced about the sitting room, nervous and anxious, the palms of her hands clammy. If she ate anything she was certain she would throw up; how was she going to be able to plough her way through an entire dinner menu?

She went into the kitchen, poured herself a large glass of dry sherry and took several large gulps. Feeling better she drank some more. She wished now that she'd accepted Toby's invitation to give her a lift to the Carters. He'd suggested picking her up and driving her there in the Peugeot, leaving his bike in the drive, but she'd refused, wanting to leave him completely free. Also, to be honest, she hadn't liked the idea of being dependent on anyone, even Toby, in case she needed to escape early. But now she wasn't so sure about driving. She looked through the French windows into the gloomy garden which had a grey, deserted look. She drained her glass quickly and went to stand in front of the glass over the fireplace.

She stared searchingly at her reflection. Was that really Laurie's mother, that painted, scented, calm-looking woman in the gold frame, that ordinary, quite pretty woman? You could see Laurie's mother if you looked closely: the pale, gaunt creature inside the exotic shell. Her eyes had the shiny, sunken look of eyes that had done a good deal of crying; those were his mother's eyes, but it wasn't obvious at first glance that that woman was a fraud who shouldn't be allowed out pretending to be real. All that pretty expanse of white bosom, those lively-looking lips, that air of grace and friendliness – they were a complete hoax. Inside the pretty doll the sawdust was being eaten away; she was liable to come apart in your hands.

She gave a deep sigh and turned away. The silence lay about her in lumps like a collapsed ceiling. Going out tonight she was leaving no one in the house; nobody needed her to come home, it wouldn't matter if she never did. And then it would be night, and dark, and she would go to bed alone.

She was beginning to be fearful of the house at night. When she couldn't sleep she would get up and wander about, cocooned by the darkness which enveloped her and seemed to drain her of judgement and will. At these times she felt she had become sorrow itself, spreading through the house like an ugly stain, concealed by the darkness which covered her like mist over a bog or the tide over quicksand. She hated herself then, her spirits were at their lowest, her senses dulled by exhaustion and the longing for sleep. She would feel her way doggedly from room to room, searching for she didn't know what, usually ending up in the kitchen where her feet echoed on the tiled floor and the fridge hummed. At least there was that. She would lean against the sink and look out to where the trees overhung the shadowy yard, their branches illuminated and washed softly brown where the light from the streetlamp across the road struck them across the garage roof.

Time to go. She stood in the sitting room, shaken by a spasm of nervous trembling, feeling evening coming on and wanting at last to be out of the house, to be active and combat her demons. She walked purposefully into the kitchen and washed up her sherry glass then put on her coat, took her black silk evening bag from the top of the bread bin and let herself out into the yard.

As she was opening the garage door Mavis' voice came out of the darkness, 'Oh, there you are, Mrs Henderson! Could I just have a word?'

Rhea closed her eyes, opened them again and slowly turned. Mavis swam up the drive, her balancing hand batting the air. She had remembered her stick and with it her progress was speedier and less precarious.

'I don't like to ask, but I wondered – only I don't like to ask.'

'Is it your wireless?' Now Rhea found she was delighted to see this human thing standing in front of her, a proof of her existence, challenging, inspiring. 'Would you like me to come over and fix it?'

Mavis shook her head. Her eyes bulged with unshed tears. One trickled down over the soft, dirt-ingrained folds of her cheek.

'What is it?' Rhea asked gently.

The words came in a rush. 'I want to have a bath, see. I'm afraid to get in, in case I fall. If you could just help me in and stay with me till I'm ready to get out again I'd be all right then.' She looked up at Rhea, wiping her face with the back of her hand. 'I wouldn't trouble you, only I'm afraid of falling. I do want a bath; I feel so unpleasant. I meant to ask Nurse but she was so rushed I didn't like to … she's got someone else she goes to as well as me, see.'

'Of course I'll come. I'll come straight away.' Mavis did smell, she had to admit. A bit. Fancy not even being able to have a bath when you want one. Compassion fretted at her. They inched their way back to Mavis' house. What a pair … both of them shaking like leaves, both of them with tears running down their faces.

The old-fashioned bathroom, built and furnished with the rest of the house in the early fifties and renovated fifty years ago, had a heartless chill about it. The lino tiles on the floor were worn, in places showing the old floorboards beneath; many of the wall tiles were webbed with hairline cracks. A faded Mabel Lucie Atwell calendar swung from a nail on the back of the door. Nurse Paul hadn't taken it down after all.

Mavis undressed slowly, as modest and flustered as a

girl. Her fingers fumbled over buttons and zips and she mumbled to herself meanwhile. Rhea stood awkwardly half turned away, not wanting to appear to be trying to hurry her by offering to help and wondering whether she should have waited tactfully outside the door, except that Mavis had seemed to assume she would be coming in with her.

'You do keep your house nice and clean; I don't know how you do it.' She looked around.

Mavis looked up, pleased. She nodded. 'I dust and do one room properly every day. Sometimes I forget which one I did the last time; I expect some of them get done more than the others.' She pulled her blouse off with a brisk, encouraged movement. 'Ideal Home 1958 this was, did you know? That was in George's parents' time.'

'Was it really? How proud they must have been.'

'George grew up here, see. He always loved this house, thought the world of it, he did.' She was down to a once white, now grey petticoat.

Rhea looked out of the window at the trees outside her own kitchen door. She really ought to wait outside. She would say something. But the old lady turned to face her and said disarmingly, with a vestige in her face of some long-forgotten power to charm, 'I'm so ashamed. I'm shy. I've never undressed in front of anybody in my life, not even George. Only I'm so afraid of falling. I'm such an ugly old sight now, look at me.' She looked down at her emaciated body. 'All skin and bone. I'm ashamed to let you see me like this.'

'Oh, don't say that ... I won't look, I promise. Don't be shy, I won't think anything about it. And you aren't ugly, you're lovely and slim, not all fat and flabby like some people. Look, I'll just help you in and then I'll leave you

while you wash. I'll wait outside the door, and you can call
if you need me.'

Yet to look was unavoidable: Mavis slipped while Rhea
was supporting her, one leg in the bath and the other
coming in over the side. The foot taking her weight slipped
and she was off balance for a moment, clutching at Rhea
with astonishing strength. Water splashed over Rhea's
chiffon dress. She caught a fleeting glimpse of small, with-
ered breasts, a patch of pubic hair sparse and grey like the
half-plucked breast of some small, grey feathered bird, and
thin white limbs like a child's flung out in an instinctive
effort to save herself. Then Mavis was balanced again and
lowering herself into the shallow water.

'I'll wait in the passage.' Rhea's skin was goosefleshed
with alarm: it had been a narrow squeak. 'You call when
you're ready. No hurry, take your time.' All thoughts of
Alice's dinner party had gone right out of her head.

In the bath Mavis sang in a reedy, childlike soprano and
Rhea, sitting on the stairs, smiled as she listened. By the
time she was ready to be helped out it was half past eight,
and by the time Rhea was able to escape it was nine. Mavis
dried herself with infinite slowness, again wanted to show
Rhea the faulty switch by the bedroom door but then
started to become confused and unhappy and Rhea, who
had by now remembered where she was supposed to be,
couldn't bring herself to leave her until Mavis was safely
tucked up in bed with a hot water bottle, a cup of Complan
by her side.

Stopping only to retrieve her coat and evening bag and
lock the door, Rhea set off, wishing too late that she had
paused to phone Alice to explain her lateness and that she

119

hadn't left her mobile on the bed. Conscious of the time and miserably aware of the water splashes darkening the front of her dress she drove like a novice, clashing the gears and stalling the car at the front of a long queue waiting at the roundabout at the T-junction with the Avenue.

Hammond House stood in its own miniature park at the end of the Avenue. The front door was white with shiny brass fittings, there were grills over the downstairs windows to deter burglars and twin bay trees in tubs on either side of the stone steps leading up to the front door. Rhea parked the car and locked it. She ran up the steps, feverish with anxiety over her appalling lateness, and knocked loudly with the lion head knocker. For good measure she rang the bell. Alice would be so annoyed. She shifted restlessly from one foot to the other as she waited ... and waited, half resolved to go away again.

The door was eventually opened by a young girl with a pink, scrubbed-looking face and hair and eyebrows so fair they were almost white. She had no makeup on and her fine hair was pulled harshly back into an elastic band at the nape of her neck. She reminded Rhea distressingly of some albino creature, a rabbit or a rat.

'Yes?' The girl's voice was uninterested and her eyes dull, like cold blue pebbles. At least, Rhea comforted herself, not pink.

Rhea smiled. 'Hello, Minna.'

Recognition dawned. 'Mrs Henderson.'

'I'm afraid I'm rather late. Alice – Mrs Carter – is expecting me.'

'She does not say.' Minna looked over her shoulder into the hall. 'They eat already.' The clink of soup spoons could be heard from behind an imposing-looking door.

Rhea said a little impatiently, 'Will you tell Mrs Carter I'm here, please?'

Minna looked at her blankly and seemed on the point of refusing when the dining room door opened and Alice emerged, clutching a pale pink napkin in one hand.

'Oh, Minna,' she said in a hushed, conspiratorial voice, then seeing the front door open she stopped. 'Who is it? My God, Rhea, where on earth have you been? We'd given you up for lost. I'm afraid we've started.' She looked at her watch. 'It *is* half past nine and you weren't answering your phone. We thought something must have happened to you. It was all I could do to stop Toby rushing off to rescue you.' She looked annoyed for a moment then smiled her best hostess smile. 'Anyway, you're here now, that's lovely.'

'I'm terribly sorry, Alice. Shall I go away again?'

'Of course not, don't be silly. Well, Minna, don't just stand there, take Mrs Henderson's coat, will you please? Excuse me, Rhea, I must just see about something. Wait, I'll only be a minute and then we'll go in together.' She hurried off down the hall, the hem of her coffee-coloured gown lifting like the floating frills of a jellyfish.

Rhea stood clasping her bag, wondering whether she ought to apologise for the water stains on her dress. Minna came back from disposing of her coat in a cupboard somewhere at the back of the hall. Not for her, late as she was, the compliment of being permitted to rid herself of her coat on her hostess' bed and the opportunity to look at herself in a glass one last time before exposing herself to the ordeal of the public gaze. From force of habit she made a mental note of her coat's whereabouts in case she might want to make an unexpected departure; she always felt a little trapped in other people's houses.

Minna hovered uncertainly, twisting her hands together

in front of her; then just as Rhea was about to try to put her at her ease with some remark about the elegance of the house and the originality of the wallpaper – a pattern of orientally inspired peacocks and flowers intertwined – she gave a startled jump, said, 'Excuse me, one of the children cry,' and made for the stairs.

On the landing at the top of the elegant flight of stairs curving up from the hall there was a sudden stampede and an eruption of shrieks and yells. Minna ran like a hare two at a time up the stairs and immediately there came the pistol shot sounds of slaps on bare flesh followed by renewed shrieks, then silence. Rhea took a step towards the stairs.

A small boy in pyjamas came around the bend in the staircase and peeped cautiously down into the hall. His pale face broke into a smile and he sat down suddenly. 'Hello, Auntie Rhea. Rosem'y dragged me on my tummy. Minna smacked her like *that*.' He pulled up the left leg of his pyjama trousers and smacked his shin, hard. He pulled a face. '*Ow!*' He put his thumb in his mouth, took it out again and said, 'Where's Laurie?'

'Laurie's gone away.' *You looked so small, and with your curly hair – for a moment – but your hair is pale, almost white, and his was a soft, dark gold, so different, and his face, so different—*

'What's gone away?' He put his thumb back in his mouth.

'Gone to heaven. Like Kippy. You remember?'

'Kippy went to heaven,' Danny said cheerfully. 'Laurie gone to heaven too.' He thought for a moment. 'Can I see him now?'

'No.'

'I want to see him.'

'I want to, too. But we can't.'

'Why not?' Suddenly, perhaps sensing her emotion, he became upset.

'Because—'

'Don't cry. Mustn't cry. *Mummy!*'

'I'm not crying, Danny. It's all right.' She hadn't meant to sound so fierce.

'*Mummy!*'

Alice came hurrying back along the passage almost at a run, her long skirts swishing, her napkin held before her like a bouquet. 'What is it? What *is* it, Daniel? Stop screeching like that, don't you know Mummy and Daddy are having a dinner party? Be *quiet,* Danny! Oh God, where on earth is Minna?'

'It's my fault.' Rhea spoke firmly into the screams.

'Want Laurie.' Danny yelled. 'Want to see Laurie *now!*'

Alice rushed up the stairs and slapped him, hard. Once she had started she seemed unable to stop; she hit him several times, then looked frantically over her shoulder at Rhea.

Rhea put her hands over her face. 'It's all my fault. Poor Danny!'

Alice, hissing, smacked Danny again. Each slap went through Rhea like a blade. 'Alice, stop that!' she suddenly shouted at the top of her voice, dropping her hands from her eyes.

'What on earth is going on?' Dick's small, scandalised voice cut into the confusion. 'What utter bedlam! Alice, have you taken leave of your senses? Have you forgotten your guests? Have you no control over your children? I beg your pardon.' He caught sight of Rhea and a look of perplexity mingled with the pained severity of his expression. 'Are you all right?' he asked coldly. 'Perhaps you can tell me what has been going on here, since no one else seems willing to?'

'Danny is being a very naughty boy.' Alice's voice was trembling. 'Minna!'

'I coming!' Minna sang from upstairs. 'Danny! Time for bed!'

'Want Kippy,' Danny moaned, sucking his thumb again. He seemed unmoved by Alice's onslaught.

Perhaps he was used to it. Rhea was still furious with Alice. She caught sight of Toby standing behind Dick in the doorway, his pale face grave. Dr Wood was standing behind Toby looking attentively straight at her (probably wondering if she was certifiable) while over his shoulder a woman peered, her face interested and amused, her dress a scarlet slash like a streak of blood over one shoulder, the other bare.

Minna picked up Danny and carried him off, still sucking his thumb. He had a red patch across one side of his face where one of Alice's slaps had landed. Rhea was pinched by a more tolerant sort of sadness. Alice had smacked him far too hard.

'I beg your pardon?' Dick turned towards her, frowning. Perhaps she had spoken her thoughts aloud.

Alice smoothed the skirt of her gown carefully with both hands, looking down at it for a few moments as absorbed as if she were alone. Reassured that the creases were only minor she gave a last pat and lifted her head. 'Thank goodness for that. Now perhaps we can get on with dinner. I'm sorry about Danny, Rhea, I can't think what came over him.'

Rhea could; it was the same thing that came over her quite regularly. She wanted to sit down on the stairs and scream, too, she knew exactly how he felt.

Dick was trying to get Alice to tell him what Danny had

said but for once his overbearing tactics were not succeeding. Alice responded by making meaningful faces at him which he was too annoyed or too insensitive or both, Rhea thought, watching this pantomime, to interpret.

'Ah well, it's all a mystery.' Bored finally, he turned his back on Alice and led the way back into the dining room, brandishing his napkin with a shooing gesture as if walking through a swarm of midges.

'Yes, do come in and sit down again, everybody.' Alice ushered Rhea in at the end of the little procession. 'We still haven't finished our soup. It will be quite cold; I'll get cook to heat it up again.' Amid the various noises of deprecation and dissent which greeted this remark she said, 'At least yours will be hot, Rhea. Polly is just bringing it in.'

Chapter Ten

THE WOMAN IN THE RED DRESS SAUNTERED AHEAD OF Rhea, a cigarette in her hand. Everybody except Dick was busy reassuring Alice that their soup, however cold, would be fine – really – it wasn't a problem.

They settled themselves again like a flock of alighting birds. Rhea found herself placed between Dick, who was seated at one end of the long, oval table, and Martin Wood. Toby was diagonally opposite her, next to Alice who was at the other end of the table, facing her husband. Dick's face was morose; Toby looked pale. Rhea wondered if he was angry with her too. Alice was talking to him in a low voice. She looked unusually mature, very slender in her pale café au lait silk dress against which her elaborate hair glimmered pale gold. Her shoulders and arms gleamed as she moved, catching a sheen of light from the beige silk wall lights and a warmer glow from the tall pink candles in two silver candelabra on the table.

Polly, whom Rhea vaguely knew because her mother was Emma at the bakery, came in and placed a bowl of soup in front of Rhea. The woman in the red dress caught Rhea's eye and nodded towards her plate. 'What an exciting evening we're having. Do start, why don't you, mustn't waste all that lovely heat.' Her voice was a low, attractive drawl. Her eyes, almond-shaped, examined Rhea with an expression of quizzical amusement, whether kindly or malicious it was impossible to say. 'I must say,' – she leaned forward with her elbows on the table, waving her cigarette in a wide arc – 'it does seem unfair that you should be the one to get the hot soup when it's your fault all of ours is cold.'

Disconcerted, Rhea picked up her spoon. She couldn't be sure that the woman was joking – although surely she must be – because her face was masked by wreaths of smoke and by the hand holding the cigarette. The hand shook a little. Rhea took a spoonful of soup, the smoke dispersed, and the girl smiled to herself. Her own bowl was still untouched.

'Lay off, Sue.' Dr Wood laid his spoon down. He touched his lips briefly with the pink napkin and bent his dark head towards Rhea. He smelt faintly of soap and pipe tobacco. 'Don't pay any attention; Sue finds it impossible to be serious; she loves to mock.' He had a calm, slightly jocular manner that Rhea found reassuring and attractive. His voice was quiet, his face good-looking with dark eyebrows and a shadowy jowl. There was a watchful expression in his brown eyes. He looked as different as possible from the angry, tense person who had rung her doorbell and told her off for sleeping. In fact, Rhea suspected he had not recognised her; she probably looked completely different too.

The woman's eyes sparkled coldly at him. 'Oh darling, that's not true. I can be boringly serious about some things. You, for example.' She lowered her eyelids and tapped the ash from her cigarette deliberately into her soup. Rhea couldn't resist glancing at Dick but he had his head down, scraping up the last smears of soup, and hadn't noticed.

Dr Wood turned away and said something to Alice. Sue's eyes, withdrawing from their absorbed inspection of his profile which she had resumed the moment he turned his head away, were momentarily desolate. She bent her head and played moodily with her soup spoon. She seemed to have no intention of actually drinking the soup, now speckled with ash.

Rhea finished her own, which was chicken with a lemony tang and delicious, in silence, bewildered by the mass of unfamiliar stimuli besieging her senses. Toby made a laughing riposte to some remark of Alice's. Alice was giving him all her attention, speaking rather low, leaving Sue at the mercy of Dick on her other side and Dr Wood free to turn back to Rhea. His soup finished, he turned his whole body around, putting his arm behind his chair as if to see her properly. Again, there was a faint aroma of tobacco.

'We haven't been properly introduced. Although of course we have met before, briefly. How is Mrs Mander doing? Nurse Paul says you are very good to her.'

Sue frowned at him. 'Oh, for God's sake, Martin. Not shop. You promised.'

'So I did. Since nobody seems to have introduced us, may I present myself? Martin Wood, at your service, and the charming lady opposite is Miss – Sue – Auberon.'

'Do call me Rhea.' Rhea's knees had begun trembling uncontrollably. At any moment the table would start shaking. She put her hands under the table and pressed them down, hard.

'And of course, I owe you an apology.'

'No no. I was rude too. Shall we forget about it? I don't

normally sleep during the day, you know. It's just—' She'd been about to explain about not sleeping at night but suddenly realised that for Martin it would constitute shop, and in any case would open up a whole basketful of worms.

'Did someone ever give that poor child back his lorry?' Sue lit another cigarette and inhaled, her eyes half closed. 'He sounded practically demented. I do hope somebody did something about it. Dick, had you confiscated it or something?'

Toby broke in, his voice louder than usual. 'Rhea, we must have a chat, I must talk to you about the Hulski development, quite a lot has happened; I'd value your opinion.'

Sue looked surprised, then affronted. Dick, having drunk his soup with single-minded attention from which he had allowed nothing to distract him, now laid down his spoon, leaned towards her and muttered something, all the while buttering the remains of his roll with small, vicious strokes of his knife. Sue bent her head – she was taller than him by several inches – evidently not having heard what he'd said, and he repeated it.

'Oh my God,' she said, glancing across the table at Rhea.

Rhea closed her eyes briefly, then opened them again. 'I'm so sorry I upset everybody's meal. Being late and everything.' She looked down at her soup spoon. She would have to stop pressing down her right knee if she was going to eat anything.

Dr Wood's eyebrows rose. 'I'm sure you had a perfectly good reason. It isn't a criminal offence.'

'That's kind of you. Are you the Carters' doctor?'

'Off duty tonight.'

'Of course.' He was so obviously a doctor, with his air of slightly defensive reserve, the economical sentences, the cheerful resigned air of assuming that the person he was talking to was probably an idiot.

'You're not going to ask me for a prescription, are you?'

'I shouldn't dream of it!' She rose to the bait indignantly.

'I am here courtesy of *la belle dame* opposite who is a bosom friend of Alice's. She is my meal ticket tonight. You?'

'I'm a friend of Alice's too.' Her eyes went involuntarily to Toby.

'And the parson? Is he a friend of yours too?'

'A very good friend.' She looked back at Martin, grateful for his friendliness and wishing she felt able to sparkle up and amuse him, to flatter him with wit, to say all the things which ought to be said at dinner parties by candlelight to an attractive man.

The doctor glanced curiously across at Toby who was listening with a slightly petrified expression to Alice. Dick turned to Rhea, wiping his buttery fingers on his napkin and allowing his eyes to slide coldly down her décolletage. 'I hope you did not have too much of a rush getting here, Mrs Henderson.'

Rhea wondered if he was being sarcastic. She said sincerely, 'I'm frightfully sorry I was so late. It was unavoidable, I'm afraid.' She had a sudden recollection of Mavis floating, singing, in her delicious bath, and smiled.

'I'm glad you find whatever it was that kept you so amusing.' Dick turned back to Sue who was staring at Rhea as if she'd grown an extra head.

Martin tipped his head towards her. 'How lovely to see you smile. Do it again. I wish you'd tell me what you were thinking about just then.'

Rhea laughed. 'I'm not sure you'd believe me.'

Dick was talking to Sue Auberon but all Sue's attention

was on Martin and Rhea. Rhea hoped desperately that she would not apologise. It had been an honest mistake; anyone could have made it. She would so much rather nothing was said.

Polly came in and began walking round the table removing the soup plates. Just as Sue was directing the falling tube of ash from her fifth cigarette into her soup plate Polly, unaware, reached over her shoulder and removed it. The ash fell in a grey feathery heap onto the white lace placemat.

'God, you idiot, look out!' Sue snapped.

Everyone stopped talking. Her face scarlet, Polly tried to put the plate back but was prevented by an imperious wave of Sue's hand. 'No, it's no use now, take it away.'

Polly's hand shook as she did as she was told.

Dr Wood said quietly but clearly enough for the whole table to hear, 'You really are a class bitch, Sue. That was entirely your fault.'

Conversation burst out all round and Rhea willed Polly to look at her. Polly caught her eye, saw her encouraging smile and pulled a despairing face. Her eyes were full of tears.

TOBY LOOKED at Rhea's animated face. He loved that aspect of her nature, the love in her that would burst out, the desire to encourage and console. He saw the doctor looking intently at her as she turned back to Dick and felt a stab of pain which he recognised to his annoyance as jealousy. Dr Wood obviously thought she was wonderful too.

Alice, leaning forward, said, 'Penny for them, Toby. You were miles away.'

'Sorry. How rude of me. It's so pleasant here, so relaxing, one forgets one's manners. The soup was delicious, did you make it?' The words sounded false and briefly he cringed inwardly. But he meant what he had said, it was pleasant here in this pretty room with the soft lights and Rhea across the table. And he was enjoying himself because she was nearby.

'Yes, I did! I'm so glad you liked it. It's full of all sorts of things, herbs and almonds and lemon as well as the chicken. Do you cook for yourself, Toby? Do you eat properly? It must be tempting to skimp your meals when there's just yourself to cook for.'

'I'm too busy to take much trouble over cooking. At least that's my excuse. I'm out a good deal. I do cook, of course, I have one staple dish I never seem to get tired of. Do you cook, Sue?' He leaned back in his chair, trying to divert Alice's attention from himself towards his other neighbour.

Martin Wood looked across at Sue. 'I'll answer for her. She's a first class cook and a courageous experimentalist which is equally important in my book.'

Sue's face softened with pleasure; her tense shoulders relaxed. 'Thank you, kind sir. It makes for a fair number of disasters too.' She looked down at the glowing tip of her cigarette.

Rhea turned to Martin. 'Do you cook, Dr Wood?'

'Martin, please. Yes, I do, as a matter of fact. Sue's better at it than me.'

Sue looked scornful. 'Men always think they can get around us with flattery. Of course, it's nonsense. They are just as capable as women of cooking a decent meal.'

Alice smiled around. 'I can't imagine Dick in the kitchen.'

Dick shrugged. 'What would be the point? I employ a

cook for that purpose. And Alice enjoys the occasional stint at the stove.'

'I love cooking, actually.' Alice smiled at Toby.

He looked away, wishing Alice wouldn't make her partiality for him quite so obvious.

Alice emptied her glass and looked round. 'More wine, anybody? I'll have some anyway. There's red, of course, but have whichever you want. Thanks, Martin. Do help yourself.'

Martin made a rueful face. 'I'm driving. It's Sue's turn to let her hair down tonight.'

Alice looked anxious as she watched the next course being brought in. 'I hope you all like venison. I asked for the joint to be carved in the kitchen.' Plates of meat in what looked like a rich sauce were handed round by Polly with graceful dexterity, and Minna carelessly, resentment spilling out of her. 'Minna kindly agreed to help Polly this evening,' Alice went on, glancing at Minna's mutinous face. 'Ron usually buttles for us but he isn't well this evening, I'm afraid. Do pass the wine around. Rhea?'

'I'll stick with white, thanks. This looks wonderful, Alice.'

Toby watched Dick fill Rhea's glass. Again. She seemed to be drinking rather a lot. Still, none of his business.

'Ron is Polly's other half,' Dick said testily as though irritated by the obligation to explain.

'Polly doesn't look old enough to have a partner,' Rhea commented when Polly had left the room. 'She looks about fifteen.'

'She's twenty, actually.' Alice looked at Minna. 'Did the children settle down all right?'

'They okay. Danny still upset.'

'I'm sure you'll manage him splendidly.'

Minna threw Alice a look of deep scorn and followed Polly out of the room. Alice turned to Toby and said gaily over the chink of cutlery and the preoccupied silence of people helping themselves to vegetables and sauces, 'What is this special meal you cook for yourself? Do tell.'

Toby said rather brusquely, 'Do go and see to Danny if you want to. Don't worry about us.' He frowned and looked down at his laden plate. Oh Lord, he'd done it again. She'd think he was accusing her of neglecting the child.

No, it was okay, Alice seemed to find his concern amusing. 'Minna will see to him, she's better with him than I am, actually.' She looked round, smiling. 'Has everybody helped themselves to vegetables?' She rang the little silver bell at her elbow.

Sue was watching Alice, her expression cynical. She was still smoking. It was a bit inconsiderate; what about the rest of them?

Polly came back into the room.

Dick looked down the table at Alice. 'My wife is drinking too much again. Here you are, Polly. Take the vegetable dishes away and keep them hot, will you? We were interrupted, Rhea. You never actually explained what it was that held you up. An emergency of some kind, I gathered. Not a real emergency, I hope.'

Rhea's voice was cold. 'It seemed to me to be an emergency.'

Sue Auberon's eyes flashed with pleasure. She obviously thrived on dissension. She extinguished her cigarette in the black Wedgewood ashtray that had appeared by her elbow and picked up her knife and fork.

Dr Wood looked at her with a slight frown. 'Could you possibly bear not to smoke anymore until we've finished our meal? I'd take it as the most enormous personal favour.'

Sue's eyebrows rose. 'It would be an enormous favour, so you're quite right.'

Rhea said more warmly to Dick, 'It really was unavoidable. I certainly didn't want to be late. I hurried as much as I could, it was the least I could do.'

'Where did you hurry from?' Sue drawled. 'Where is your abode?' She made it sound as though Rhea had come crawling from some den in the woods.

'Not far. Only about seven minutes by car. It's more suburban than here, but quite pretty.'

'I'll vouch for that,' Martin said.

Sue's eyes flickered over Rhea's wedding ring. 'How do you know where she lives?'

Alice said quietly to Toby, 'Do tell what this dish is you like to cook for yourself. I'd really like to know.'

Toby told her, with one ear open for Martin who was saying, 'Rhea's neighbour is one of my patients. I was there yesterday. Poor old lady, she's in a bit of a state. No family to speak of.'

'Curried omelette!' Alice screamed suddenly. 'How perfectly foul!'

'It's delicious,' Toby said into the surprised silence.

The doctor looked amused. 'Is this something you like to cook? Do divulge the recipe. Something new for us to try.'

Everybody was looking at him except Alice who was giggling and sipping her wine.

'Well, you peel an onion and fry it.' He hesitated, embarrassed. 'It's terribly simple, you just bung it all in and cook it. Onion, curry powder, spices, eggs. That's all.'

'You must show me later,' Alice enthused. 'You must do it yourself and I'll watch. Will you? I want to know how you do it.'

135

'How everybody else does it, I should think,' Sue murmured. 'Priest or no priest.'

Alice broke into giggles. 'Sue, you're outrageous!'

Toby glanced across at Rhea and saw a blush forming. Perhaps the safest thing was to pretend he hadn't heard.

Dick appeared either not to have heard or was taking no notice.

Sue, looking a little subdued, was lighting another cigarette,. She seemed to have lost interest in her food. The doctor turned to Rhea and Toby heard him ask, 'What do you do? Do you live alone or do you have family? Alice is dreadfully bad about introductions.'

'That's because the only person she's interested in is herself,' Sue said under her breath.

'I heard that,' Alice snapped, and turned back to Toby.

'If you can't behave yourself,' Martin hissed between clenched teeth, 'I'm going to have to insist you go home.'

'You can't speak to me like that.'

No, you can't, Rhea thought. *Bossyboots.* She wondered if she was a bit drunk.

'I just have. Now behave.' Martin turned back to Rhea. 'Believe it or not, she thinks this kind of talk is amusing. Now, tell me about yourself.'

'I am a writer. I live alone. I have no family.'

The feeling of betrayal was complete and shattering. She blinked. Her carefully manufactured calm began to dissolve, and she started to shiver uncontrollably.

He was looking at her, frowning. 'Are you all right?'

Her teeth chattered. Claustrophobia knotted around her, tying her in. Her feet felt icy cold, the food sat like a stone in her stomach, she was terribly afraid she was going to be sick. She took in lungfuls of air, desperately trying to hide her distress.

Sue was talking animatedly to Toby, and Dick as usual was concentrating exclusively on his food. The room felt stuffy and overwarm, the air laden with the aroma of food. Rhea put down her fork; her discomfort increased and she turned to Martin with an unconscious gesture of supplication. She had to get out. She sat back in her chair, pretending to rummage in her bag for a tissue.

Suddenly she felt a little better, safer. She breathed in, relaxed slightly and felt better still. It was going to be all right. She felt inexpressibly relieved and started to giggle helplessly. She couldn't help it and she couldn't stop. Dick lifted his head with his loaded fork halfway to his mouth and switched his attention to her. He always had to pick the wrong moment. She giggled some more. She felt a rush of panic as the gusts of laughter swept through her.

'It wasn't that funny,' Martin said quickly, laughing himself.

Oh, the perfect gentleman ... Rhea tried to catch her breath. She gave him a grateful look and set herself off again. Dick, losing interest, switched his attention to Sue whose voice was now raised in a tirade against the inefficiency and duplicity of her local garage; Alice's voice joined hers in heartfelt agreement and Toby leaned on one elbow, listened and said nothing.

Rhea's eyes filled with tears of irrational mirth.

Martin shifted his chair slightly round and leaned towards her. 'Shall I tread on your foot? Or would a glass of cold water – thrown over you of course – be better? Or should I smack your face? That works, sometimes, in the face of unexplained laughter.'

Rhea looked at him and took a few breaths. 'I think it's

gone. I haven't done that since school. How simply awful. Perhaps if you threaten to take five pounds off me if it starts again, I'll stop. That works with hiccups.' She felt slightly less pallid, as though the laughter had done her good.

'It's nerves, of course you know. Yours, if I may say so, seem pretty far gone.'

She tried to make a joke of it. 'Lucky I'm not your patient then.' She sat back and exhaled. What a way for a doctor to end up on his night off, sitting next to a candidate for the loony bin. She sat quietly, giving herself time to calm down. It was a relief to be with a stranger, someone who meant nothing to her and who knew nothing of Laurie. To him she was simply an ordinary girl, not a person marked by tragedy.

Toby turned to Sue, interrupting Alice quite rudely, Rhea thought. Although you couldn't blame him for trying to deflect her: Alice had been so obvious, concentrating almost exclusively on him. After all her plans and schemes she was making a mess of it.

Dick had lapsed into a morose silence, apparently unwilling to exert himself beyond advising Sue that the obvious thing to do was to change her garage.

'Do you – what do you do for a living?' Rhea heard Toby ask Sue.

'I?' She turned on Toby with large, surprised eyes. Her mouth pouted with unconscious sensuality. Alice had turned her attention to Martin, so Rhea was able to relax for a moment and listen. 'I design clothes.'

Surreptitiously Rhea examined Sue's high, arched eyebrows, the deep-set blue eyes, the aquiline nose and drooping, disappointed mouth. Handsome rather than beautiful; attractive, certainly. Her skin was brown and clear, her hair a dark auburn with a pale pink streak in the front.

'You, I take it, are a parson. Much more interesting.'

'I dispute that, but yes, I'm the curate at St. Andrew's.'

'Wherever that it. I'm afraid I don't subscribe to these outlandish superstitions. What on earth are you doing in this den of thieves?'

Toby laughed.

Alice interposed, 'Sue, that's rude.'

Toby looked surprised. 'I like people who are honest about what they think. I'm here because Alice invited me. I met Alice through Rhea. To be honest, I think I'm making up numbers.'

Alice straightened her back. 'Nonsense. You're guest of honour.'

Sue's eyebrows rose. 'Why?'

Toby looked as though he'd like to know the answer to that one too.

'Does there have to be a reason?' Alice rang the little silver bell at her elbow. 'Rhea darling, will you have some more?'

'For your pretty blue eyes, is my guess,' Sue said under her breath.

'Grey.' Rhea spoke half to herself.

Meat and veg were brought in again by Polly and offered round. Presumably Minna was upstairs with the children.

Toby shook his head. 'I had an enormous helping the first time. It was delicious.'

'Quite the little courtier,' Sue said, very low.

He turned and grinned at her. 'I'll give you a job as my conscience.'

Rhea felt a little disturbed. Toby obviously liked Sue.

Perhaps she was saying things he rather wished he could say himself.

'Now that might be a lot of fun.' Sue looked at him from under lashes thickened with blue mascara.

'What kind of clothes do you design?'

'Is this genuine interest or merely politeness?' She leaned back with a tired sigh and fitted another cigarette into a long black holder.

'Both.'

Polly came in with a pile of plates and distributed them around the table.

Sue smiled, squinting down at her cigarette as she lit it with her small blue enamel and gold lighter. The lighter had lain beside her wine glass since the last cigarette and seemed as much a part of her as the bright red lipstick and the gold snake necklace with the ruby eyes encircling the strong brown column of her neck. She narrowed her eyes and inhaled deeply. 'I've been working freelance for a while, but I've just burned my boats and signed a five year contract with Ina Jones. You won't have heard of her. She supplies Liberty's, Fortnum's, all the big stores. She's on the up as a name in the fashion industry. I like her, she likes my work and she says I can have my head, so how could I refuse?' Her eyes sparkled briefly; it seemed to Rhea that she deliberately extinguished the glow.

Toby looked impressed. 'You must be good.'

She looked at him mockingly and he said, slightly exasperated, 'You don't trust anybody, do you?'

Everybody at the table was now listening. Sue shrugged. 'In my business, you don't, you rely on yourself absolutely. Other people either want to make money out of you or stab you in the back. Nobody cares if you succeed except you yourself. You learn to rely on your own judgement, not other people's. You wouldn't last a week, otherwise.' She tapped ash into the ashtray.

Toby leaned sideways to let Polly put a wine glass by his place.

Alice was trying to attract his attention. 'Do you like chestnuts, Toby?'

'I love the roasted ones, anyway.'

Alice spooned glistening brown lumps from a silver dish Polly was offering her onto Toby's plate and gave it to him.

Toby thanked her and accepted the plate. Alice served herself and Polly moved on. Toby turned back to Sue, evidently unwilling to snap the delicate thread of understanding they were weaving between them. Sue was being offered the chestnuts by Polly. Toby turned back to Alice and said, 'Thanks Alice, this looks wonderful; you're looking after us extremely well.'

She looked pleased and watched anxiously as he helped himself to cream. The chestnuts, gleaming in a syrupy sauce, looked rich and delicious. The others were still being handed theirs; Rhea watched Toby's face as it dawned on him that Alice had served him personally, before anybody else.

Martin had turned back to Rhea again. 'Do you often dine out? Do you have a madly busy social life? I imagine you do.'

He had spoken almost without thought and Rhea felt rebuffed, wondering how he could have formed an impression of her that was so ludicrously wide of the mark. He clearly had no interest in what she was really like. Well, in view of her performance this evening she could hardly blame him. 'Absolutely not. I hardly go out at all.' This could sound like self-pity but she didn't want to start explaining about Laurie so she said quickly, 'I like my own company. I'm a quiet sort of person.'

'What a waste.' He looked at her teasingly, eyebrows raised.

'I go to parties now and then and people come to supper. That's my favourite kind of evening, a few friends for a fork supper on our knees in front of the fire in the winter or in the garden in the summer: wine, you know, and something substantial to eat, and lots of conversation. I don't mean – I mean this is lovely but—'

'I know exactly what you mean. No need to explain.' Polly intervened and he helped himself to chestnuts.

Rhea was flushed with the effort of trying to appear cheerful, sociable and above all, normal. 'Of course, my social life is a bit spasmodic. I'm a writer, and at certain stages of the book I don't do anything else at all.'

'You're a writer! How interesting. Tell me about it.'

She felt suddenly exhausted. She had already told him she was a writer and he had forgotten already. Or hadn't been listening. She leaned back in her chair with a little sigh. 'I haven't been doing much lately. I'll be into it again soon.' Liar, liar, pants on fire. She felt the same cringing sensation she used to feel in those distant days before her first novel had been published, when people who knew she was writing were always expecting something dramatic to have happened and nothing ever had. She had felt that she was constantly disappointing people. She had almost forgotten those tense, more or less unhappy days when she had been struggling, at the beginning, before Tom, before Laurie.

Martin, who had finished his chestnuts, was examining her face again. 'You're looking very serious. Do you want some cheese? Or a biscuit?'

'Not for me. You have some.' She watched him pass the cheese board on to Alice. He turned back. 'Don't you want to talk about your work?'

'I'd rather talk about yours.' After a pause she went on, 'I'm so sorry, I'm being a most awful bore. I shouldn't have come. I wouldn't have, only Alice insisted.' She wondered what had prompted this outburst of honesty; perhaps it was because he was kind and had been nice to her.

He was looking at her with a puzzled expression, his eyes curious and sympathetic. 'My God. I've just realised who you are.' He turned away as though embarrassment had deprived him momentarily of speech. He turned back. 'Alice told me about your little boy. I am most terribly sorry. What a dreadful thing to happen.'

She swallowed. 'Thank you.' She looked at him. 'Are you sure this doesn't constitute shop?'

It had happened, somebody had mentioned Laurie and she hadn't collapsed, she hadn't fainted, she had coped. She'd even made a kind of a joke. She glanced at him but the compassion in his eyes almost undid her. 'Could we talk about something else now?'

'Yes, of course.'

'Please don't bother about it. Don't say anything. Please.'

'I won't, of course I won't. It's just—'

'Nothing at all or I won't be able to stay. Perhaps I should go home anyway, I really don't know what on earth I'm doing here.'

'Do you want to go home? I'll take you if you like.'

'You're very kind. I'm not usually like this, honestly, I can be quite good company, so I've been told.' She was beginning to feel rather drunk. 'Goodness, you might have to! I drove here. I shouldn't have been drinking at all. I forgot.' She looked at him, biting her lip. 'What an idiot.'

'Don't worry about it. Do you good to relax. I'll take you home.'

'I can easily walk, it isn't any distance. Anyway, what about Sue?'

'She can take my car.'

Rhea drank some more and became aware of a feeling of pleasant lassitude. She smiled at Martin, who was watching her thoughtfully, and put her glass down with great care. Her head spun a little. She drained her glass and the top of her head drifted off somewhere. Perhaps she could leave through the gap and float around for a bit. 'This really is the answer; whyever didn't I think of this before? Wine ... beautiful, beautiful wine.'

'Perhaps you'd better not drink anymore.'

'I wonder what will happen when I have to stand up.' She realised suddenly that Sue and Alice were on their feet. Where had all the time gone? The cheeseboard had apparently done the rounds of the table without her being aware. The men were all standing up too. Toby was looking at her anxiously. Everybody was waiting for her.

Martin was holding the back of her chair. She tried to stand and was greatly amused by her failure to succeed. The faces seemed to be registering surprise and a certain amount of frost. There was anguish on Toby's followed by relief as she managed it at last, holding onto the table's edge, and slowly followed the other women to the door, swaying gently. At the door she turned and waved not to Toby but to Martin who was watching her with an expression of stoical resignation as though he had seen all this many, many times before. She resisted a strong impulse to thumb her nose at Dick who was looking even more po-faced than usual.

Dick the Prick, she thought, giggling to herself. Dick the Prick. She froze for a moment, wondering if she had spoken out loud. Nobody fainted so she couldn't have done.

Alice was moving towards the stairs, 'We'll go upstairs and refresh for a moment. They'll be a while so we have time. Dick still likes to do the port and nuts thing; it gives them a chance to get to know one another, I suppose.'

Sue turned to Rhea, trailing behind. 'Are you okay?'

'Yes, I think so, thank you for asking.'

When she reached the bottom of the stairs, Sue was waiting for her. 'I hope Martin hasn't been lacing your drinks.'

'No no, I'm fine. Ooh, look, I'm floating. My feet have disappeared.' It was true, she couldn't feel her feet at all. She skimmed effortlessly up the stairs. 'Where's Alice?' she called over her shoulder to Sue when she'd reached halfway.

'Alice has gone ahead.' Something was amusing Sue. She started to laugh.

Rhea laughed in sympathy. It was nice when people were happy.

Alice was waiting for them on the landing.

Sue called up to her. 'Do you think she's all right?'

'Who?' Alice peered over the banister. 'Oh. Rhea, are you okay?'

'I'm wonderful, thank you so much for asking.'

Rhea stumbled on the top step but righted herself. Alice was standing outside an open bedroom door, frowning. 'Oh *Rhea*,' she said. 'How on earth did you manage to get into this state?'

Rhea scampered along the passage towards her. Alice snatched at her as she passed but Rhea evaded her, giggling, and rounded the corner.

Alice called after her, 'Rhea, come back here.'

Rhea stopped laughing and began to feel sad. Alice needed her and she wasn't sure she'd be able to help, she was starting to feel a little sick. She mustn't be sick here. She turned round and trotted back around the corner.

Alice had stepped out to try to catch her. Oh dear, she ought to stop but unfortunately she couldn't, not just at the moment; there was something she absolutely had to do. Only problem was she couldn't exactly remember what.

Home, that was it, she was supposed to be going home. She scurried round Alice and made for the stairs. Actually, she was *longing* to go home. There was someone else who wanted to go home, too, but who on earth was it? It was really important to remember so she could help them. You couldn't help someone if you couldn't even remember their name. She came to a halt, frowning. Who was it?

Ah yes. Mole, that was the boy, the little chap with the black coat and the pink nose in Laurie's *Wind in the Willows*. Her eyes filled with tears. Mole wanted to go home really, really badly. Poor little Mole. And Mole was quite right, home was the best place in the whole world. It was where the heart was. Wherever you wandered, there was no place like it. Home sweet home. 'Mole,' she said aloud, and set off again.

Sue, at the top of the stairs, put an arm out to stop her but Rhea dodged past.

Sue peered down the stairs and started to laugh. 'She's sliding down the bannisters. She's come off the end and now she's sitting on the floor.'

'Oh God. I'd better get her back up here before the men come out. I don't want Dick to see her like this.'

'Or the parson. I don't think he'd approve.'

'Come on, Rhea.' Alice ran down the stairs and helped Rhea to her feet.

'Mole,' Rhea said.

'Up you come. Up the stairs, come on, up, up, one at a time.'

'Are you my mother?' Rhea said.

'Of course I'm not your mother. Honestly, Rhea.'

They reached the landing again. Danny appeared in a doorway. 'What's going on? You woked me up.'

'What are you doing here?' Alice demanded. 'Why aren't you in the nursery?'

'I been asleep on your bed, with the coats.'

'Oh, Danny.'

'And Benjie.'

'Oh, Danny. Whatever would Dadda say?'

'And Benjie's had kittens.'

'What?'

'I counted them. Six. I can count up to six.'

'Super dooper,' Rhea said. 'Can I see 'em?'

'No,' Alice said. 'Anyway, he can't possibly have had kittens.'

'Why not?' asked Sue.

'He's a gerbil.'

Sue gave a little scream. 'I can't stand gerbils. They're rats in disguise.'

Rhea started screaming too, to keep her company. Danny joined in. Alice, completely losing her cool, started screaming too. They all stood on the upstairs landing and screamed their heads off.

The dining room door opened and Dick shot out like a torpedo, his napkin dangling from his hand. 'What the hell is going on?'

Alice stopped screaming. 'There's a gerbil and six babies in the coats,' she called down to him.

'There can't be. All right then,' – he started to climb the stairs – 'out of my way, I'll get rid of them.'

Danny started yelling again. 'He's going to kill Benjie! Don't let him kill Benjie, Mummy!'

'Who's Benjie?' Dick stopped halfway up the stairs.

'My gerbil!'

Dick turned round. 'This is a madhouse. I am going to the library. Alice, this is all your fault. Tell me when they've all gone home.' He went back down the stairs, turned left and disappeared from view.

Alice's mouth fell open. Rhea giggled. Alice looked like the rainbow fish in Laurie's story book.

'What about the others?' Alice said. 'Rhea, this is all your fault.'

Sue laughed. 'Never mind them, I'll go and keep them company. Let me know when you've found the gerbils and I mean all seven of them. I'll come to the christening.'

Rhea began laughing immoderately. 'Toby can christen them.'

'Minna!' Alice shrieked. She opened a door and shoved Rhea through it. 'Go in there at once and lie down. Stay here till I come and get you. Don't move. Thank God Dick didn't notice how drunk you are, we'd never have heard the end of it. There's a bathroom through there. Where's Sue? Oh, she's gone downstairs. Right. Danny, you come with me. Come on, show me Benjie. Minna!' she yelled again, closing the door.

Rhea lay on a bed that felt like clouds, her head whirling round and round, only dimly aware of the voices in the passage outside the door. The voices faded and she lay cocooned in silence, soothed by the pearly light from the bedside lamp and the apricot softness of the walls and ceiling. Her mind reeled delightfully. She forgot Laurie, she forgot everything in a blissful melting of body and bones into air. She was never going to move again; she was floating in a warm sea, cushioned inside this apricot warmth that reminded her of the inside of a Chinese lantern.

Perhaps she had died. But in that case, where was Laurie? She could try to look for him here on this astral plane but her head felt so heavy she couldn't move it. Later, she thought, later; there's no hurry. She drifted into sleep.

She dreamed that Laurie was standing beside the bed waiting for her to wake up so he could speak to her. He had one of his model boats in his hand. She couldn't see which one because the light was too dim. He held it up so she could see it properly and he smiled, a happy, loving smile.

When she awoke she was alone in a strange room. Still wrapped in her dream, she held her arms out for Laurie, but he wasn't there.

Chapter Eleven

RHEA STOOD IN THE KITCHEN, ONE HAND PRESSED against her temple where a chorus of drums beat a reproachful *chamade*. Last night at Alice's she'd been discovered by Toby tiptoeing across the hall towards the front door, her shoes in her hand. Toby had insisted on driving her home since, as he rightly pointed out, she was in no condition to drive. In vain she'd protested that she had no intention of driving, she had decided to walk. Toby would have none of it; he would take her home. He promised Alice that he would return the next morning for his bike and with that, though clearly resenting his being whisked away, she had to be content.

Rhea had looked forward to walking home, to the peace, the silence and the opportunity to clear her head. Being baulked of it annoyed her and in the car she was ungracious. Toby, ignoring her bad mood, told her that Dr Wood had gone upstairs to look for her but finding her asleep in Alice's spare room had come downstairs again. He'd been concerned about her, Toby said.

She wasn't surprised Martin had been concerned; he

was a doctor after all – probably thought she'd be better off in a loony bin. She yawned; her head ached; it felt too heavy for her neck; when she moved, bright stars like the sparks from a bonfire leapt and sank inside her skull. *A bonfire of the vanities.* She filled the blue mug with water from the tap, drank deeply, then wandered around the house, stunned by the silence, the noise and tumult of the evening before reverberating through her.

In the breakfast room she leaned against the windowsill, recalling a summer night when she had danced with Laurie in her arms to lull him, wakeful and anxious with some inexplicable foreboding. She had held him and hummed a tune he loved – something cheerful – Glen Miller – *String of Pearls*? Something like that.

She was afraid that she was beginning to lose her grip on him. She could feel him retreating further and further away. She foresaw with terror the inevitable end, that he would be lost to her as completely as though an ocean divided them.

She hurried up the stairs and along the passage to his room. This time she didn't hesitate; she pushed open the door and went straight in. She went to his chest of drawers and began to wrench open the drawers, pulling out clothes in armfuls, his denim dungarees, his jerseys, pants, socks. She looked wildly around, and her eyes met the cold, beady stares of the silent, stuffed toy animals ranged along the window ledge.

She began to panic; her heart started to pound. She took deep breaths to steady herself. It was all dead! It was all – nothing. Nothing but bits of cloth and stuffing and wool ... it was all rubbish ... Laurie wasn't here; he had gone.

A coldness settled over her like a coating of ice. She sat down on Laurie's bed. Complete silence descended but she wasn't aware of the silence nor of herself sitting on the bed. Only of the extraordinary coldness which gripped her and started her shaking as if in the grip of a rigor, so that soon she was sitting there in the silence, her teeth rattling like castanets, startlingly loud, the only sound in the empty room.

SPRING TURNED to summer without her being aware of it. The trees filled out with greenery, the delicate sprays of pale young leaves darkened and thickened among the branches; the garden was full of sunlight and the song of birds. Her thoughts still groping in darkness, her body cold, Rhea weeded the flower beds obsessively, only vaguely aware of what she was doing, tormented by the fear that his face was fading from her memory.

Halfway up the tiny garden, set into a niche between two rose beds, the sand pit, wet with dew, lay dishevelled, still scattered with Laurie's toys, his bucket and spade and the bright pink elephant watering can. Mostly she pretended the sand pit wasn't there and noted these relics warily out of the corner of her eye, but one morning with no forewarning she approached the sand pit as though drawn by a magnet, dropped onto her knees on the wet grass and picked up Laurie's red and yellow whistle. She heard the note the whistle made. She heard it play. She saw Laurie stomping around the garden path, tummy sticking out, head up, marching in time to the music.

'Laurie,' she said aloud, her rigid self-discipline deserting her. 'Laurie.'

He was with her again, inescapably. She sat very still and felt the small head tucked under her chin, the cloud of soft hair, the weight on her lap and under her left ribs. Now it was bedtime and they were reading *Appley Dappley's Nursery Rhymes*, Laurie's favourite book. When they came to the poems he liked best he wriggled, stroked the pages ruminatively with his fingertip and threw his head back to grin at her, his eyes shining. At the end he closed the book with a little sigh.

'Bye-bye Appy Dappley. See you mornin'.'

She held him in a long hug before lying him down to sleep.

'Kiss Teddy too.'

Teddy lay down with him. Laurie's eyes were dreamy, his thumb hovering near his mouth. His soft gold hair curled like vine tendrils; she would have to cut it soon. It was too long, but so pretty and so soft, like fine spun, honey-coloured silk. She stroked his forehead and his round cheek and ran her finger down his tiny nose.

'Knock at the door ...' She tapped his forehead. 'Peep in!' She touched the corners of his eyes. 'Lift up the latch.' She touched the tip of his nose. 'Wipe your feet,' – she stroked her finger this way and that on his upper lip – 'and walk in!' Her fingers walked up his chin. 'Shake hands,' – she pinched his left cheek – 'and *how* do you do?' She pinched the other one.

He dissolved into giggles, his eyes shining, hunching up his shoulders, head sideways, ticklish.

'Knock a-door *again*!' His voice was unsteady with laughter; he caught his breath. That had been a mistake, he was sleepy before and now he was ready for games but still open to suggestion.

'More in the morning. Laurie go to sleep now like a good boy. Teddy's sleepy too – look! Teddy's lying down too.'

'Teddy smilin',' Laurie said happily.

She was kneeling on the grass by the sand pit, and she was alone. Laurie was not here. Laurie was nowhere.

'Laurie?' she said, her lips dry as dust.

Her heart began to beat very fast, her stomach churned. She rushed back to the house and into the downstairs lavatory and sat with her head bent over her knees, waves of sickness washing through her and her stomach dissolving.

IT WAS WORSE than she could possibly have imagined, this terrible letting go. She would fight it tooth and nail, she told herself, it would happen despite herself, without her permission. This feeling of exclusion from him was almost too much to bear, especially as she was haunted by the maddening suspicion that this was something he wanted, that he was deliberately pushing her away. She didn't know where this idea had come from, but she couldn't get rid of it.

She was becoming confused about the order of events in his short life and this was another weight on her mind, the speed with which she seemed to be forgetting isolated incidents or, worse, his particular mannerisms and expressions. Why hadn't she written them down, the verbal absurdities she'd laughed over, the day and hour that each important step forward had been taken, the first tooth, the first word? She had kept no record of these things anywhere. She asked herself whether such records would have delayed the fading of his bright image.

There were digital photos of him on her iPad but she couldn't bring herself to look at them; they were the last ditch, the last outpost of her experience of him. Once that boundary had been crossed there would be nowhere else to go. Once she stood with the iPad in her hand, her stomach full of butterflies, on the point of pressing the photo icon, longing for the momentary ecstasy as an alcoholic yearns for a drink. But she was scared. She had read somewhere that if you looked at a photo for too long it would superimpose itself on your memory of the real face so that you would never again be able to recapture the living image. So resisting the temptation she sat in his room, looked at his clothes, held them, pressed them to her face, breathed in what was left of his little-child scent. She sat on the floor and played with his toys; she looked at his scribblings, held his worn crayons and the china piggy bank with his 'savings', a few pence, rattling round inside.

But the room was beginning to go cold on her, to lose its evocative power. She had known this would be the inevitable end; the pain she had felt in his room the morning after Alice's dinner party had ushered in a clearer vision of the future. Full of resentment, she accepted that there would be change. But in calmer moments the room gave her a sad kind of comfort.

She weeded the garden, cleaned the house and sat like a convalescent for hours on end in the orchard under the apple trees, her thoughts moving in an endless spiral with no beginning and no end. Sometimes she thought about her situation, about how far she had progressed on this journey … where to? To the other side of grief? She felt in a kind of limbo, a little removed from the immediate agony but nowhere near acceptance and resignation. The sharpness of the first anguish had been in its own way a reassurance, a proof of Laurie's existence. Now she seemed to be in a void created by the passing of time.

She began to doubt herself. She didn't know what to do, how to fill her time. She didn't want to change. She didn't want ever to feel any different from the moment of that first bitter knowledge, that realisation. It had come when she had been sitting on the back doorstep in her dressing gown that morning when Toby had come. That moment was the closest connection she had with Laurie. Why would she want to change when to change meant to leave him behind to be folded gently, step by inexorable step, back into the womb of time, until one day he would be completely gone?

If she could keep the poignancy of her grief at its most intense even once in a while, then she might keep him with her for ever. Her instinct was to build a shrine, to cover a wall of his room with photographs of him and pile up his clothes and toys underneath it. The temptation to do this was almost overwhelming but when it came to the point she was stopped by her conviction that this was not what Laurie wanted, in fact was the opposite of what he wanted.

Once he had fallen down and grazed his knee on the terrace. He'd rebelled against the pain which was considerable as the graze was deep; he'd screamed and thrown himself about, shocked and outraged, even hit her at first when she went to comfort him. But eventually he let her hold him in her arms and acknowledge the hurt with him and he'd seemed to be comforted by not having to bear the pain alone.

Who would bear this pain with her – God? But he was the one who was responsible. If He created everything then he created this too. They said that in His inimitable way He suffered with you. How did that work, then? Also, how was it supposed to help?

Did He disapprove of pain? If He did, of what aspect of it? Of suffering itself, or of humanity for being the sort of people for whom suffering was necessary? Buddhists said that suffering was caused not by the experiences we have but by our reaction to them. This made more sense but how did one learn, how could one teach oneself to react in the right way? Her yearning for Laurie often brought about a savage, frustrated fury. It was her will that was being broken as much as her heart.

She began to go for long walks every day. Walking relieved her restlessness and exhausted her physically so that she slept better at night. Often, she turned towards the river. She walked for miles along the riverbank watching the seagulls, circling idly on the tide foraging for scraps among the houseboats moored along the bank or perched impassively on mast heads and buoys. She was soothed by the water itself, by its brilliance, the limpid reflections of the clouds, its drifting motion. Sometimes she crossed by the ferry and walked along the muddy footpath on the other side where anglers fished and fewer people came.

She cut herself off deliberately from parks and playgrounds where small children skipped and chattered, pulling at their mothers' hands. She felt that she would taint the children if she went near them. When she couldn't avoid them, every sight and sound pricked her like a thorn, the pain immediate and physical, bringing a sharp constriction of the heart, an agonised longing leaving her depressed and weakened. So she brushed past, eyes down and ears deliberately closed, and when she had passed by her heart ached because perhaps there might have been a child who looked a little like him; she might have been able to persuade herself, just for a moment ... but no. She pulled herself up firmly. She didn't want to end up snatching babies out of prams.

After a while she gave up trying to remember him. She shut the door of his room and tried to forget him even though doing this woke in her a bitter sense of betrayal and a feeling of absolute loneliness. This loneliness was recent. Too preoccupied before with the violence and passion of her feelings, now in this period of depression and the flat, unhappy acceptance of his absence it invaded her days and nights like a sickness.

Alice dropped in more and more often. She seemed restless, she either talked too much or sat in unresponsive silence. Rhea found her tenseness and dissatisfaction unsettling and wanted to help her, but she didn't know how. So she waited.

'Martin phoned,' Alice said one morning, sitting as usual on the kitchen table swinging her legs while Rhea did the ironing and waited for the kettle to boil. 'He asked about you. He wanted your phone number. Are you ex-directory or something? Has he phoned? He said he was going to.'

'No, he hasn't. I shouldn't think he will, either. It was probably about Mavis.'

'Who, her next door? No no. He fancies you, I know he does. I'm amazed he hasn't rung.'

'He may have done. I don't always answer the phone.'

'What, you mean you sit there and let it ring? I couldn't do that to save my life, I'm far too nosy. Anyway, don't you like him? It looked as though you were getting on like a house on fire at my dinner party.'

Rhea looked at her dubiously.

'Oh well.' Alice jumped down from the table and watched Rhea spoon coffee grounds into the cafetière. 'I'd be flattered if it was me, I think he's heavenly – don't you, Rhea, don't you think he's good-looking?'

'He could be Brad Pitt and I don't think I'd notice at the moment. Anyway, what about Sue?'

'That's all over. Everyone's amazed it's lasted this long, they've been at each other's throats for such ages.' Alice reached up for two mugs and set them down by the cafetière.

'Poor Sue. She loves him, I'm sure she does.'

It amused Rhea that Alice now made herself so much at home. Once she caught herself thinking that if she started working on a new book she wouldn't be quite so happy then about Alice breezing in and out the way she did. Then she wondered, her heartbeat quickening, whether this meant that she thought there was a possibility that she might actually start to write again one day. She had been considering doing something else – anything, stacking shelves in Tesco or trying for a job in the library; she had assumed that writing for her was now a thing of the past and she would have to do something soon; her meagre capital was dwindling fast.

Alice watched as Rhea filled their mugs. 'You are funny, Rhea, don't you want – are you really not interested?'

Rhea sighed. 'I don't know.' She carried the mugs over to the table. 'I don't know about anything anymore.'

'Aren't we going in the garden?'

'Sorry. I wasn't thinking. Of course.'

'I'll get the chairs out. Do you really want one of those horrible uncomfortable ones? I want my super long one. Aren't you going to be too hot in those jeans?'

'I'm never too hot. I'm never hot enough.'

Alice dragged the garden bed out of the shed. As soon as the warmer weather had come she had adopted it for herself. Rhea preferred to sit upright in a position of preparedness. For what? She didn't know. All she knew was that there was no way she could relax and lie prone in the sun as Alice did.

Alice settled herself and took the mug Rhea held out to her. 'I wonder if Toby will drop in.'

'What's today? Wednesday. He might. Perhaps this afternoon.' Now Alice would stay, but it didn't matter. The days when time had been so precious and her need to get on with the writing so urgent that she couldn't have borne this kind of interruption, seemed part of another life.

'How is he?' Alice lifted her face up to the sunlight. 'I don't seem to have seen him for a while.'

'He's been away on a conference; he only got back yesterday. I thought he said you were helping with the transport for the senior citizens' evenings at the vicarage. Don't you see him then?'

'He hasn't showed up. I didn't know he'd been away. Anyway, we can't really talk with all that going on. I thought he looked a bit tired the last time I saw him. He had that drawn look he sometimes gets.'

Rhea hid her surprise. 'He does get tired.' She sipped her coffee. 'Will you be helping tomorrow night?'

'I said I would; might as well, I've precious little else to do. Dick's away so much and Minna can look after the children, it isn't her night off.'

'I'm sure he appreciates it. And Phil too, of course.'

'It's really Toby's thing. Still, Phil's okay, for a vicar.'

'Will you be going to Spain again this year?'

Alice stirred restlessly. She flung one arm over her head as though striking a pose. But Rhea had felt recently that Alice was losing some of her affectation, had even become more sincere in her reactions, which she felt was an improvement: the old Alice had been fun but awfully tiring. Perhaps Toby was having some influence.

'Dick did bring up the subject the other day. We might, I suppose. I don't really want to go away just now, though.' She lowered her arm and sighed. 'I don't think I can face being stuck in a hotel with Dick all day while he eyes the women up and complains non-stop about everything. Perhaps Minna might take the children and go with him.'

'And leave you on your own?'

'I shouldn't mind. It would be a relief, actually. That's not a bad idea. I might try to have a talk to Dick about it at the weekend.' She sipped her coffee.

'Won't he mind if you don't go?''

'Who, Dick?' Alice threw her an astonished look then leaned back and closed her eyes, balancing her mug between her hip bones. Rhea noticed suddenly how thin she had become. 'He'll be delighted. When I'm there I hardly see him. There's the colony, you see; there are at least two women he gets off with every year. Someone told me people take bets on which one it will be this time. He does stick to one at a time. So far. I suppose that's something.'

Rhea frowned. 'Won't the children miss you?'

'With Minna around? They won't miss me a bit.'

'Oh, Alice.'

'Oh, Alice.' She made a mocking face, her eyes still shut. 'Oh well. I've made my bed, I must lie on it, I suppose.'

After a pause Rhea said, 'Are you awfully unhappy?'

There was a long silence. Alice opened her eyes and burst out, 'You've no idea how much I envy you. Nobody to consider but yourself, free to do whatever you like, whenever you like. If you knew what hell my life was ...'

Rhea started to laugh. She couldn't help it. Alice banged her mug down on the terrace beside her chair. She sat up and looked at Rhea, her mouth a round O of indignation, swung her legs round and planted her feet on the ground. 'How dare you laugh! How *dare* you! You say you want to help me and then when I confide in you, you have the brass nerve to *laugh!*'

'I'm sorry, Alice.' Rhea spluttered to a stop. 'I'm not

laughing at you ... but don't you see? No, you don't.' She shook her head. 'Look. I'm sorry if I offended you.'

'Your nerves are in rotten condition, Martin's quite right.' Alice swung her legs back and settled down again. Not so dreadfully offended, then. 'You are so odd sometimes, Rhea, I just don't understand you.'

Rhea took a moment to collect herself. 'Look, I'm really so sorry you aren't happy with Dick. I wish there was something I could do to help.'

They sat in silence for a while. Alice said, 'I've been thinking a lot recently about my life and the way it's gone, the choices I've made. My marriage is a complete farce. I don't love Dick anymore and he sure as hell doesn't love me. Even the kids don't like me much.'

Rhea frowned. 'Of course they do, they love you.' She finished her coffee and put her mug down.

'They prefer Minna.' She looked at Rhea with bright, panic-stricken eyes.

'You can't really believe that. You're their mother; children always love their mother best, no matter what. They're just used to Minna looking after them, that's all. She won't be there for ever.'

'Rose is so like Dick. She looks like me but she's just like Dick inside. She's beginning to despise me, like he does. She's dreadfully rude sometimes, God knows what she'll be like when she's a teenager. Sometimes I feel I just can't be bothered with it anymore. Dick encourages her, he uses her to get at me.'

'Surely not.'

'Oh yes. You don't know him, Rhea, he's a monster in his own petty way. Danny loves me I suppose, that's why I take it out on him, because he doesn't argue back. It breaks my heart inside but I do it anyway. Sometimes I think I need help. I don't mean to get so mad with him.'

'Would it help if you set aside some time to do something special with the children on your own without Minna? Say a couple of times a week? So it's like a treat for them?'

'You're saying I don't spend enough time with them too. You're as bad as Toby.'

'That's not what I'm saying at all. I just mean—' Rhea gave up.

Alice was staring intently ahead at the twisted branches of the fig tree rearing up against the fence. 'If only I were free ...'

Rhea stood up and began to walk about.

'Do come and sit down,' Alice said. 'Whatever is the matter? You look so fierce.'

'Do I? I was thinking about Toby.' She came to a stop at the foot of Alice's chair.

'You don't look very happy about it.' Alice pulled a tissue out of her sleeve and blew her nose.

Rhea turned away. 'I was trying to work out how I feel about him.'

'Why, is he in love with you or something?' She tucked the tissue away again.

'I shouldn't think so.' She noticed that Alice was gripping the sides of her chair.

Alice darted a look at her. 'He worries a lot about you.'

'Does he now?'

'Don't be cross.'

Rhea strolled back. 'I'm not cross. I know he worries about me as I do about him. That's what friends do, they worry about each other. There's no more to it than that.'

Alice sat up, swung her legs round and put her feet on

the ground. 'Perhaps you should ask him. Perhaps you should think a bit harder about how you feel about him, so he won't keep wasting his time coming around all the time, if you don't want him.' Avoiding Rhea's eyes she burst out, 'Why don't you get out a bit more and meet other people instead of moping here all the time? Then he wouldn't feel he had to keep hanging around, he'd be able to get on with his own life, find someone who *does* want him.'

Rhea stared at her, open mouthed. 'Alice.'

'*No.*' Alice's face contorted. She looked as though she was about to burst into tears. 'He never gets a minute to himself what with all his visits and all he has to do. He's always dashing off somewhere. It's people like you who make his life so impossible.' Her voice rose. 'Why don't you get a life? Tell him you're okay and he doesn't need to worry about you. Let him off the hook, give him a chance. Why don't you *back off*,' she suddenly shouted, glaring at Rhea, colour rushing up into her face.

Rhea stared down at her, astonished. 'He's told you all this himself, has he?'

'No, of course not.' Alice glanced at her, slightly shame-faced. 'He doesn't need to, it's just so bloody obvious.' She swung her legs back onto the long chair, the colour in her face already fading. She lay back and closed her eyes and said more calmly, 'Why don't you go out with Martin? He's fed up with that Auberon creature, everybody knows that. She's making a complete fool of herself hanging onto him, poor fool. Everybody's talking about it.'

Rhea took a deep breath and tried to speak calmly. 'Alice. Nobody forces Toby to come here; I don't invite him, he invites himself. I'm not going to stop him coming if he wants to come. We're friends. It has nothing to do with raging lust or ulterior motives. We care about each other.

He is welcome to go on coming here as long as he chooses and it has *nothing,* Alice, to do with you.'

She felt lighter for standing up for herself. She left the terrace and went into the kitchen. She filled a mug with water from the tap and stood sipping it, astonished by the sweeping potency of her anger. You could run cars on that. But was there something in what Alice was saying?

She heard movement behind her and turned round. Alice was leaning against the door jamb, looking mutinous. 'You're so tetchy at the moment,' Alice said. 'I don't know what's the matter with me either, I seem to lose my cool over every little thing.' She blew her nose and looked around for somewhere to dispose of the tissue. 'I think I'm getting a cold.'

Rhea tipped the remains of the mug of water down the sink and rinsed it under the tap. She opened the door under the sink where the refuse bin was, then stepped past Alice out into the yard.

She walked down the garden. How flat everything was. Everything seemed shaded, even the sunlight, as though it was the start of an eclipse. She so hoped Laurie wasn't frightened, wherever he was. Would he grow up in heaven, if there was a heaven, or would he always be two and three-quarters, nearly three?

He had been so looking forward to his 'three birthday.' He loved birthday cards. He had spent hours with the pile of cards he'd been given on his second birthday, looking at the pictures and sorting them into piles based on a system only he could understand. Months ahead of time Rhea had bought the card for his third birthday. She'd hidden it in her desk and laughed over it, looking forward to his reaction when he saw it.

Perhaps she might find some other child to give it to.

Only a few weeks ago such an idea would have horrified her but now she was in a strange, impatient mood. It was as if she was sick of waiting. That was what it felt like, this endless, timeless suspension: like waiting for something to happen. She held onto the metal rung of the climbing frame and thought, this is real, I can feel it and see it, it is hard and cold. I am real, this is my body walking about, missing Laurie. This is my hand, holding onto this bit of steel and this is my mind, suffering.

'I am Laurie's mother,' she told herself. 'I am the mother of Laurie.' But with Laurie gone, was she still his mother? A mother's role involved care and he was beyond her care. She wanted desperately to believe that she had not lost the ability to care for him. She felt so useless ... her hands, her feet, her voice ... with the point of her existence gone.

She had given up trying to pray for him. Her prayers were a farce. God was, in relation to Laurie, irrelevant. There was nothing there but a vacuum, a black hole into which Laurie seemed to be being sucked more and more completely. Laurie was dead. His body had been burnt and he was dead. But where was his mind, had that gone too, his consciousness?

Were all the things human beings felt, purely chemical reactions? All the loving ... the pain, the hate, the despair? Was it really all just – biology? Surely there must be more to it than that?

If she could accept that his body had gone, then what she was left with was his mind, which was as much a part of his reality as her mind was a part of hers. But what was a mind? What did survive, if one believed in survival? Was it his mind, his unique – she was going to say, personality, but that was different again. It was a minefield. Did Laurie exist somewhere out of time, freed in some way by death?

Was he with God? But what did he know of God, her little helpless boy who never thought about such things in his life, although his passionate interest in the universe might be said to be an interest in God ... sun, moon, stars, animals, birds, trees, flowers ...

Rhea jumped. Alice was standing behind her.

Alice hopped from one foot to the other. 'There's an old lady at the door. I think it's the batty old woman from next door. Shall I say you're busy?'

She hadn't heard the bell ringing. 'I'll come.'

They walked together to the front door which stood open. Mavis hovered on the doorstep peering anxiously into the hall.

Rhea stood back. 'Hello Mavis. Do come in.'

'Oh, hello dear.' Mavis looked as astonished as though she'd been expecting someone else to be there. She stood for a while leaning on her stick, looking down at the hall floor and reassembling her thoughts. At last she looked up and said hesitantly as if still not sure she had come to the right house, 'It's my wireless. I wonder if you could – I can't get a word out of it and I'm so worried. I've only just had it mended, see. Aren't these workmen dreadful? They just don't care nowadays, do they? I wanted to listen to that funny fellow I like – George loved him, you know, used to split his sides – what was his name? I'll recall it in a minute. Anyway, I switched it on and nothing happened.'

'I'm off,' Alice said into Rhea's ear. 'Bye darling, see you soon. Bye bye, Mrs – Mrs. I must pop off home now – the children, you know.' She slipped past Mavis and tripped down to her car which she'd parked this time in the drive.

Rhea felt unexpectedly calm. She nodded at Mavis. 'I'll come back with you.'

Mavis brightened. 'Will you really, dear? I'll go on

ahead then so as not to hold you up. I remember the name of the funny fellow now. I do hope we won't be too late for his show ... Tommy Cooper, that's the one. Him with the fez.' She looked at Rhea, triumphant. 'If we're quick, we might just be in time to hear the end.'

'You don't get out enough,' Toby said. It was early evening and he had persuaded Rhea to come for a walk with him along the river.

'I do go for long tramps almost every day.' Rhea walked quickly by his side, her hands in her jacket pockets, her head down.

He had forgotten that she had begun to go for walks. 'You're still avoiding people.'

'Does it matter, really?' They passed a young couple entwined on a bench. 'I went to Alice's dinner party and look what happened then.'

'You weren't ready. You shouldn't really have gone.' He remembered Alice's behaviour that evening and the next day when he had gone back to pick up his bike. Despite her vivacity there'd been an edge of desperation that had made him uncomfortable. Still, Alice wasn't his concern; Rhea was.

'Maybe I'll come to Evensong one Sunday.' She strode along by his side, setting the pace. Toby, relishing her company, would have preferred to linger,. 'Perhaps you'll believe now what a heathen I am; I don't turn to God even when I need him the most. Does he expect me to grovel?' She smiled to take the sting out of the words. Not altogether serious, then.

'Sometimes we're least able to find God when we need

Him the most. It's as if our desperation deafens us to His voice and He can't get through to us.'

'He doesn't want to get through to me. I've tried.'

'Perhaps you shouldn't try so hard.'

Rhea looked down at her trainers. 'I think I've come to that conclusion myself. Or perhaps I'm sick of shouting at somebody who so obviously can't hear me. Or isn't interested.'

He wondered if she was annoyed with him. She must know that talking like this hurt him.

'Anyway, there probably isn't any answer, or not one he's prepared to give. So what do I do?' She looked at him, her eyes momentarily bleak and hostile.

He could feel her dejection, an almost palpable cloud around her reaching out to him but at the same time repulsing him, warning him not to get too near. He raised his hands in a gesture of futility. 'Endure. Put up with it. Wait patiently. Try not to get cynical.' He dropped his hands by his sides. 'Suffer.'

'That's cool. I don't mind suffering.' After a long pause she said, 'I really *need* to suffer. It's proof to me that I love him and that he's still my child. What's so awful, terrifying and awful, is the absolute blankness when I try to pray to God or to reach Laurie. There's this huge, deaf emptiness. There simply is nobody there.'

'Just try to be patient.'

'I still worry that he's too little to think of trying to reach me. If he was older he might try to make some attempt to let me know how he is. No.' She pulled herself up short, glanced at him with an expression that was almost humorous. 'That's rubbish, isn't it? What am I thinking of? I keep pretending, that's the trouble. I can't seem to take in that death isn't the way it is, an inexorable cutting off.' She strode on.

Toby's insides contracted. How had he had the audacity to tell her she had to wait? He didn't even know what she was supposed to be waiting for. It was just a feeling he had that if she just hung in there ... but perhaps he was kidding himself as well.

He nerved himself to speak. 'Don't stop believing in the bond of love that holds you together. It's stronger than his absence, stronger than death.' Death, he thought. End of life, annihilation, ceasing to be? No. Death was not those things.

They came to the marketplace and turned and began to walk back the way they had come.

Rhea glanced at him. 'I'm sorry I keep going over the same old ground. Boring, boring, boring. It's never exactly the same for me, some new idea seems to come each time, but I do realise how incredibly boring it must be for you.'

Toby felt an inarticulate longing to tell her that nothing could be further from the truth. You are my beloved, he longed to say: my darling, my precious one. He succeeded only, he guessed, in looking fervent. Rhea wasn't even looking at him now.

She said, looking up at the seagulls wheeling overhead, 'You know, you mustn't feel you have to come and see me so often.' Her voice sounded gruff, a bit embarrassed. 'Of course, I love seeing you but I think I've been making unfair demands on your time. I haven't meant to. I've been worrying a bit about this, actually ... I do know how busy you are.' She gave him a bright glance and went on. 'I know I went to pieces for a bit but I'm all right now. I can never thank you enough for all you've done for me but—'

He glanced at her. There were tears on her cheeks. She

was letting them dry naturally rather than wipe them away; she was too proud to let him see. He strode on, an overpowering emotion building up inside him like a volcano preparing to erupt. He walked so fast for the next fifty yards that she had to skip to keep up. His thoughts flapped in circles like a flock of birds in the middle of which a cat has suddenly appeared. He strode ahead, burning with impatience.

Rhea, breathless, caught up with him. 'You're walking terribly fast. Have you suddenly remembered an appointment or something?' She caught at his jacket as he raced ahead.

He slowed down. 'Running away from myself!' He swept his hair back over his head with both hands, giving the momentary impression of somebody tearing their hair. The words burst from him. 'Don't tell me not to come to you. I couldn't bear it.'

They walked home in almost total silence. At her gate they paused. Toby said, as though determined to ignore what he'd just said, 'You look better for the exercise. All this walking is doing you good, you've got some real colour in your cheeks.'

'Have a cup of tea before you go,' Rhea said as they approached her front door. 'It won't take a minute Your helmet is inside anyway.' She'd spoken from habit, but after what he'd just said perhaps inviting him in wasn't such a good idea; it might look like encouragement, when she had no idea how she felt. She needed time to process what he'd said.

She led the way round the side of the house to the kitchen door, her heart beating faster than usual, her thoughts in confusion. Her nervousness grew as she filled the kettle at the sink. Alice was right, she'd become horribly selfish where Toby was concerned. She'd wanted their relationship to stay the way it had always been; she hadn't wanted to have to think of him as a person with feelings and desires and problems. How stupid was that? He was a man like other men.

Toby leaned against the dresser, looking at the floor, his feet crossed at the ankle, his arms across his chest. His heartfelt words resounded in the silence, filling the space between them, binding them together. She watched the steam begin to curl gently from the spout of the kettle. Absorbed in her thoughts she splashed hot water into the teapot. She threw out the water and dropped teabags into the teapot.

Why couldn't he have left things as they were? He had changed everything by saying what he'd said. She poured boiling water onto the teabags, put the kettle back on its stand and stood waiting for the tea to brew. She had never deliberately led him on, but now she knew how he felt she was terrified of hurting him.

'I've taken the mugs over and I've got the milk.' He had opened the fridge door and closed it again without her hearing or seeing. He carried the milk jug over to the table in the annexe. 'Shall we sit here? I can't stay long.'

She followed him, carrying the teapot, her eyes on the dark blue pullover and the graceful, trousered legs beneath. It was nearly the end of June: he had been nearby all this time and she had simply taken him for granted.

When they were sitting down she snuck a look at his face. He was such an attractive man; why couldn't she feel anything? She sat sipping her tea with lowered eyes, resenting both her discomfort and him for being the cause of it. Why had he made his feelings so obvious? They'd been perfectly okay as they were. No, she reminded herself again with a twinge of guilt. *She* had been perfectly okay. She hadn't been thinking about him or cared about his feelings. She'd been so selfish.

She looked past him out of the window at the evening sky, as blue as irises, and the quiet stars beginning to appear. What a perfect evening.

She leapt to her feet, almost knocking her chair over. What did it matter to her what kind of evening it was? How could she have allowed such a thought into her head? She moved rapidly round the table and stood looking out of the window, breathing fast, her eyes burning. She gazed at the sky, tense as a soldier facing an indomitable enemy.

Were her memories of Laurie fading? Was this how it was going to be from now on? Moments becoming more and more frequent when she would be – how was it C.S. Lewis had put it – *surprised by joy*? How could she resist time itself? She heard the grate of chair legs on the quarry tiles and turned to find Toby standing beside her. She blinked in surprise. She'd forgotten he was there.

'Am I really going to get over it? Am I going to forget him?'

The sorrow on his face almost undid her. She turned to him and let him put his arms around her. He held her rigid and shivering until gradually she became calmer. She pushed him away, her palms flat against his chest. Almost in unison they turned inwards and stood shoulder to shoulder, leaning their backs against the windowsill, facing the now shadowy room.

She shook her head, feeling the need to deflect him in some way. She should not have allowed him to take her in his arms, but she had needed comfort so badly. 'I don't understand any of this. Now you see why I can't face coming to church: I'd feel a complete hypocrite. People would think I was coming because it comforted me, and nothing could be further from the truth.'

'You might find it soothing, if nothing else.'

She gave a huff of laughter. 'It isn't meant to be soothing. And how could I take Communion in this frame of mind?'

'What is your frame of mind?'

'Well, certainly not resting on God or whatever you're supposed to be doing. Talk about being in love and charity with your neighbour, I'm not even in love and charity with God.'

She felt suddenly sick of tragedy, exhausted and longing to be rid of the weight of this burden. She glanced sideways at Toby who was staring down at the floor – and she remembered what she had forgotten: how things had been before all this had happened. A memory had been triggered by the smell of his skin, the feel of his arms around her. She'd been mistaken in thinking that she hadn't fancied him.

It came back to her now that before Laurie's death, the event that had brought her life to a shuddering halt, her feelings towards Toby had started to change. She had started to fantasise about relieving him of some of that tension and restraint, that nerve-wracking saintliness. She had quivered inside when he touched her hand by accident. She had daydreamed that one day he would take her into his arms and kiss her mouth and fall in love with her.

Her lips formed themselves into a tremulous smile. She had forgotten how powerful the attraction had been. Would it have lasted? Had she looked beyond that first kiss, that embryonic satisfaction?

Following him to the front door she crushed the back of

her hand against her mouth in a half-hearted attempt to punish herself. Her teeth bruised the inside of her lip. Serve her right. To think of that, now! That was all over, of course. There was no possibility of those lost feelings being recaptured.

She watched in silence as he hauled on his boots and reached for his gauntlets. They kissed, the perfunctory contact of cheek with cheek that had come to be their customary manner of greeting and parting. He reached for his helmet and pulled it on, buckled the strap under his chin. She stood at the door and watched him stride to his bike, mount and wave goodbye.

When they had kissed, for the first time she had been uncomfortably aware of the intense emotion under the rigid control. Something had been roused, in herself or in Toby, something she didn't want, that her whole being rejected.

Chapter Twelve

June 20TH: Laurie's birthday. Rhea took his birthday card out of her desk and wrote in it exactly as though she would be giving it to him in person. She had been so dreading today that now it had come she felt relieved, but still sick with foreboding.

She planned to drive out as far as Midhurst or Haslemere with a packet of sandwiches and a drink and her paperback of Emily Dickinson's poems. She had taken to reading poetry again and was finding solace in quiet country places where she could sit reading to the sound of bees and grasshoppers and the vibration of minute wings in the heather; and sometimes a lark.

The day was fine and sunny. She walked in a wood near Haslemere where the air was dusty and tomblike, the trunks of high Scots pines rising like thin red flames from the sombre floor. She walked until the pines gave way to avenues of beeches, shady giants set far apart, their trunks rising out of the dead leaves of years, soft piles into which her feet sank. The ground between the trees was mossy and dark and smelt of fungi.

She came to a small clearing and looking around, knew she had come to the right place. The sun sparkled through the lofty canopies of leaves, its rays striking off at angles as the wind shifted the branches in slow, languourous movement. In this small, circular, almost chapel-like space there was airiness, movement and light under the high green vault. She took Laurie's card out of the rucksack where she had put it carefully between the pages of Emily's poems, and read it for the last time:

To Laurie,
from Mummy
with all her love xxxxx.

On the front of the card was the bold red letter **3**; inside, the caption over which she had so often laughed in secret:

'WHEEE! You're THREE!'

She held the card and read it slowly several times. Then she said aloud, 'Happy birthday sweetheart. Happy birthday, Laurie.'

She took a trowel out of the rucksack and began to dig. She dug a hole about twenty by twenty-five centimetres. She laid the card tucked into its envelope in the earth dark and rich with leaf mould and began slowly to fill the hole in again. The spadefuls of earth rattled on the white envelope, then as the card was gradually covered over the earth fell silently, heavy and as rich as fruitcake, and she pressed it down with her hands, securing Laurie's card in that place forever or until it rotted away. It was the burial service she couldn't remember, without which the earthly part of Laurie would never for her be truly laid to rest.

Perhaps a tree would grow. A card tree. He would have

loved the idea of a card tree. She finished the job, patting the earth down flat and finally covering the spot with a few handfuls of dead leaves. When she had moved away it would be indistinguishable from a thousand similar spots at the root of a thousand almost identical trees. She didn't want to be able to find the spot again.

She had hoped to talk to him here. She had fancied that at last her searching would be rewarded and that he would come to her here in this lonely place, even if only for an instant, and comfort her. But he had not come. She had known as soon as she reached the place that there was no one there. The air of solitude, of desertion, was so strong as to almost be a presence. This space among these trees was as empty of any human or spirit life as the remotest mountaintop.

She stood up, wiping her hands on her jeans, and looked steadily down for several minutes at the place where the grave was. Her hands were filthy, her face soaked with tears. She dragged her eyes away, lifted her rucksack off the ground and forced herself to walk away. For ten minutes she didn't look back, not even slowing her pace while she rummaged for the small plastic bag she had tucked into her jacket pocket before leaving the house, and dropped the filthy trowel into it.

It was midday already but she didn't stop to eat. She paused to put the trowel into her rucksack then continued walking all afternoon and into the evening in a great arc, cutting back across country to the place where she had left the car. When she finally opened the car door she was so exhausted that she had to sit for several minutes slumped in the driver's seat before she found the energy to start the journey home.

It was after nine. Daylight had turned to twilight and

stars glimmered in the gauzy sky. Her nostrils were full of the scent of wood bark, her hair tangled, her cheeks cold; with sunset the air had grown cold. Her jeans were torn where she had plunged through dense thickets of brushwood and hedges of gorse. Her feet were wet from a shallow, icy stream where she had found watercress growing. She was almost totally done in, but she was conscious somewhere on the margins of her mind of a faint feeling of triumph.

Just before starting the engine she whispered aloud, her hands tense on the wheel, 'I'm here, darling. See? Not despairing. This sad thing isn't going to beat us. I won't let it. It's going to be all right. I love you,' she said fiercely. 'I love you.' Just to say the words was a reassurance, like a promise to him which she felt that surely he must hear.

SHE WOKE around five the next morning and was immediately aware of a sense of lightness and alleviation. She lay for a few minutes listening to the birds, testing the feeling and gradually relaxing, for once unquestioning. Perhaps the need for questioning might be coming to an end. The feeling of relief stayed with her as she ate a slice of bread and an apple in the kitchen, her heartbeat quickening at the thought of the river awaiting her, its calm, flat surface opalescent in the early morning light with that particular muted pearliness she loved, grey then stroked with pink and yellow as the sun began to pierce the overlying mist.

She remembered the evening, only a few days ago, when she had stood with Toby in her kitchen looking out at the beauty of the night. She remembered the heartbreak she had felt at rejoicing in it. Now she couldn't think how she could have blamed herself so bitterly; now she felt the need to find joy wherever she could and draw strength from it.

Laurie had been so full of joy. This was what he was nudging her to do. The change didn't surprise her; she was changing all the time. She was not the same from one week to the next. She told herself now to go with the flow, to respond to every inspired impulse that came.

She stole down to the gate, walking on the grass beside the path in case Mavis should be up and about, hear her feet crunching on the gravel and intercept her. This was her most precious time; she thirsted for the sheer joy and physical delight of striding in blessed silence through the enchantment of the natural world. She longed for it and dreaded interruption.

She reached the gate – there was a movement, both gates clicked simultaneously and hope was gone.

'Oh, there you are!' Mavis shuffled eagerly towards her, her left hand circling in the air, her right clamped firmly round the handle of her walking stick. 'I was hoping – I hoped I might see you. My wireless has gone wrong. So annoying ... I wonder if you could ...'

Rhea said coldly, 'I might just have time.' Immediately ashamed, she hurried to make amends. 'I was just off for a walk.'

'Where, dear?' Mavis peered up at her, radiating goodwill. 'Where did you say? Off to church, were you? It said it was Sunday on the wireless.' She wheeled dangerously and set off towards her own gate. 'I haven't been inside a church for a long time. George didn't hold with that sort of thing. Couldn't stand all that preaching. Said it gave him indigestion. Telling him what to do. Said they hadn't got anything better to do and he had.' She inched up the path ahead of

Rhea. Mumbling to herself she fumbled in her bag for her keys.

Waiting behind her Rhea fumed and suffered. She longed, longed to be striding off down the hill towards the river. Soon it would be too late, the water dulled to pewter or else too bright. She fidgeted and glanced at her watch, fighting down the urge to snatch Mavis' bag from the shaking old hands and find the key, easily, in a fraction of the time.

It struck her suddenly that Laurie might sometimes have seemed irritatingly slow to someone who was not his mother. Mavis had had a mother once. Slowly her feeling of frustration subsided.

Mavis turned to her with a stricken expression, her face waxy, the tip of her nose pinched and yellow. 'I can't find them.' Her voice rose alarmingly. 'My keys – look – they're not in my bag.' She pushed the open bag into Rhea's hands. 'Can you see them anywhere inside there?'

Rhea peered inside the bag and dug her fingers into the pockets in growing disbelief. The bag was completely empty. 'They're not, are they?' She thought for a moment. 'You'd better come to my house and have a cup of tea while we decide what to do.'

'Whatever can have happened to them?' Mavis gazed at Rhea as if hoping to read the answer in her face. Disappointed, her gaze dropped. 'I'm sure they were in my bag when I came out. I always put my keys into my bag then; I hang my handbag on the door handle inside, so I'll remember it, and I always put the bunch of keys inside so I can get back into the house again. I wonder if I dropped them on the path ...' Without warning she turned, arms scarecrow-spread to balance herself, and lurched down the steps. She set off towards the gate, hunched over and peering at the ground. Rhea followed her down the path. Idiot. Why hadn't she asked Nurse Paul for a spare key?

After five minutes she persuaded Mavis to give up the search. She guided her back along the pavement. 'We'll get the fire brigade if necessary. We'll soon have you back home again.'

Seated on a chair in the kitchen, Mavis began to cry. She rummaged in the empty bag for a handkerchief. Rhea fetched a box of tissues from her bedroom. 'Please, Mavis, try not to worry. As soon as you've had your cup of tea I'll see if I can get into your house. I might be able to climb in through a window or something, it will be easy, please don't upset yourself. Have you been up long?' she asked, to distract her.

'Up? Is it the morning?'

'It's a quarter to six on Sunday morning.'

'Oh – well then – I don't think I went to bed. It's Sunday morning, is it? Oh dear. I missed my dinner yester-day, too. Got along there and the whole place was shut up. I think they've closed it down. I came and rang your bell, but you didn't hear.' Her voice was laden with grievance.

'What a shame. Didn't you have any dinner at all?'

'Not a mouthful.' She shook her head mournfully. 'And Nurse didn't come and see me yesterday either. They don't bother, you know. They don't care about the old people, they only come when it suits them. You never know where you are.' She blew her nose lustily, a trumpet sound of disgust. She shifted in her chair, sighed and wiped her mouth with a tissue. 'Do you know,' she said as Rhea set down a cup of tea at her elbow, 'I've not heard a word from my son Brendan, not in six weeks – not a word. He doesn't take the trouble to write, and the children have never written to me, not once, not even to say thank you for their birthday presents, and me their only granny! Nona's parents are both dead, you know. Killed in a car crash they were. No, they're an uncaring lot, they just don't care. I've a good mind to write to Brendan and tick him off good and proper.' Tears of weakness and disappointment trickled down her face. 'I'm going to tell him how disgusted I am with him, tell him he bloomin' well ought to make the children write, out of respect if nothing else. Don't you think that's right, Rhea? Don't you think it's disgraceful that they don't take the trouble to write? I tell you, I do. I've got a good mind to tell him he won't see a penny of my money after I'm dead: there are others who deserve it a lot more than he does – you, Rhea, for one. All the kindness you've shown me and the things you've done for me ...' She looked cunningly at Rhea out of the corner of her eye.

'I shouldn't at all like you to give me any money.' After a pause Rhea went on, 'I'm sorry if that sounds ungrateful but what I meant was, blood is thicker than water and I don't need any more money, I have my writing and teaching, which I'll be getting back to soon, and a grant I got from the Arts Council last year. There are lots of charities that do need money, of course, but I'm sure it would be a mistake.'

Mavis, not in the least interested in leaving her money to charity but only in getting her own back on Brendan, sat with her eyelids lowered, her face wearing the caustic expression it always wore when money was the subject of the conversation. She drank her tea and made no reply although Rhea thought she looked slightly relieved. She put her cup down with a determined clink. 'Well, it would serve him right. And that hulking wife of his, scheming great woman that she is.'

'You know, kids nowadays don't really write letters

anymore. Well, hardly any of them do. All they know is texting. Email, at a pinch.'

'Email ... what's email?'

'It's ... when you have a computer. You type letters on that and it goes off in a flash. You don't need to post it. Only thing is, you'd have to have an iPad, or a smart phone.'

'A smart phone?'

Rhea gave up. 'Tell me about Nona. Is she really big?' Rhea had always imagined Brendan's wife as small and quick, like Mavis in her heyday.

'Oh, she's a great big woman. Big boned and tall – shapeless. No figure. You could put two of me inside her. And she's one of those colourless women – you know – drab. Mouse face and mouse hair. She caught my Brendan all right, silly little fool. Oh well, he got what was coming to him and he's stuck with it.' Her expression was now positively evil. She had revived in an extraordinary way and was sitting crouched over her cup of tea with an expression of gloating satisfaction, her mind dwelling with pleasure on the reaction of her son and his wife if she were to cut them out of her will.

You couldn't really blame her. Rhea poured her another cup of tea.

Mavis' expression changed in a flash to one of pathos. 'Will you write the letter for me?' Her lips quivered. She took a sip, then looked up at Rhea with a determined but hopeless expression as though expecting her to refuse. 'My eyesight is so poor I can't seem to get my handwriting straight on the page and then I can't see what I've written, to go over it, see ... it's a terrible strain on my eyes. I thought, if I told it to you what I wanted you to say, you could write it all down for me. I've got to give that boy a piece of my mind.'

Rhea shook her head. 'I'm sorry, I can't possibly write that kind of letter. I'd like to help but think of the consequences! I could be accused of all sorts of things, trying to get hold of your money, for a start.'

Mavis, evidently unaccustomed to such frankness on this sacred subject, looked at her sharply, then her eyes slid away, plainly bewildered by the unexpected firmness in Rhea's face. 'You'll not help me then.'

'I'll help you to write it. I'll do everything I can to help except actually write it. But don't you think you ought to think about it a bit longer first? It's so easy to write something one regrets later.' She sighed. Mavis wasn't listening.

'I want to do it now.' She handed Rhea her cup and started to pull herself out of her chair. Her stick, resting against her bony knees, fell to the floor with a clatter.

'You can't!' Rhea momentarily lost her head. 'You can't go back now, you're locked out of your house!'

'What! What did you say? Who's locked out of the house? Whose house?'

'Yours!' Catching her panic, Rhea flapped her hands about. She forced herself to calm down. 'Don't worry about it, I'm going to find a way to get in. Now, sit down again.' She dived to retrieve Mavis' stick and pushed her gently back into her chair.

'But who's locked me out of my house? Who would do such a thing?'

'I've just remembered. Nurse Paul comes earlier than usual on a Sunday, doesn't she? She's bound to look in soon. She'll have her key.'

'She hasn't been for days. She's getting slack. You can't rely on anybody these days.'

'We'll wait until she comes. Now, can I boil you an egg

or make you some toast or something? I'm sure it would do you good to have something to eat, not just tea.'

'I wouldn't mind a nice soft-boiled egg.' Mavis had subsided obediently into her chair again and now sat leaning forward on her stick, a woebegone expression on her face.

She became more cheerful as Rhea cooked the egg and buttered a slice of bread for her. She was just putting the first spoonful of egg into her mouth when the doorbell rang. Alarmed by the sudden loud peal she looked up at Rhea with a vacant expression, egg yolk trickling down her chin.

Nurse Paul stood on the porch, her face anxious. 'Have you got the old duck in here?'

Rhea rolled her eyes and beckoned her in. 'She came out without her key.'

'Holy Mary, she can't have. I made her put it on a chain round her neck so she couldn't lose it. Oh, the silly old dear.' She clumped through into the kitchen. 'Hello, my dear.' Her voice was as cheerful and bracing as a draught of fresh cider. 'Who's lost her front door key then?' She reached familiarly down inside Mavis' shirt collar and hooked out a silver chain on the end of which dangled a Yale key.

Mavis' face was a picture. Nurse Paul hooted with laughter. 'We'll be giving her a collar and chain next! Oh well.' She rubbed her hands together as though they were cold. 'You'll know next time. Sorry. I ought to have told you. Was she wandering about again?'

'We met in the road.'

'Oh well, better the deed, better the day.'

Oblivious, Mavis went on eating her egg. Watching her, wondering with every wavering spoonful whether it would find its way to her mouth, Rhea became aware that her mouth was opening and closing as it had when she was feeding Laurie before he was old enough to manage a spoon himself.

Nurse Paul shouted, 'Would you like me to see you home when you've finished, dear? We've got a few things to sort out and I expect Rhea has things to do, too.'

'Do have a cup of tea, Nurse Paul.'

'Thanks a lot.' She leaned against the sink, breathing heavily. She laid a hand over her heart. 'Whoops! Been up most of the night with one of my mothers. Gorgeous little chap, eight and a half pounds, quite a whopper ... oh!' A red flush spread across her neck. To watch her confusion was painful.

'It's okay, don't worry about it.' Rhea unhooked another mug from the dresser. She smiled at Nurse Paul and began pouring her tea. 'Is she thrilled to bits?'

'It's always lovely when a baby's really wanted.' Puffing, she took the proffered mug. Relief made her garrulous. 'Thanks love. Dad was there, hoppin' about in his excitement like it was a football match. He kept rushing down to the foot of the bed to see what was happening and then flying back up the other end to egg his wife on – laugh! It was a scream! Never saw anybody so thrilled. We all had tears in our eyes, I can tell you.'

'Like that Frank Spencer, when Betty had her baby,' Mavis said suddenly. 'Lived up the road there, they did. Lovely boy he was, Frank. Do you remember? "Ow Bettee, it's got the Spencer nose!" Ooh I did love that Frank. Funniest programme I've ever seen.'

Rhea and Nurse Paul exchanged looks.

'Only I missed most of it because my wireless went wrong.'

Rhea remembered why Mavis had accosted her in the first place. 'Is it okay at the moment?'

'Oh, it's all right now,' Mavis conceded, her mouth perilously full of bread and butter. She swallowed. 'I had it mended of course but it kept going wrong. But it's all right now. My clocks all need mending though. Somebody keeps hiding the keys so I can't wind them up.'

'Now don't go working yourself up, dear.' Nurse Paul drained her cup, set it down on the draining board and came to stand with arms akimbo in front of Mavis like Goliath confronting a very small David. 'Now, can I help you up, dear?'

Mavis struggled to her feet, Nurse Paul's supporting hand under her elbow.

Watching Mavis' struggles, Rhea smiled. Nurse Paul was kind to her, whatever Mavis said. Mavis probably complained about Rhea too behind her back. She walked with them to the front door. 'I'm glad about the key, what a relief. Good idea, Nurse Paul.'

'Well, we don't want to lose her, do we?'

On the doorstep Mavis turned, her arm gripped firmly by Nurse Paul's strong hand, and gazed imploringly up at Rhea. 'You will come and help me with my letter, then?'

'What letter?' Nurse Paul said sharply.

'I promise.' Rhea stood on the porch watching their slow progress down the path. She called after them, already regretting her offer, cornered and unwilling, 'I could come after lunch, if you like.'

'She's got a nice bit of lamb for her lunch today, haven't you dear? Always lamb on a Sunday.'

'Have I?'

'They'll be round with it near dinner time. After dinner you'd better have a lie down, dear, your colour's not too good this morning. Got up a bit early, didn't we? Nice smooth gravel on this path, eh dear? Not like yours, dear, all those uneven paving stones. Break your neck one of these days if you don't watch out.' She grinned over her shoulder at Rhea who had come out of the house and was wandering slowly after them.

Rhea called after them, 'I thought your sister was coming, Mavis. I thought you were going out to lunch today.'

The procession slowed to a halt.

Mavis looked up at Nurse Paul. 'What's that, what did she say?'

'Rhea thought you might be going out with your sister today. D'you think she's really going out?' she called over her shoulder to Rhea.

'There was a note on the windowsill, last time I looked.'

'Whose handwriting?'

'Mavis', I think.'

'Hm ... s'pose they could have phoned. Bugger, I've asked them to bring her dinner. Roast lamb today, too. Just have to cancel it I suppose. Can't ring this time of the morning, they'll all be snoring their little heads off.' She looked at her watch. 'Glory be, it's not eight o'clock yet.'

'I'll have it if she doesn't need it. If you tell them to bang on my door instead if she isn't there.'

'And pay for it?'

'Of course. I rather fancy a nice bit of lamb.' Her mouth was watering already.

'Save a deal of trouble. Are you sure?'

'Positive. Let's hope she goes out.'

'You've got to eat, Rhea. What you need is protein, I can tell just by looking at you.'

'I do eat, I eat like anything.'

'Come on then.' Mavis tugged at Nurse Paul's arm. 'What are we waiting for?'

'Patience, patience. We're trying to sort out your royal highness's meals on wheels. We're trying to make sure you don't go hungry.'

'But I'm going out to lunch.'

'If you say so. How do I know you haven't invented the whole thing?'

'I've lost all my money again.'

'Oh gawd.' She rolled her eyes in Rhea's direction. 'See what I mean? P'raps you're going out today with the fairy queen. Perhaps *she's* got all your money. Oh well, let's get on then. No peace for the wicked.'

Rhea watched them go, Mavis hobbling along, her stick dabbing at the pavement, Nurse Paul supporting her, leaning slightly towards her like a great tug nudging a little ship into port.

Chapter Thirteen

Rhea straightened the duvet she'd thrown over the bed. She ought to do something about Mavis' garden; it was full of weeds. But if Mavis saw her weeding she'd think she was trying to steal her plants.

Her glance fell on the pink shaded lamp beside her bed. Immediately Laurie was there, his hand on the switch, his face rapt, watching the circle of rose blossom on the white wall then disappear, then blossom again.

Alice arrived. She stood on the porch looking tidy and subdued, holding a prayer book in her hand. 'Are you busy?' She stepped into the hall. 'I've been to Communion. God, what a bore. I couldn't make head or tail of it and my back nearly broke in half with all that kneeling.'

'At least you did kneel. Most people don't bother nowadays.'

'I thought you had to.'

Rhea shook her head. 'Come and have some coffee. You do look nice, like a primrose. How are things?'

'Oh, awful. As usual.' Alice put her prayer book on the

hall table as though glad to be rid of it and followed Rhea into the kitchen. She went through the arch to the annexe and sank onto a chair. 'Rose and Danny fight all the time. It drives me round the bend the way they pick on each other constantly about nothing at all. It must be the heat or something; I don't think this weather suits the kids. Not like me, I love it.'

Rhea switched the kettle on and spooned coffee into the cafetière. 'It's good you've got Spain to look forward to. You are going, aren't you?'

Alice shook her head. 'I think I've persuaded Dick to take Minna and the kids without me. I'd much prefer to have a holiday here by myself. Isn't it a fab idea?' She looked at Rhea then glanced away quickly as though to hide whatever it was giving her eyes that warm, disturbed glow. 'Dick thinks I've gone potty, going to church all the time. He says I'd be just as well-off consulting astrology or tarot or something. He's so prejudiced. And he never listens. He just picks up the paper and says um, and I know he isn't listening.' She banged the table with her fist. 'Honestly, he's so rude. He gets cross with Rose for cheeking him and answering him back but she's only doing what he does. Have you noticed how like him she's getting? In the end he won't be able to handle her either. I've given up with Rose, she has no respect for me; it's his fault, he's always putting me down in front of them. Sometimes I hate him.' Her face was a complicated mixture of bitterness and disgust. She sat back and clenched her fists in her lap. 'How can I possibly be expected to love somebody who's so horrid all the time?'

'Who, Rose, or Dick?'

'Dick, of course. I can't help loving Rose, even if she is the most spoilt little bitch in the world.'

Rhea went through to the annexe, put Alice's coffee down at her elbow and drew out a chair for herself. 'Have you talked to him about it?'

'I have tried. I told you.'

Rhea watched the light dancing on the quarry tiles. The day was windy, the sky overcast with thin sunlight filtering through. The leaping shadows on the floor, thrown through the open back door by the swaying branches of the trees in the yard, reminded her of the shadows of clouds moving across a hilltop and over fields. She gazed at them half hypnotised, longing to be out there on some cloud-shadowed hill being blown along by the wind, alone and free.

She forced her attention back to Alice.

Alice's face was stony. 'I don't love him anymore. I just don't.'

'What will you do?'

Alice shrugged. 'What can I do? I don't have any money of my own.'

Rhea leaned her elbows on the table. 'You could get a job. You're a trained secretary, aren't you? And Dick might have to give you something to help with the children. You're not really thinking of leaving him, are you?'

'Isn't that what I just said?'

'Not exactly. Why did you marry him if you feel like this about him? You were his secretary, you must have known what he was like.'

'He was different then. He was always respectful to me in the office. I think if he would even just be polite to me I could stand living with him, it's the awful sarcasm and snide remarks I can't stand. If he despises me so much, why did he marry me? I can't bear being treated like that, especially in front of other people. It's embarrassing.'

'I think it's easier to divorce since the new ruling came in. I think you only have to say that the marriage has irretrievably broken down.'

'How do you know so much about it? You're not divorced are you, Rhea? You've been on your own as long as I've known you.'

Rhea looked down at her coffee cup. 'I looked into it recently, because – well, I don't know if I ever told you about Tom ... Laurie – Laurie's father.' She swallowed. 'He walked out when I got pregnant. It's just, he's been gone so long—'

'You mean you need to know if he's coming back – because of Toby.'

Rhea frowned. 'It's got nothing to do with Toby. For me. So I know where I am.'

The doorbell rang.

Instantly, Alice's whole being changed. Hope flooded through her, warming her face, smoothing her creased forehead and softening her mouth. She put her mug down on the table.

Opening the front door, Rhea took one look at Toby's face and knew from his expression that he had decided to pretend that his outburst following their walk along the river had never happened. Rhea must have made her troubled reaction more obvious than she had realised at the time. Whatever the reason for his tactfulness, she was thankful. They could return to the way things had been before, she didn't have to worry about it just at the moment; she could go back to being selfish and Toby would go back to pretending that all there was between them was a warm friendship. He was tough. He would cope.

She was so happy to see him. She smiled, radiant with relief. She guessed that Alice had flown to her handbag and was examining her face in a little mirror, curving her lips in an experimental smile, reassuring herself. When she came back to the kitchen with Toby walking behind her Alice was back in her chair, her cheeks faintly flushed. She smiled at Toby, radiant, waiting for him to say hello.

Toby raised his hand in casual greeting. 'Hi. I saw your car outside.'

Now Alice would think that's why he came in; perhaps it was. Rhea unhooked another mug from the dresser.

'I won't stop for coffee, thanks.' He came and stood by her. She hooked the cup back. 'I've just had some at Miss Carey's, that's why I'm in the neighbourhood.' He turned to Alice. 'Are you still on for Thursday?'

'Sure, if it would help.'

'It's a terrific help, we need all the transport we can get.'

'Fine. Well then—' Alice shone as though a lamp had been switched on inside her. Rhea thought, awed, this is what it does for you, it's better than any beauty treatment. She looked curiously at Toby who was smiling benignly at Alice. Men. He hadn't a clue.

'How are the children?'

The glow vanished. Alice's mouth drooped, she averted her eyes and said, 'Feeling the heat rather.'

'Dick?'

Rhea turned away. Couldn't Toby see that Alice didn't want to talk about Dick? Perhaps she ought to leave them alone together. She walked to the back door and looked out into the yard, at the crumpled brown flowers still clinging to the lilac tree and the thin, wind-sprung branches of the prunus. She saw Laurie pedalling his tricycle across the yard, his knees working up and down, his elbows sticking out. It wasn't a tricy-cle, it was a coal lorry, and he was delivering coal to someone who lived behind the dustbin which stood in the angle formed by the tool shed and the fence. Behind him he dragged an old satchel of Rhea's, full of bricks.

She heard Toby say, 'I haven't seen Dick to speak to for a while.'

Alice stood up, smoothing down the skirt of her yellow linen suit. She looked around for her bag. 'He's the same as usual.' She had shrunk into herself like a snubbed child, all her radiance, her delight in him gone.

Rhea, her back turned, rolled her eyes. Talk about a disconnect. Couldn't Toby see? Alice didn't want him to think of her in connection with Dick, or the children. She wanted him to think of her as a person alone, individual, free. She said, 'Do stay awhile, Alice.'

'I have to get back.' Alice's eyes darted round the room. She stood poised as though wanting to leave but rooted to the floor. Her face was pale and her skin had an ethereal transparency. She looked ill.

Rhea noticed again how thin Alice had become, her face no longer full but fine drawn, her body's softness shaved away so that her suit hung loosely over her tiny waist and slim thighs, over bony shoulders and invisible breasts. She said quickly, 'I'll come to the door with you. Don't forget your prayer book, you left it in the hall.'

By the front door she touched Alice's arm. 'Are you okay, Alice? You don't look well.'

Alice put her arm around Rhea's waist, clung to her for a moment and laid her head against her shoulder. 'No, I'm not all right, not a bit.' She gave a little sob.

'Do you really have to go? Come back and talk to us. Toby won't mind.'

Alice shook her head. 'I don't want him to see me like

this.' She pulled a tissue out of her bag and dried her eyes with small, stabbing movements. 'I don't want his pity.'

Yet she had invited his pity. Rhea recollected the soulful, directionless gaze, the sighing. She said, 'You're going to have to do something, Alice. You can't just struggle on with things getting worse and worse. Don't go, not like this.'

'They'll be gone soon to Spain. I shall have three whole weeks on my own to do as I like. I'm living for it ... you can't imagine.'

Rhea watched her drive away, her face smooth and composed again. She came back into the kitchen. 'She's so unhappy, Toby, I can't bear it. It makes me itch with pity, just being with her. She used to be so complacent and casual, it was part of her charm.'

'She did seem rather down.' Toby was leaning against the dresser, one foot crossed over the other, playing with two teaspoons.

'She is. I'm worried.'

'What's the matter with her?'

Rhea looked at him consideringly. 'Unhappy marriage.' She took Alice's mug over to the sink to wash it up.

'Seriously?'

'It sounds awful. She's really unhappy, Toby. She keeps saying she wishes she could talk to you about it, then in the next breath she says she doesn't want you to see her when she's down.'

'Of course she can talk to me, everybody else seems to. Not that I can do anything, except listen. That's usually all people want anyway, nobody wants to be told what to do.' He banged the spoons together experimentally. 'It seems to me Alice is the sort of girl who knows exactly what she wants and usually gets it.'

'You're always so hard on her.'

'Am I? It isn't intentional.'

Rhea put Alice's mug on the plate rack to drain. She turned, drying her hands on a drying-up cloth, and leaned against the sink. 'Toby, what's Alice like when she's with you? Alone, I mean. Is she all over you the way she was at her dinner party or does she behave quite normally? I do have a reason for asking.'

'Goodness, I don't know, Rhea. What is this? What's normal, if it comes to that? I don't know her well enough to know what she's *normally* like. You tell me.'

'My guess is that she's got a huge crush on you and it's making her unhappy.'

'What? Don't be ridiculous.' He uncrossed his feet and turned his back to put the spoons back in their drawer. 'What on earth gives you that idea?'

'Haven't you noticed? You must be blind if you haven't. Perhaps you like it, perhaps you're flattered.'

He turned to face her again. 'Rhea!'

'Well? You're being deliberately obtuse and I don't know why. Perhaps you like women fawning all over you with their tongues hanging out.'

He frowned. He leaned against the dresser with his hands behind his back. 'Of course I don't. What's got into you?'

'What's got into you, you mean? I know what's got into me – Alice has. I'm worried about her. I keep telling you.'

'I thought the problem was her marriage.'

'Hasn't it occurred to you that the two things might be connected? When a person is unhappy they grasp at every little straw – you know that.'

'What are you saying?'

Rhea came up to him and stood in front of him, looking him full in the face. 'I'm saying that Alice is in a hell of a mess and you're not taking it seriously. And it could partly be to do with you.'

'But I hardly know the girl!'

'I'm not saying it's your fault, I just want you to be aware and not make things worse.'

'Are you saying I've encouraged her?'

'I don't know – have you?'

He threw up his hands. 'Of course not. She's married. I don't think of her like that, she's a parishioner, that's all. She's started coming to church ...' He began to walk about, thinking. 'She hasn't made it obvious, not to me, anyway. She's offered to help, but a lot of people do that. I know she was a bit silly at the dinner thing, but I put it down to her having too much to drink. Look, you've got quite enough on your plate without finding something else to worry about. She'll be all right.'

'She's talking about leaving him. I think she feels ganged up against by the family. They're going off on holiday to Spain without her.'

He stopped beside her. 'Her choice?'

'Apparently.'

'Might give her the break she needs.'

'I hope so. I don't like to think of her rattling around inside that huge house all on her own.'

'Still, as you say, her choice.'

Rhea sighed. 'I know.'

Toby put out a hand and touched her forehead. 'Stop worrying, you'll get frown lines.' He turned away. 'I'm due in church for the midday stint.'

Rhea walked behind him to the door. 'They're going to put Mavis in a home. Oh look, Alice has left her prayer book. I wonder if I'll see her before you will.'

'I'll take it. When are they – Mavis, I mean? What's her

family got to say about it? It could be the best thing for her, you know; it depends on the place. Where's she going? Does she have funds?'

'She's got plenty of money. I don't think they've decided yet. She's furious with her son, she says he neglects her, she's writing him a horrible letter to tell him off for neglecting her. As though that will do any good. I'm trying to make her see that it won't help.'

'She could be happier with people around her. She must get lonely.'

'I realise that. It's just – to have to leave her home that she's so proud of – her last contact with George – she'll probably forget all about him. And to have it all arranged for her over her head as though she's a child ... it's so insulting.'

'You're too soft-hearted. And do stop worrying about Alice. If she wants to talk about her domestic problems I'm always available, although I don't think I'm the best person, especially if she's been getting silly ideas about me. What about Relate?'

'Yeah yeah. I'll talk to her.'

'This whole thing is an attention-seeking storm in a teacup, if you ask me.'

'Good thing I'm not asking you then, isn't it? Bye, Toby.'

Later, she sat at Mavis' dining room table with the light from the lamp directed full on to the block of thin blue writing paper under Mavis' trembling fist. Rhea had switched on the lamp because the day was still overcast and the light, filtering in between the heavy woollen curtains and overcrowded sill, was gloomy and dull. Mavis was trembling so violently that she was barely able to hold the pen between her arthritic fingers.

Rhea frowned. 'Look how cold your hands are. Can't I put the electric fire on? I know it's summer but it's freezing this evening. This is silly, you can't write when your hands are stiff with cold. Come over to my house if you don't want to put the fire on here. Please come.'

'No. No, I must write the letter here.'

'Then let me put the fire on.'

'The electric is so expensive – should I?'

'I can't believe you don't have central heating. You can't let yourself get this cold, Mavis, you'll make yourself ill.'

'Well, just one bar.'

Rhea switched on the fire. The power strip, bristling with plugs, hissed and crackled. The place was a death trap; it was a miracle Mavis hadn't burned the place down before now. Rhea pulled up a chair beside her and sat down.

Mavis looked at her. 'It's my nerves. Always go to my hands my nerves do. And my stomach. Butterflies, you know. Used to get dreadful nerves I did, before going into company. Tiny little thing I was then, took a size three in shoes, did I ever tell you that, Rhea? Very small feet I had. I worked in an office for a while before I went in for nannying, and the lads used to tease me something chronic about my size. Used to offer to carry my handbag for me in case it was too heavy!'

The word handbag touched some chord in her memory and brought the look of desolate anxiety, never far away, back into her face. She looked at Rhea, her rheumy eyes perplexed. 'All my money's gone out of my handbag. A whole wad of notes, gone. Somebody must have taken it.'

Not again. 'Couldn't you have put it somewhere for safety?'

'Where would I? Only got it out of the bank Monday morning. Somebody's taken it.' Her eyes ranged round the room and came to rest on the sheet of blue airmail paper on which she had already inscribed her address, the date and the words, *Dear Brendan*.

'Are you sure you want me here, Mavis? Wouldn't it be easier for you to say the things you want to say if you're by yourself?'

'No, I need you here for when I start to write. The light's awkward. Move the lamp over a bit.'

Rhea moved the lamp a fraction of an inch. Mavis bent over the page and began laboriously to write:

I was Heart Broken when I received your last. There was not one Word in it of how I might be in Health or how I was getting along here all on my own with no one to care for me by night or by Day. If it were not for Nurse coming in I would not see a Soul from one Day to the next. I had lunch with Auntie Edna who was in good spirits even though she is Blind, only she has her family to look after her which makes All the difference. She is full of talk of her grandchildren and I could of died of shame having to tell her I have not once seen George's and mine with them being so far away in America. You would do well to get the Children to write me a letter sometimes Brendan. It is an absolute Disgrace that they never write a letter to me even though I am their Gran. You would think they would be glad to have a gran. Some people haven't and would love to have. And you Yourself never write. I want to ask you what I should do about the furniture, and do you know they are thinking of putting me in a Home?

Tears falling freely over the page, Mavis ploughed on. 'Where am I?' She rubbed her face piteously with a hand-kerchief. 'Where have I got to?'

'Putting me in a home,' Rhea said sorrowfully.

Goodness knows what kind of place it may be. They will take away all my money and my keys. And the clock. Could you come over and sort it all out for me? It will cost a lot of money, too, hundreds of pounds a week. Still what have you done to deserve my money. I might as well use it up before I die. Anyway I am thinking of leaving it all to Mrs Henderson or to a charity. She has done more to deserve it than any of you. Unless I hear from you By Return,' – she deleted *by return* and put in *soon* instead – *'I shall see to this right away. I have an appointment to see my solicitor Friday next.*

'You can't put that in about me. It could be very awkward for me if you do.'

Mavis stared at her wildly, the tears pouring effortlessly down in runnels through the thick white mask of powder. 'Oh, but I must! It's the only thing he will understand. He was the same as a boy. The only thing that had any effect was to stop his pocket money. He's as mercenary as Old Nick. I bet he's mean fisted with that poor Nona, too.'

'No, Mavis. You have to scratch that bit out. And the bit about deserving it. Brendan will think I'm after your money. Cross out the bit about me. You could leave in about leaving it to charity, that's fine. That will bother him just as much.'

Obediently Mavis scored two heavy lines through the offending passage. 'He'll have to come now, won't he, Rhea?' She turned her whole body to face Rhea and banged the table with her fist, tilting her chair sideways so that two of its legs left the floor. Rhea's hand shot out to grasp the back of the chair to stop it falling over. 'He'll know I mean what I say. I've never threatened anything I haven't been willing to carry out. You can't with children, you know, they don't respect you if you don't do as you say you will. I dare say you do that with your little fellow too. How is he, by the way? He'll know what I mean all right. Never go back on your word. He'll have to do something.'

Her chair crashed back onto all four legs as she bent over the letter again. All but the half inch at the bottom was covered with her fine, almost indecipherable scrawl, the black lines crossing and intercrossing like tracer fire against a blue sky.

Chapter Fourteen

THE BLUE VAN ROOF SLID IN UNDER THE HEDGE. RHEA ran out to catch Nurse Paul before she could disappear inside Mavis' front door.

Nurse Paul climbed out of the van. 'We've found a place for her.'

'Oh! Where?'

'Greyfriars in Thames Ditton. Cost her a bomb but she can spare it. Mrs Deal the matron is a good sort, all the old dears like her. I think she'll be okay there.' She put up a hand to forestall the protest dawning in Rhea's face. 'I know what you're going to say. It's a shame, nobody's pretending any different but what else can we do? We haven't got time to be coming in all hours of the day and night. She needs full time nursing care, you know that, you know how wretched she gets, particularly weekends when the shops are shut and there's no one about. It would be much more unkind to leave her here getting worse and worse. In any case she'll set the place on fire one of these days. Or electrocute herself.'

'I know it isn't safe her being on her own. And I know

she gets unhappy. But on her good days she's so normal, and so independent by nature, she's going to hate being shut up in a care home.'

'Well, think of something else then,' Nurse Paul snapped, opening Mavis' gate. 'It isn't prison, Rhea.'

'I suppose at least she'll have a room of her own and her own things round her?'

Nurse Paul shook her head. 'Probably share with two other oldies. They don't like them having their own things, it unsettles them. Besides, there isn't the room.'

'But all her beautiful things! There are nursing homes where they let them have their own rooms and their own furniture, aren't there? I'm sure there was one my mother used to visit—'

'The old dear's much too dotty for anywhere like that, Rhea. She'd upset all the other residents; you know how peculiar she can get.' Suddenly enraged she snapped, 'She's damn lucky not to be ending her days in a geriatric ward, I can tell you. If she didn't have all that lolly that's exactly where she'd be.' She turned her back on Rhea and slammed the gate impatiently behind her.

'Nurse Paul?'

'What is it now?' She turned, halfway up the path, and stood holding her hand to her side as though she was in pain.

'That's what I wanted to tell you. She wrote to Brendan yesterday. You will wait till she hears from him, won't you? He might say she could go out there to live.'

'Chance'll be a fine thing, knowing him.'

'You've met him?'

'Selfish as all get out. Couldn't care less about his mum. Anyway, we can't wait more than another week or she'll lose the place. We were thinking of Friday. Could make it

Friday week, possibly. I suppose I can stand another week of this.'

'Oh, do try! She's written him such a letter! He's bound to reply soon, he couldn't help it.'

'Showed it to you, did she?' A flicker crossed the large, plain face, of malice? Jealousy? She turned away.

RHEA AND TOBY had picnicked in the shade of an oak tree at the top of a little hill. Rhea had brought their lunch, rolls stuffed with ham and cheese, apples and a bottle of cider, and now they were walking. It wasn't proper walking, it was too hot for that and the grass and bracken were knee high which made it impossible to keep up a proper pace. This was more of a scramble, an explore.

Down the other side of the hill and through a little plantation they wandered, Toby leading and Rhea following.

Rhea kept stopping to look at ferns and fungi, to listen to the grasshoppers and birds and to overturn small rocks and examine the beetles that ran out.

'We might see a snake, it's so hot.' She felt disarmed by Toby today. He was at his best, contented and not looking at her as though he'd like to eat her, the way he still did sometimes. She caught up with him. 'I shan't have Mavis next door after next weekend. Unless Brendan replies to her letter before then to suggest something else, they're moving her into Greyfriars on Friday.'

Toby bent and pulled up a handful of grass. 'When did she write?'

'Ages ago. He ought to have replied by now; he must realise how urgent it is.'

'You can't force love,' Toby said.

'She's still his mother.' Rhea jumped off a fallen log.

207

'Doesn't that count for anything?' Her feet landed on a cushion of sphagnum moss and sank into its sponge-like softness. 'Oh look, Toby, look at all these different kinds of moss! Laurie and I used to make little houses – I believe we came to this exact spot once. I must take off my sandals.'

'Watch out for thorns.'

She kicked off her sandals and knelt on the little carpet of moss, pressing her hands into it and examining each variety in turn. Suddenly she stopped. She began to look intently around at the little patch, at the bracken, a fallen log, a tangle of blackberries, the knotty roots of a huge beech tree. Was this the place where she and Laurie had built their own version from moss and twigs of the *Mossy Green Theatre*, the tiny theatre that was the subject of one of Laurie's favourite books? She'd forgotten all about it but now memories came flooding in, filling her with excitement. The remnants of the theatre might still be here!

She searched among the roots of the beech tree, lifting tiny curtains of moss, poking at anything that looked possible, conscious that Toby was waiting, that she couldn't take too long. Eventually she paused, sighing with frustration. It was hopeless; she'd known it would be. She must stop before she exhausted even Toby's unending good humour. She felt a moment's irritation. If only she was alone, she could have stayed longer, kept on looking.

Oh dear, she was getting so selfish, she had to pull herself together. Poor Toby. She was being so unfair on him. She abandoned the search, stood up and began to tread up and down on the soft moss, smiling with pleasure at the feel of it under her bare feet.

. . .

LOOKING AT HER, so beautiful and as liberated by her brief happiness as though she had suddenly sprouted a pair of wings, Toby's heart went out to her completely. She trod up and down on the moss with her feet bare, holding her skirt away from her legs with both hands and circling round, looking as though she was treading grapes. She was wearing a yellow cotton top and a green skirt that came down to her calves. Her feet were rather large, shapely and bony and her long hair hung down her back, reaching almost to her waist.

'Rhea,' he said, unable to prevent himself. He took his foot off the log he had propped it on and approached her. Instantly she stopped moving. Standing sideways to him she turned her head and watched him warily as he approached, an anxious look replacing the joy in her eyes. Wafted towards her on a gust of feeling he noticed her withdrawal but would not be put off. He had made up his mind; he would ask her.

He said, brushing all doubt aside, 'Rhea, darling Rhea, will you marry me? Will you think about it? I love you so much. I have – for a long time – it feels like always.' He didn't touch her but stood near her, his arms by his sides, his heart throbbing, waiting to see what she would say. He waited, but she said nothing. His heart sinking, he said more hesitantly, 'I think – we've got to know each other so well.'

She had turned her face away as soon as he had started to speak and now she stood with her head bent, seemingly incapable of speech. The silence stretched.

Immense disappointment flooded through him. She gave not a sign, said not a word. She stood as though hypnotised. Embarrassed now, he moved to turn away and then, without turning her head, she put out a hand to prevent him.

'Toby. Wait a minute. Please. I don't know what to say.'

. . .

WHY DID he have to spoil it – this first moment of happiness, a moment she wanted to treasure, to marvel over and over again in the dark times she knew lay ahead, when happiness would once again seem the most inaccessible thing on earth? Times like last night when woken, she imagined, by a cry from Laurie's room she had rolled out of bed half awake and stumbled along to his room, already comforting him.

'It's all right, Laurie. Mummy's here. What's the trouble – did you have a bad dream?' He had sometimes had nightmares of animals chasing him, foxes or bears.

She had seen the empty bed and no child there.

How could Toby possibly understand what it was like for her? He tried, he really tried, but he couldn't see what was going on inside her head. Sometimes he forgot, of course he did, he was only human, and someone else's grief was just so boring, it never let up. She turned to him, put her hand on his arm. 'I'm sorry.'

He recoiled as though she'd hit him.

She looked at him, dismayed by his reaction. She gave his arm a little tug. 'No, wait. It's just, I really need to give this some thought. I didn't realise – it's come as a bit of a bolt from the blue.'

She wasn't even sure if this was true. She could feel the extra heat coming off him, his whole body shaking with the thumping of his heart. She looked up for inspiration at the patches of blue sky showing through the branches of the oak trees. She let go of his arm and clasped her hands together in front of her, still not looking at him.

She shook her head. 'I'm not ready to think about marrying anyone yet. It's too soon. In any case,' – she gave a little laugh to take the sting out of the words – 'I'd be an absolutely hopeless vicar's wife. There's too much I can't subscribe to. If I'm perfectly honest I don't think it probably matters two pins what faith you follow, as long as you believe in God. It's nonsense to say you can only be forgiven your sins if you're a Christian, or a Moslem or whatever. And anyway, what is sin, exactly? What matters is love, that's all. Love and kindness and gratitude. I don't think I'm really a Christian at all, and you can't possibly marry someone who isn't even a Christian. God is what matters. God, and love. I don't approve of religion.'

'I don't have to be a vicar. I could leave the Church.'

'Oh Toby! I couldn't possibly be responsible for that!'

'I've been thinking of applying for a college chaplaincy. My old college is asking for applications and I've already written to them about it. I haven't been convinced for a long time that parish life is for me. If I got it, that would suit you better, wouldn't it, Rhea? Cambridge would be a good place to live, there's so much going on, music and art. Lots of writers live there. You would be among your own kind.'

'How thoughtful you are ... you've worked all this out. But I can't get married anyway, I'm still married to Tom. I've no idea if he's alive or dead. I'm not free to marry anyone.'

'You could get divorced. You've been apart long enough. Do you still love him? Would you want him back?'

'I don't know, I've never considered the possibility that he might come back. When he left he went so completely, there's never been a word or a sign. He could be anywhere – in China or Afghanistan. He could be living in a shack in the Caribbean somewhere, like Gauguin. He isn't in the UK – I'd know. I'd hear, if he was working. There's been nothing. I suppose I ought to start trying to find out.'

'You can't love him still. He left you. He never even saw Laurie.'

'I know. I know.'

'You can't love him.'

'Oh Toby, it isn't just Tom. I love you to bits, you know I do, but that's the trouble really, I'm so used to the way we've been, kind of – best friends, not – not lovers. We'd have to start all over again. And what if it didn't work out? We'd have lost what we have, which is wonderful, Toby, it means the world to me. I know it isn't what you want, but ... real love, the needing and sharing for ever and ever, I don't know if that's for me. I'm too solitary. Too selfish, probably. My work matters terribly to me, at least it did and I'm hoping and praying it will again, some day.' She frowned fiercely at a clump of bracken and sat down suddenly on a fallen tree trunk. She motioned for him to sit beside her. 'It's quite dry, I think.'

Toby stayed standing where he was. 'You loved Laurie.'

She frowned. That was completely different – he wasn't making sense. She stole a glance at his cold face. What had he expected, for her to fall into his arms? Had she misled him so totally? 'Perhaps I've just got too used to my own way of life.'

She had thought she would never write again, but the prospect of having her choice in the matter taken away from her was concentrating her mind wonderfully. She felt the familiar stirring of excitement, like something coming alive inside her, wings preening experimentally, stiff from long disuse.

She said, 'I got into really unsociable habits after Tom left. There were times when I'd wake at two in the morning and write till dawn. A normal day for me started at half past four: I'm freshest then, my internal critic is still half asleep.

Nothing else mattered as much as work. Apart from Laurie, of course, but he was asleep when I was working. That would make you unhappy. If I started writing again I would want to write every day. Being your wife would be a job in itself, wouldn't it? The phone would have to be answered, there'd be people around all the time. It wouldn't work for me and then I'd feel guilty and be unhappy. It wouldn't work.' While she was speaking, she was becoming more and more convinced.

Toby had been fidgeting throughout this speech. Now he looked straight at her. 'I don't believe any of this. At least, only the thing you haven't said, which is that you don't love me enough. You're not in love with me.'

Rhea sat still with her hands in her lap. It was awful, hurting someone so badly. She wished she felt able to love him the way he deserved. 'We've grown so fond of each other. I'm so sorry, Toby.'

'D-don't be silly.' He moved away, not looking at her. 'Perhaps we ought to get back. I've got to be back soon, anyway.' Without looking to see if she was following he began to move off quickly down the hill towards the car park where Rhea had left her car.

Rhea started to pull on her sandals. Her legs were trembling. He had stopped and was waiting for her to catch up. As she drew near he turned away and set off again at a good pace, and she followed behind.

RHEA TURNED the car into the drive. A police car was drawn up outside Mavis' house. Nurse Paul was standing with one hand on the gate in earnest conversation with two policemen. As Rhea's car approached they turned towards it, their faces grave.

Rhea climbed out. What now? She had driven Toby home in almost total silence, and after what had happened she was feeling the need of some peace and quiet. 'What's up, Nurse Paul?'

Nurse Paul's forehead puckered in a frown. 'It's Mavis. She stepped off the pavement in front of a car and caused an accident.'

'Oh my God. Where?'

'Upper Brighton Road.'

'Was she hurt?'

Nurse Paul snorted. 'Not her, she's as right as rain, it's the other poor bugger that isn't. Swerved to avoid her and drove straight into a car coming the other way. He's dead, the other car's a write off and the driver's got multiple injuries.'

'My God.' She bit her lip and stood with her hands clasped tightly at her waist, staring at Nurse Paul.

'Now perhaps you'll see why it's so important for us to get her into safekeeping as soon as possible. We can't have this kind of thing happening.'

'No ... of course not. Where is she? Is she in the house? Can I go and see her?"

Nurse Paul shrugged and took her hand off the gate. 'Yes, okay, go on.'

The two men, both of them young with grave expressions on their faces, moved to let her through, looking at her with curious eyes.

Nurse Paul looked grim. 'I haven't seen her to talk to today. I rang her bell about two, but she didn't answer so I let myself in. I was worried in case she'd collapsed or something. We do our best,' she said to the officers.

Rhea turned away and set off up the path. Nurse Paul's

voice followed her. 'We can't be here all the time. There wasn't a sign of her. God knows where she went this afternoon. I looked all over. She hadn't been to the centre for her dinner or to any of the shops she usually visits. Nobody'd seen hide nor hair of her. Then we got a call from you guys.' She raised her voice and called after Rhea, 'She knew she'd caused the accident. They found her sitting by the side of the road crying for her son.'

The front door stood open. The stairs rose steeply from the centre of the tiny hall. Rhea looked up at them. They must look like a mountain to Mavis when she was feeling tired and wobbly.

Mavis sat perched on the edge of her high iron bed, her thin legs dangling like wind chimes in the little breeze that blew in through the open window. The stale odour of unwashed body and old clothes hung about the bedroom, the stagnant smell of sad, unkempt old age. Drab and depressing, the antithesis of the youth Rhea had felt burgeoning in her again among the sharp, fresh scents of the young, green bracken and the feel of the damp moss under her bare feet, so achingly fresh in her memory. For an instant, faced by the tiny huddle of bird-light bones and darned grey flesh that was Mavis, she baulked at the sight of such uncompromising misery; she could hardly bear it. Outside the sun shone, but distantly, as if it had nothing to do with this room and the people in the room, the musty smell and the old woman sitting crying silently and hope-lessly on the edge of the bed.

Mavis was clutching a blue air letter crumpled up in her fist as though she wanted to destroy it but could not bring herself to do so. Her eyes tight shut, she gave a little moan, whimpering as though she was in pain, and tears trickled down the grooves in the fragile skin of her face.

Rhea approached cautiously. 'You've heard from him, then. He answered your letter.'

Mavis lifted the hand which held the letter in a little indicative gesture which was at the same time a gesture of despair. 'And what a letter. You've never seen anything like it in your life. Callous, he is. Callous and cruel.'

Rhea sat on the bed beside her. 'What does he say?'

'He doesn't ask anything about me, about how I'm feeling, whether I'm being looked after properly or how I am in my health. Never asked about my back even. Doesn't mention me at all. It's all about him, his troubles, his family, his goings-on. Might as well not have taken the trouble to write to him or him to me. I might as well be dead for all he cares. Even asks me for money. Says he's hard up. I've no use for that letter; it's no use to me.' She sobbed quietly and hopelessly, pressing a greyish handkerchief to her nose.

Rhea put her arm around her. She felt too big, too healthy and strong beside Mavis' frail, tiny body. She hugged her tight. 'Don't take on so.' That was what people said, wasn't it? *Don't take on so.* 'You'll make yourself ill.' She willed some of her strength to infuse the thin body pressed up against her side. She felt Laurie creep into the cavern of her ribs and curl himself there, content.

'What am I going to do?' Mavis rubbed her red-rimmed eyes with the back of her hand, like a child.

'You'll feel better in the morning. You're tired tonight. You've had a shock and it's making you depressed.'

She shook her head, whimpering. 'I wish it would all end. Perhaps God will be merciful and take me in my sleep tonight.'

'Oh Mavis, don't. Nurse will bring you up some Complan. You'll feel better in the morning, you'll see.'

She said to Nurse Paul in the kitchen, 'She seems to

have forgotten all about the accident. All she's thinking about is her letter from Brendan. Does she know she's going to Greyfriars on Friday?'

'What's the use of upsetting her, dear?' Nurse Paul had undergone one of her lightning changes of mood and was now more unbending and cheerful than she had been for weeks. Perhaps it was the prospect of having this burden taken off her shoulders. Rhea frowned. She was a nurse. It was her job.

Nurse Paul took the milk pan over to the sink. 'You know how worked up she gets. She'll go spare.'

'What about her clothes? She'll have to pack. Would you like me to help?'

The haunted look came back into Nurse Paul's face. She rinsed the pan under the tap, stabbing at it with the ancient washing-up brush. 'This bloody thing's completely knackered. Look at it. I can do all that after she's gone. She'll just need her overnight bag to start with.'

'But her treasures,' Rhea went on doggedly, quaking slightly. Nurse Paul's back had a belligerent, uncompromising stiffness about it. 'Everyone has treasures and secrets. She may have things in a special box somewhere that she doesn't want anyone to see. Love letters. Private things that are important to her. You must ask her. You mightn't recognise them for what they are. They might not seem valuable to anyone else but her.'

'All right, all right.' Nurse Paul turned and gave her a very nasty look indeed. 'All right. I'll ask her. Now are you satisfied?' She banged a teaspoon down on the tray beside the cup of Complan. 'Never mind that she'll get all upset again. I'll ask her, if that's what madam wants. Not tonight though, we've had enough trouble for one day, thank you very much. I should think even you,' – she gave Rhea another venomous look – 'ought to be able to see that. Thank God there were witnesses, that's all I can say. Can you imagine her in court? She may have to go yet ... Holy Mother, I can't stand much more of this,' she muttered under her breath, picking up the tray and kicking the door open with one foot. 'Roll on Friday, that's all I can say. Roll on the day.'

Chapter Fifteen

Rhea leaned against the windowsill, looking out at the quiet street, the trees opposite and the lamppost. Moonlight lay over the road, the pavements and the garden, every surface gilded. The lawn lay like a silver pond between the rose beds. There was no colour, only this strange and radiant light. The sky behind the pulsing moon shone like a skating rink of polished obsidian, radiant with glittering stars.

She had been unable to sleep, tormented by the knowledge that tomorrow Mavis would be driven away from the house that had been her home all her married life, without ceremony, with barely a soul to care or to witness, and become a person in an institution. She had lost with her faculties any control over her own destiny.

It was her dottiness that was the problem. She had to be incarcerated to keep her and other people out of danger. There was really no other solution, or only one, which didn't seem to be available, which was love. Love would have wanted to look after her, would have rejoiced to do it.

Love always had time, was never too busy, was prepared to make sacrifices.

Rhea sighed. She herself seemed to be barren of the sort of love it would take. Love had run out.

Was what she had felt for Laurie, love? It had never involved sacrifice, had never given her anything but joy. In time she might have had to make sacrifices, and it was impossible to believe that she would not have made them with equal joy. Now she ought to be prepared to have Mavis live with her, to love and care for her and be for her the daughter she'd never had. But she couldn't do it – because she wanted to write.

Perhaps she was simply using work as an excuse. Perhaps she would spend the rest of her life saying she couldn't do things because of work and never write another word. Perhaps these intermittent longings were not the beginning of something but its dying convulsions, like the flapping and leaping of a fish dying at the bottom of a boat. Perhaps her ability to write, booby-trapped by Laurie's death, was dying too.

Sitting on the edge of her bed she watched the moon-light spilling over the sill and onto the floor, over her bare legs and the white duvet. She felt cut off from reality, imprisoned in this eerie overspill of light. She lay down and pulled the duvet up. She relaxed at last. She imagined herself enclosed within two huge soft wings and slipped at last into sleep.

At noon the next day she stood at her front gate watching Nurse Paul's van drive away, Mavis seated bolt upright in the front passenger seat, refusing to wave, maybe not even realising she was being waved to, her expression quite cheerful. She probably thought she was going out to lunch somewhere. Rhea turned away with a feeling of emptiness and regret and walked up the path to her front door, pausing to put her nose inside a coral rose under the forsythia hedge.

She was trembling. The rose was so soft and cool and smelt – of rose perfume, sweet and delicate, wafting, breathing – alive. Mavis was going to a noisy prison where she would never have any privacy, ever again. For the rest of her life she would be imprisoned, captive, already buried in her grave.

She would take Mavis roses from the garden every week; Mavis loved her flowers so. Perhaps Greyfriars would have a garden she could walk in. In Mavis' own garden huge white lilies grew under the windows. She and George had been founder members of the local Horticultural Society. George, irritated by Rhea's haphazard method of gardening, had long ago given up trying to persuade her to join.

She stood aimlessly in the hall. Strange to realise there would never again come the imperious rat-tat-tat on the door, the quavering 'Are you there?' What would Mavis do without a wireless to go wrong? Would they let her listen to the radio in that place?

She would look into these things. She would make an absolute nuisance of herself to see that Mavis was as comfortable, as happy as possible. She would fight them, them and their tidy little solutions.

An hour later she saw that the van had returned. She'd been half looking out for it; Nurse Paul had said she would come back sometime to pack up Mavis' things and Rhea was determined to see that she took the things that might be special to her, not just bung anything in all anyhow. In any case she wanted to hear how it had gone, whether Mavis had jibbed and made a scene or accepted her new home.

She walked round to the house and up the path; the

front door was ajar and stepping into the hall she saw that the dining room door was open too. Nurse Paul was bending over the table with her back to the door. Rhea opened her mouth to call out but shut it again. What on earth was she doing?

Rhea blinked, unable at first to believe what she was seeing: Nurse Paul was picking up wads of ten and twenty-pound notes and stowing them away in the lining of her regulation navy mackintosh. More notes, bundles of them, lay in piles on the dining room table. There must be hundreds of pounds there ... thousands. Nurse Paul's hands moved swiftly and efficiently, as though she had thought this out in advance and had carefully planned where each bundle must go.

Rhea stood completely still, not daring to move for fear of alarming her. She would have liked to back off without being seen or heard, but that was impossible, the floorboards in the hall all creaked; she couldn't imagine how Nurse Paul hadn't heard her arrive. Steeling herself, she coughed gently.

Nurse Paul turned around in one violent movement, throwing one arm up over her face as though to protect herself. Rhea, horrified at being the cause of such irrational terror, gave a little exclamation and in a moment, realising who it was, Nurse Paul dropped her arm, straightened her back and stood upright, her arms hanging by her sides. Light from the window gleamed across the lenses of her flesh-pink spectacles and it was as if a shutter came down over her flushed face; her eyelids lowered, flickered and lifted again over a look that was determined, defiant and anguished.

'Oh bugger.' Her body seemed to slump. She had been active, inspired, and now for a moment she stood utterly still as though the shock of discovery had poleaxed her. Slowly she took off her spectacles and turned to glance regretfully at the table. 'Another few minutes and I'd have been done.' She sat down suddenly on one of the dining room chairs. 'Oh dear.' She blinked several times and began to massage her eyes with the thumb and middle finger of her right hand, her elbow resting on the table. Her spectacles rode up and down on the hinge of her fingers. The corners of her mouth drooped. After that initial moment of terror she didn't look frightened, or ashamed; only immensely tired.

'I'm sorry.' Rhea wasn't sure whether she was apologising for catching her red handed or sorry because Nurse Paul looked so tired, disappointed and defeated. 'Look. Can we talk about this?'

'Nothing to talk about.' Nurse Paul stared straight ahead. 'I took it. A few notes here and there over the months. She never missed it. She was always thinking people were taking things; she didn't need the money. I began taking more when I realised it was on the cards that she'd be moved out of here. I knew it was bound to happen before too long and I didn't have much time. I got a bit nervous once or twice, she began noticing when I took too much at a time – fifty pounds once. I hid the cash inside the books on the shelves there.' She indicated the bookshelves facing them. 'If anyone found them I could always say she'd hidden them there herself, dotty old cow. Just the sort of thing she would do. I wrote down the titles of the books I'd hidden the money in, in case I forgot when the time came to collect it all. I wanted to take some of it away before now, but I was frightened.' For the first time her lips trembled. She pressed them together. A bewildered look had come into her eyes. 'She might have cottoned on, and there was nowhere to hide the money in the nurses' home. I had to choose a time when I was just going off duty. I've got the weekend off, see. I was going to my sister in Angmering.'

'But what's it for? Why did you need it?'

Nurse Paul shrugged. '*She* doesn't need it. She'll only leave it to a cat's home or that awful son of hers who doesn't deserve it. She'd never have missed this lot; she'd never have known. Oh, Rhea, don't make me put it all back. I can't. It's taken months to get this lot together. I'm sure I've suffered enough, the worry I've had and the guilt – I did feel guilty – but not now, not now it's done. Can't you just go away and pretend you didn't see? I know it's wrong, I know it's stealing but I don't care, I'll answer for it if anyone finds out, I'll take the responsibility.' She stared at Rhea, her pale blue eyes magnified behind the pink-tinted lenses, her eyelids red. She looked almost insane.

'But I can't pretend I haven't seen. You must see that; it would be condoning what you've done, and I don't.' She wished Toby were here. He would know the right thing to do. She wished she didn't feel she was being priggish and unkind. But she couldn't just turn her back, the money belonged to Mavis. It was stealing.

The house seemed to sigh and creak as they waited uneasily each for the other to take the initiative. Rhea leaned against the door jamb, her hands behind her, one under the other, crushed against the wooden post. She felt like a policeman on duty guarding a prisoner. It wasn't a role she relished. All her attention was focused on Nurse Paul sitting solidly with her feet planted apart, staring straight ahead. There was something massive, stubborn and implacable about her that Tom would have relished: *Study of a District Nurse Faced with a Conundrum*.

It struck her that Nurse Paul might possibly be danger-ous. If she decided to go for Rhea there was little doubt what the outcome would be, but after a moment's thought she dismissed this idea as melodramatic and unlikely. If she'd been going to do anything like that she'd have done it already. And why on earth had she left all the doors open? Had she wanted to be found out?

Several minutes went by. It was ridiculous, they couldn't go on sitting there forever, frozen in mutual embarrassment like lumps of meat grown cold and congealed on a plate. She said suddenly, 'Count it.'

'What?'

'Take it all out and count it. All of it. Come on, I'll help. Hurry up, someone might come.' She backed into the hall, keeping her eyes on Nurse Paul, and pushed the front door shut with her foot.

Looking dazed, Nurse Paul started to pull wads of notes from their hiding places in her mackintosh and throw them down on the table. Some of the bundles were secured with rubber bands but most of it was loose.

Rhea looked around. 'We need a pen and paper.' There was a pad and a biro on the windowsill. 'We'll make piles of a hundred pounds in tens. Five hundred in twenties. Come on, this is your mess, you have to help clear it up.'

They worked in feverish silence. The total amounted to three thousand, six hundred and thirty-five pounds. Rhea's lips were determined, her face set. 'Now we'll put it back where it was, inside the books. Come on. Come *on*, Nurse Paul, we must hurry, someone might come.'

'I can't ... please don't make me.' Nurse Paul's eyes filled with frustrated tears. 'Look. You can have half. Go on, take it.' She pushed bundles of notes towards Rhea across the table. 'Please.'

Rhea looked at her in amazement. 'Don't be idiotic. Now come on, get on with it.'

Nurse Paul moved wearily from table to shelves and back again, her head bent, her lips moving soundlessly. Her face was grey. She looked ill. But she was lucky Rhea hadn't called the police. She was lucky. It was no good her looking like that.

When the money was all dealt with, Rhea said, 'Come home and have some coffee with me. We'll phone Mr Perry and tell him we've found money inside one of Mavis' books and we're concerned there may be more. We'll ask him to sort it out. He'll understand that you have to be careful of your reputation. You found it and you came next door to get me so I could be a witness. He's an honest sort of person, it will be safe with him.'

She picked up Nurse Paul's attaché case and led the way out of the house, closing the front door behind them. Her mind leapt ahead to when this was over, when she would be free again. She would go for a walk, far away, into the countryside. She was already there in her mind, walking across quiet fields where cows swished and ambled, heavy-shouldered, where birds sang in the yellow evening light.

She would have her supper under a tree. She would take sandwiches and chocolate and apples and a can of cider and sit in the dappled shade. She would watch the sun set and the moon rise.

Her heart beat faster. She was already striding away downhill, over the stile, down the stony ground at the edge of the cornfield, poppy-splashed, towards the river. A lark sang.

She opened the kitchen door. 'Come in, Nurse Paul.'

LAURIE CAME and stood beside her bed that night. He seemed to her to have grown a little. His face shone like a cameo in the near darkness. He stood quietly for several seconds before speaking, the way he always had in the early mornings when he had come into her room. He had hovered like a little watchful bird, waiting to see if she was awake.

He spoke softly and she heard each word with complete clarity. He said, 'My head is better now, Mummy. You're better too.'

The words came before she was fully awake, and when she woke up and looked for him he was gone. But she lay on her back, her arm flung out towards the place where he had stood, and let the new knowledge grow and spread through her, the absolute certainty that for a few moments he had been close to her. She felt his presence still, happy and confident, reassuring, encouraging, infinitely comforting. In an extraordinary way making her grief seem for a moment completely meaningless.

She whispered, 'Laurie, is that you?'

The answering silence made no difference. She said slowly and emphatically to herself, to make quite sure she wouldn't forget and that in the morning she wouldn't talk herself into thinking that this had been a dream, 'You came. You were here. You haven't gone away at all.' She turned on her side and slipped into a deep and refreshing sleep.

In the morning the comforted feeling was still with her. It hadn't vanished with the little figure by the bed. It had become part of her. It was as if Laurie himself had climbed into the cavity formed by her ribs and had curled himself up in her heart; that was how it felt, as if he had come back to her in spirit and was there to stay.

Could she trust it, this new life resting inside her as content as a wanderer come home, as incapable of leaving again? Dressing, she thought with a surge of regret, *I wish I could tell Toby. I wish I could see him.* But in the ten days since the episode in the park he had not been near her. They had parted with hardly a word. She thought about phoning him to see how he was, but hesitated; perhaps that wasn't what he wanted, perhaps he'd rather forget about her.

If only they could pretend it had never happened and go on as before. She wondered how he would be when they did meet again, as they were bound to; whether he would still be cold and distant or whether his generosity was capable of overcoming even this. But all the same she felt a tiny lifting of relief when she thought of him as if a minor burden had been taken from her shoulders. She felt bad about this but in her defence, she argued with herself, how could she be expected to grieve over what had happened with Toby when as the result of Laurie's visit she was finding herself so unexpectedly uplifted by these waves of sheer joy?

She asked herself why she had ever been afraid. Why she had assumed she had lost Laurie. She walked about in the garden, letting the summer weather nourish and revive her, pushing her hands in among the silky leaves of the plants in the flowerbeds, letting her fingers explore the soft petals of roses and nasturtiums and laying her palms on the warm earth moist with the frequent rain. She put her arms around the slender silver birches in the copse beyond the apple trees and held them as if they were people. The renewal of the boundless love she had always felt towards these growing things sprang directly from the deep well of joy that had opened up inside her. She was overflowing with love. It filled and spilled from her, just as her grief had permeated her at the beginning leaving no room for love.

She was not exactly happy. What she felt was too intense, too vivid, too much like delight. She steeled herself against disaster. Maybe this wouldn't last. Maybe she was being taught another lesson. But she felt sure that Laurie would not leave her. He was there, she could feel him close inside her. She accepted her belief in his presence just as she had accepted the fact of her pregnancy in the early weeks when there had been nothing to show that she was pregnant. Inside, she had known.

And the joy didn't last. It slowly died, leaving her yearning again for what she had lost, not sufficiently grateful for what she had found, stranded between two peaks of emotion, unable to reach either, lost again.

Chapter Sixteen

THE THIN, BROWN MAN STANDING ON THE PORCH WAS young, in his early thirties or thereabouts. His hair was dark and tousled. He wore scuffed jeans and a denim shirt frayed at the cuffs. He was holding a cap which he passed from hand to hand as though it was red hot and he was trying not to drop it. His face was gaunt with anxiety.

Rhea tried to remember where she had seen him before. He was nervous, he shifted from one foot to the other, his eyes flicking from her face to the hall behind her, round the roof of the porch and onto the forsythia hedge in Mavis' garden.

At last, he seemed to make up his mind. 'Mrs Henderson?'

'Yes?'

Where was it? He had been different then – not nervous, then. He had emanated strength ... he had helped her, supported her in some way. Where? The memory of a hand came into her head, a sunburned hand with dirt-rimmed nails, the back of the hand streaked with oil. She remembered the smell of oil from a machine pumping by the side of the road, mixed with the smell of sweat, of fear – she remembered—

He looked down at his fingers twisting and rolling the cap into a long sausage shape. 'I asked up at the hospital. They told me about your littl'un ... I meant to come before.' He stopped, as though he felt the pointlessness of embarking on long explanations. He had been too embarrassed to come before. He had got her address from the hospital and had put off coming again and again.

'Me and the lads ... we were just ... we were that sorry.'

And she remembered. The gang of workmen round the pumping, oil-smelling machine, the gaping hole in the pavement. They had been repairing something, pipes or drains. They had turned and watched her as she approached along the icy gutter, barefoot, with Laurie in her arms.

'It was you.' She stood with her eyes fixed on his face. She put out her hand wonderingly and touched his shirt sleeve. 'You.'

She was back again in the freezing January afternoon, the tarmac icy and gritty under her bare feet, a splinter of glass in her heel, Laurie a dead weight in her arms. She had walked a good quarter of a mile past several people, but no one had stopped her or spoken to her before this man.

He had supported her arms and the child together. She had refused to let him take Laurie from her. He had shouted to someone, someone had gone running, and he had held her, talked to her, soothed her all the while, and when the police car had arrived she wouldn't let him leave her. He had left the gang of labourers mending the road and had stayed with her until the ambulance came.

She remembered the smell of oil and sweat and the current of concern that had come surging from him, surrounding her like a warm sea, almost palpable, warmer than the thin sunlight which seemed to leave her aching body cold as ice, which couldn't stop her shuddering or the chattering of her teeth.

'It was terrible.' He looked at her, his face twisted into an expression of pity and dismay, his nervousness gone now that she was not about to collapse or weep or shout at him and tell him to go away. 'I thought, what if it was one of my own kids.' He paused, shaking his head. 'Couldn't stand it. Kept seeing you and the littl'un ... the wife said, why don't you call the lady, see if there's anything you can do, like.' He shook his head again and looked down at his hands and at the cap twisting and turning this way and that. 'I knew it would do no good o' course but I had to come for my own peace of mind. See if you was all right. That beautiful little kid. Couldn't stop thinking about it and the pity of it ...' He stopped and stood rigidly still for a moment, glancing anxiously at her and then away again as if afraid he might have said too much.

Rhea stared at him, unable to utter a word. All this time when she had thought she was grieving alone and being gawped at by strangers, this total stranger had been sharing her grief. When afterwards she had sometimes seethed with resentment and bitterness, remembering the group of silent men with their staring eyes ... ghouls, she had thought, unfeeling ghouls ... all the while they had all, including this man, been feeling the utmost pity and sorrow. They had cared that Laurie had died.

She had got it so wrong.

She burst out, astonished and humbled, 'Don't you see what this means for me – what you've done for me by coming here?' She went on, speaking quietly, 'He didn't suffer, you know. They said so, at the hospital. It was so sudden, an aneurysm, a sort of haemorrhage. He wouldn't have known anything about it. He was in the sand pit, playing. I was standing there watching him.' To speak of it brought enormous relief. Now she couldn't get the words out quickly enough. 'We were lucky; we were spared so much. Think of parents who have to watch their child die slowly of some painful illness, that must be so much worse. But this just – happened.'

He stared down at the porch floor. The quarry tiles needed polishing. Dead leaves had drifted in and come to rest in the corners under the stone seats and beneath the overhanging doorstep. He stared at one of the seats as if it fascinated him.

He shook his head once or twice while she was speaking and when she stopped he cleared his throat. 'I got a lot of time for kids.' He shifted his weight onto his other leg. 'I'd like us to have another but the wife says it'd kill her.' He smiled, a twisted, dry smile, still avoiding her eyes. 'I think I'd do my nut if anything happened to one o' them.'

She wanted to reassure him. Between them stood the gulf of her experience and the wall of his fear. 'I'm all right now, you know.'

He looked at her as though he didn't believe her. She stepped out onto the sunlit porch and sat down on the tiled step. She patted the step beside her and put her elbows on her knees. She stared thoughtfully at the lawn, her chin in her hands. After a moment the man sat down beside her, carefully as if afraid of causing offence. The tiled step was hot, almost scalding. The sun blazed all about them.

Rhea smiled at him. 'This is the best place to sit in the morning. The house faces the wrong way ... I often have my coffee out here. Or tea. Would you like some tea?'

He mumbled something about getting back to his

dinner but seemed in no hurry to move and they sat for a while in a peaceful silence.

Rhea said, 'After a while you come to realise that it isn't the way you imagine it, people you love dying and leaving you behind. Laurie hasn't really left me. I know that now but it took a long time for me to realise it. I mean, not to grieve is impossible but grief is only a process, the first step to a different place. I've got to that place at last and now I'm – not exactly happy – of course I miss Laurie terribly – I haven't quite got peace of mind again – but I know it will come eventually and it's right that it should. It's like a journey. It's nearly eight months now. I've come this far and have further to go but at least I know that I'm facing in the right direction and that the place I'm in is real and not an illusion.' She glanced at his bewildered face and smiled. 'At least that is how it is for me. It could be quite different for someone else.'

He shifted his feet on the gravel. She imagined him saying to himself, too polite to contradict her to her face – poor cow, the kid's death has turned her brain.

She longed to convince him, to take away his fear. But it was hard to explain in words something that she knew with her heart rather than with her head. She tried again. 'The physical person you could see and feel is gone, of course.' She forced herself to say it. 'Their body is buried or burned.' He made a little clucking noise which she ignored. 'But the inside person is as alive as you are. You thought they only existed in your memory, that their survival depended on you, but that's not right.' She looked at him, willing him to understand. 'It's a kind of resurrection.'

He burst out, 'But how do you know? What makes you think—' He stopped, looking down at his feet. 'It's not likely, is it?'

'Isn't it? It's not something that can be explained. It's a kind of insight that comes – when it's needed, I suppose. It's something that perhaps can't be explained, only experienced. That's why—' She turned to him on impulse. 'That's why you really don't need to be afraid for your children – the people you love – or for yourself. There isn't any end, the way we think there is. There is no death. There's life. As real as here.'

Why was it so difficult to put into words all she felt – all she knew? She said with a little apologetic laugh, 'I wish I could convince you to stop worrying about Laurie. And about me.' She leaned back, her hands linked round her knees. 'I must sound completely nuts.' She hugged her knees to her chest and said in a rush of exhilaration, 'I can't tell you what it means to me, your having taken the trouble to come. You've helped me so much.'

How could she make him understand what it meant to her, him coming here? How another part of the horror faded away when she realised that the faces dimly remembered, the onlookers with their staring white faces, the people without names ... that some of them, most of them perhaps, belonged to people like this man – people who cared, who were feeling real anguish for her in her pain. They were not voyeuristic ghouls at all but people full of love.

'Of course it's been dreadful.' She swallowed, holding onto herself with difficulty. 'I miss him always, always. But I'm not lost or angry or confused anymore.' She said softly after a pause, 'I want to thank you, more than I can say, for doing what you did to help me, and for coming here today.'

She felt that he was pleased although he shook his head and frowned fiercely, forbidding her by his expression to say any more. He sat slapping his cap against the palm of his hand, looking restlessly about him as though irritated by a new and unfamiliar idea. 'It's all a bit above me,' he said at last. 'Never was one for thinking deep about things much.' He turned to look at her fully in the face at last and she caught a glimpse of puzzled, warm brown eyes. He promptly withdrew his glance and sat brooding for a while, frowning and looking down at his worn black trainers, shifting them fractionally as though tempted to draw patterns in the gravel with his feet.

Rhea looked down at his shoes and he glanced at her quickly and pulled them in under the step as if embarrassed. 'The wife said I ought to have tidied up a bit.'

'Oh no.' Rhea looked down at her jeans. 'I hardly ever dress up myself.'

'Well.' He put his hands on his thin knees and pushed himself slowly to his feet. 'Suppose I'd better be getting along.' He looked down at her and said, hooking his thumbs into his belt, 'The name's Lewis. Pete Lewis.'

'Rhea.' She smiled and held out her hand and he unhooked his thumbs and shook it hesitantly.

'I'm right glad to have seen you again.' He let go her hand and she stood up. He seemed about to touch her arm or her shoulder but changed his mind. His hand fell to his side. 'Thing is, I can't get over you being like this. So—' he shrugged. He shook his head and looked away. 'The wife'll be tickled pink. I mean … terrified I was, not knowing what to say. And look at you.' He looked almost indignant for a moment, then he raised his eyebrows and shrugged. 'It's good. It's great.'

Rhea followed him down the steps. 'Oh, by the way, you don't know any kids who could do with some toys, do you? Little kids – two or three or so. Are any of yours—?'

'Well … dare say we might.' He stood still, awkward again.

'Only I've got these toys.' Rhea, dismayed too, hurried on. 'I haven't packed them up yet but – do you think you could possibly drop by sometime to pick them up? Do you live far away?' She noticed a small black van parked a little way down the road. 'Is that your van?'

He thought for a bit. 'I could come by this evening. I only live the other side of the railway. Crid Road, just over the roundabout.'

'I know. Oh, thank you! Could you? There are some clothes too. Could you see that somebody gets them who could make use of them?'

It doesn't matter, she told herself, it doesn't matter. He'll know somebody. Better not to know. And best they should be used. She tightened her lips, felt herself grow pale and stiffened herself against mounting panic and indecision.

'The wife would know somebody, I dare say. She'd be able to sort it out for you.' He hesitated. 'If you're sure.'

'Yes.' She felt her face set tight. She stopped halfway down the path and waved as he swung himself into the van.

She stood quite still until the sound of the van's engine had died away to nothing. She turned back to the house, walked across the hall, up the stairs and into Laurie's room.

She began to sort his belongings into three piles: soft toys, other toys and clothes. She kept her mind deliberately blank, her imagination strictly under control, but her heart beat violently. Waves of nausea came and went. Her stomach churned. She found cardboard boxes and black plastic refuse bags stacked in the garage and packed everything as neatly as she could. She felt torn apart as she looked at each beloved object for the last time. Everything she put in she longed passionately to keep. I must not, she kept saying to herself, over and over. I must not.

It took all afternoon and by the time she'd finished she

had reached a plateau of mental and physical exhaustion. The room was stripped. She'd unhooked the pictures from the walls and taken the Peter Rabbit curtains down. She'd even remembered to fetch his mug and his knife and fork and the Beatrix Potter nursery rhyme china from the kitchen. She lugged the boxes downstairs one by one and stacked them in the hall against the wall. She made a cup of coffee and drank it sitting on the stairs looking at the pile of boxes.

She longed for Pete Lewis to come. What had he meant by 'evening'? Did he mean five o'clock, or ten? What was evening anyway?

She couldn't face him, after all. She wrote a note saying she'd had to go out then dragged the boxes outside one at a time and left them stacked on the porch. There were seven. She lifted the lighter ones and set them on top of the heavier ones. They seemed fewer, arranged like that. She closed the front door on them and went upstairs to wait by her bedroom window for the sound of the van's arrival.

She braced herself against the ring of the doorbell which she felt would be bound to come. He mightn't notice the note, at least not at first, although she had laid it conspicuously on top of one of the boxes, held down by a stone. Sitting upright in a chair with her head resting against the window curtains, she slept.

She was woken by the sound of voices. Standing hidden behind the curtains, her shoulder pressed against the wall, her startled heart jumping and her mind still numb with sleep, she watched as the boxes were carried to the van by Pete Lewis and someone else, a slighter man with a jaunty step whose face she never saw.

They were like seven small, misshapen coffins. *Laurie.* She wanted desperately to call out, to stop them. She put her hand into her mouth and bit it hard, to stop herself. The skin of her forehead burned, the blood pulsed behind her eyes.

The van door slammed and the engine started up. There was a stinging pain in her hand where she had bitten it.

They had gone. Everything had gone, there was nothing left, no relic, no symbol. She thought miserably – how could I do it, voluntarily give it all away?

She sat on the edge of the bed and reached for her phone, then withdrew her hand. She looked down at the hands lying in her lap. The one she had bitten throbbed and stung. She could imagine no boundary now, no limit to her horizon. She had come to the other side of grief. She had struggled, endured, survived what felt like unendurable pain, and beyond it there was nothingness.

She felt unable to trust her most steadfast beliefs. Meaningless pain had come and gone, meaningless joy. It was all so much incomprehensible folly. She had believed that she had hit on some gigantic and miraculous truth, but for the moment that truth, real or illusory, escaped her. Now she understood nothing at all, in spite of all her brave words to Pete Lewis. She felt herself falling into the blackest depression; there was nothing in the world that she wanted to do.

Chapter Seventeen

ONE MORNING, OUTSIDE THE POST OFFICE, SHE RAN into Toby. She had parked the car in a side street and was walking along the High Street when she saw him coming out of the tobacconist next door. He stopped at the pillar box to post a letter and paused, frowning, looking up the street as if he couldn't decide which direction to go in.

When he bent forward to post the letter his hair flopped forward as usual and now on straightening up he swept it back with a swift, haphazard gesture instead of the usual slow, careful sweep of his hand, giving from this distance an impression of irritability and impatience. He stood on the pavement, tall and thin, slightly stooped and lost looking.

Facing in her direction he stared ahead gravely, his eyes blank and unfocussed, his eyes scored at the corners with tiny lines of care. For a brief instant Rhea saw how he would look when he was old. Her insides pinched with an intense pang of fondness. With a graceful movement he zipped up his anorak and began to walk in her direction.

He saw her and stood still. He came on more slowly, lifting a hand in greeting. There was no time to prepare

240

herself; she felt a confusion of panicky sensations like a film spool spun too quickly: the noise and petrol smell of the traffic pouring past them, the heat of the sun rebounding from the hoardings bordering the pavement on her right-hand side, Toby walking inexorably towards her. Her nerves tensed for the encounter. She felt a cowardly desire to avoid him which was now impossible, then an equally foolish longing to run towards him and fold him in her arms and tell him how much she had missed him.

Their steps slowed; they met. Rhea stopped, avoiding his eyes, and stood back against the hoarding to be out of the way of passers-by, her palms flat against a poster advertising Silk Cut, the hot paper curling at the edges where the glue had come unstuck, its riotous symbols too large for decipherment at such close range.

She felt the constraint in him, the tongue-tying force of some strong emotion – resentment, probably. She didn't blame him. Her own knees were shaking and her heart thumped. She narrowed her eyes against the sun and stared across the road at a plate-glass window behind which an impressive range of car accessories was displayed. Beside them two men seemed to be arguing. One of them was talking nineteen to the dozen, jabbing his forefinger at his opponent, his speech accompanied by wild gesticulations; then as she watched he ran out of steam and dived into his pockets for cigarettes, searched around for matches, lit one and inhaled while the other man began to speak.

She looked at Toby at last. 'How are you? I haven't seen you for so long.'

He said in a firm voice which had a cool, unfamiliar edge which hurt her, 'Fine. And you?'

The sound of his voice, so unusually clipped and cold, carved a hollow place in her stomach. He moved out of the way of a young mother pushing a baby in a pram and stood back beside her against the hoarding. 'Are you going to the Post Office?'

'Yup. Stamps. Thought it was time I wrote some replies to all the kind cards.'

'Right. Good.' He glanced at her quickly with a look in which she detected a flash of approval, then looked away.

This was awful. Her mind whirled in confusion, unable to find any foothold or launching pad. There seemed nothing to talk about anymore. He was so cold ... he was still angry. She looked down at the pavement. 'How have you been?'

What she longed to tell him was how much she had missed him. She drew in a breath and looked away from him again. Across the road the second man was still talking rapidly; he bent and took out a box from under the counter, put it down on the countertop and lifted the lid. The first man took a long drag on his cigarette then bent to examine the contents of the box.

A bus intervened, chugging laboriously past. The shop window disappeared from view.

Toby said, 'I've been seeing quite a bit of Alice lately.'

'Oh, how is she? I hope she's okay.' She didn't like to say that Alice had fallen out with her too. Or rather, that Alice seemed to be avoiding her. She glanced at him swiftly and saw the raw emotion in his eyes before he closed his face again. She ran her tongue over dry lips.

'She seems okay. What about you?'

'I'm fine. Fine.' She glanced at him, sensing a hesitancy in him now, a softening. The tension inside her dissolved in little bursts of slow, melting heat. If only she could take his hand and not say anything. If only there was no need for words.

She watched the wheels of a passing car, her head turning as the car progressed, her eyes losing the car then picking up another as it approached. Dust blew in the gutter, eddied in the small breeze from the wheels of the cars as they streamed past, then settled again. She wanted to tell him about Nurse Paul ... about Pete Lewis coming and how she had cleared out Laurie's room. So much had happened since that day in the park. But he wouldn't be interested now, he had washed his hands of her and no wonder. She raised her hands and dropped them in a little unconscious gesture of despair.

She looked away from him again. 'Well, I mustn't keep you.'

Had she made the most awful mistake? She could have made up her mind to love him. They could have made themselves some sort of relationship – only not on his terms. She could have warmed and melted him with passion, with tenderness and all the good things she felt for him ... but it wouldn't have done.

She was lonely. Not just for Laurie but for herself. She wanted to give herself passionately in love again ... perhaps she might find herself then, retrieve what was left, what hadn't been swallowed up in Laurie's grave. She might manage to make something of what was left of her life, learn to live again, to love. Otherwise, if she went on like this she'd swallow herself whole. Self, self, self. Writers were self-centred at the best of times. Bereaved writer – there was a recipe for disaster.

She said with pretended lightness, her eyes once more on the passing traffic, 'Have you forgiven me?' She turned and looked him full in the face and saw that he was looking at her, startled, his eyes voluble, some struggle going on. She shook her head. 'Toby, I honestly wouldn't have been good for you. We see things differently. I would corrupt you.'

He looked away. He said, his voice choking, 'How could you ever corrupt anybody?'

'Anyway, I can't marry anybody, not for a long time. I think I'm meant to be by myself.'

'Is it Laurie?' He reached for her hand and held it at last and she turned her palm into his and laced her fingers between his and held them tightly.

'I don't know.' She felt almost tearful with relief. 'It might be. I'm too inward. I want to write too much. It's dehumanising. I haven't time to concentrate properly on people, not when I'm in such a muddle still. I can't even write yet!' She gave a little laugh and said rather wildly, afraid of all the words and of committing herself to anything, 'Did you see the rainbow round the moon last night? Wasn't it beautiful? All the way round, a proper halo, and all the colours distinct, like stained glass. Did you see it against the clouds? It showed up beautifully there ... against the black sky you could hardly see it at all.'

Toby held tightly onto her hand while she talked about the moon, as excited as a child, the words falling over each other.

When he let go of her hand it would be over. This was the end. The sound of her low voice had struck a deep, poignant chord inside him. When she had first spoken to ask how he was he had physically shivered with the delight of hearing it again.

He missed her so much. Even now, feeling her close beside him, he was missing her. He yearned for the old, easy relationship; even more for the new one he had longed for, the shared life, the promise of the companionship he found so delightful. No, he had not forgiven her. It was not a question of forgiveness.

She didn't love him. It wasn't her fault, nor was it his. He honestly believed she might have come to love him in time. He would regret for ever the impulse that had compelled him to speak – too soon, he was now convinced.

He suffered through being near her. It was a kind of torment, especially since she knew how he felt and somehow had become more provocative as a result. It was a kind of pride, he supposed, a feeling of power, unconscious because she wasn't cruel or vain, but hurtful all the same.

He had been offered the Cambridge chaplaincy. Now that his curacy was coming to an end it was time for a radical change. It was also the right time to move. If he stayed near her he would never be able to get her out of his mind, never belong entirely to himself again. He hadn't asked himself whether one of the reasons he had applied for it was because it would suit Rhea better than if he were in a parish job. If he admitted this to himself, he would have to admit that he hadn't completely given up hope, after all.

He was deeply unhappy; there was no comfort to be found anywhere. It was a bad patch. He would get through it; things would probably improve – they could hardly be worse. He would always love her.

He heard her say, withdrawing her hand gently and smiling at him, 'Can we be friends again one day?'

His sense of her loneliness made it worse. Why, when she was so alone, when they understood each other so well ... why? She didn't seem to understand how overpowering his need for her was. How could she stand there and look at him like that, otherwise?

'Do you really think that's possible?'

She looked hurt. She blinked and looked away again at the streaming, ever-moving traffic, the cars and lorries and buses slowing and starting, braking and revving up again for the pedestrian crossing a little way down the street.

'Perhaps one day, when I've got over you a bit.' He let go of her hand and strode away down the street, not looking back.

ONE NIGHT RHEA was woken by the phone ringing. Reaching for it, dazed with sleep, she thought, *Laurie,* then, *Toby – there's been an accident—*

His voice sounded loud in her ear. 'Rhea? Sorry to wake you so late.'

'Are you okay? What's happened?' She looked for the clock in the pitch darkness, knocked over a bottle of hand lotion and eventually switched on the lamp.

'I know it's late. It's Alice. I'm afraid something may have happened to her.'

'What sort of thing? What's happened?'

'I left her an hour ago ... she was in a bad way. I should have gone back straight away. Could you come with me to the house? They're all away so she's on her own. There wasn't anyone else I could think of to ask. Could you come?' She heard the agitation in his voice.

'Of course I'll come.'

'I'll be round in fifteen minutes. Wait by the gate.' He slammed down the phone.

She hurled herself out of bed and into her jeans and sweater, then rushed downstairs to get the car out of the garage and into the road. She sat in readiness behind the wheel, her eyes fixed on the lamp-lit road, waiting for the familiar sound of the Honda, her mind full of foreboding for

Alice and a passionate desire to see Toby again. Her heart was beating like a drum.

It was a warm, still night, the sky full of stars. She hadn't been in touch with Alice for far too long. Since Toby and she had quarrelled she hadn't gone out of her way to seek Alice out and Alice's dropping in had slowed to a stop, as though she knew what had happened and been offended by it. Perhaps Toby had said something, though Rhea rather hoped he hadn't.

She heard the Honda's engine in the distance and saw the beam from its headlight glance over the trees bordering the road. A moment later it roared up out of the darkness. Toby wheeled the bike round the side of the house and came hurrying back. She had the passenger door open for him and started up as soon as he was belted in. She glanced at his face. 'What happened?'

'I went round to hers this evening.' Toby raked his hand through his helmet-flattened hair. 'She said she was having people round and invited me. For a drink, she said.' He paused and looked out of the side window. 'When I got there she was alone. That was okay, I knew Dick and the children were in Spain. We had a drink. No sign of the other guests arriving. It got later and later ... still nobody. I asked her straight out if anyone else was coming.'

'And of course they weren't. Poor Alice.' The oldest trick in the book. 'Then what happened? She threw herself into your arms and declared passionate love?'

'It isn't f-funny.'

'You can't say I didn't warn you. I told you she had a crush on you and you took not a blind bit of notice.'

'I know. You did.'

'So then what happened? What did you do?'

'It was awful. She put on some music and suggested we

dance. She said she was going to leave Dick but she was afraid of losing the children. She said a lot of horrible things about him and then,' – he paused and Rhea sensed his deep embarrassment – 'she said she was in love with me. I mean, she'd been drinking. A lot. You have to understand that. When I told her I didn't feel that way about her and never could, she lost it, she started hitting herself in the face with her fists ... it was awful ... honestly, Rhea, it was as if she loathed herself. She just lost it.'

'Oh dear, how ghastly. Poor Toby. Have you had that kind of thing happen to you before? I've always thought you must be a sitting duck in your job. Like a doctor.'

'Well, in a way, but never like this.' He let out a long breath. 'It isn't usually people you know; it tends to be comparative strangers. People who know you tend to get disillusioned pretty quickly.' He glanced at her and shook his head. 'I said all the wrong things. I panicked. I couldn't wait to get out of there to give her a chance to cool down but she'd locked the door. Of course, she'd had too much to drink. She was like a different person. She started tearing off her clothes and throwing herself at me. It was a nightmare; I couldn't calm her down.' He paused again. 'To be honest I started to think she might say I'd beaten her up. I'm ashamed of that but honestly, it did cross my mind. She was making such a mess of her face. She seemed almost insane.'

'Oh, poor Alice.'

'That's why I thought I'd better not go back alone. I got out by tricking her; I said I had to go and lock up the bike. I felt terrible but there wasn't any other way to get out.' He looked down at his hands.

'Are you thinking she may have done something to harm herself?'

'I suppose that is what I'm worried about.'

'How soon after you left her did you phone me?'

'The minute I got home. Quarter of an hour?'

'I can't go any faster, there's a police car lurking down that side road. We're nearly there. I do hope she's okay. I wish I'd been keeping an eye on her; this is my fault too. Who would have thought she'd try and pull a stunt like that?'

'She probably wouldn't have if she hadn't been drinking. She was pretty high when I arrived.'

'I expect she's missing the children too, whatever she says. Here we are. Look at all the lights, she must have put on every light in the house. Go and try the door while I park.'

Toby knocked on the front door and rang the bell. Rhea joined him and they tried again. Nothing. A paved path led round the side of the house to the back. They hurried down it and peered through the clouded glass panes in the back door.

Rhea tried the handle. 'This opens into a passage. That's the kitchen, through there. This door's locked, we'll have to break in. We have to get in, now.' She tugged at the door handle.

Toby picked a loose brick up from a little wall edging a raised herb bed. It came away easily, scattering mortar on the path. He pulled a handkerchief out of his pocket and wrapped it round the brick. He aimed it at the glass panel nearest to the door handle.

The thought flashed through Rhea's mind that there was no way Dick wouldn't have installed an alarm. She held her breath, tensed for a cacophony of sound – but none came. Silence, apart from the glass shattering and splintering on the passage floor.

'My arm's thinner.' She put her arm gingerly through

the jagged-edged hole in the glass panel. A shard of glass sliced the flesh of her forearm as she twisted her wrist in her efforts to her. to locate the key but she hardly felt the pain, With a further effort she turned the key and cautiously pulled her arm back.

Toby winced. 'Your arm's bleeding.'

'Doesn't matter. Come on.' She turned the handle and opened the door. 'Alice! Alice?'

'I left her in the drawing room.' Toby strode along the passage towards a swing door at the end and pushed his way through into the hall with Rhea close behind him. 'Alice?'

No reply.

Rhea made for the staircase. 'You look in the drawing room ... I'm going upstairs. She could be anywhere.' She ran up the stairs, two at a time. 'Alice! It's us, Toby and Rhea. Where are you?' Louder she called, 'Alice, are you okay? Toby was worried about you.'

She heard the faint sound of music and ran along the landing towards the sound, flinging open doors as she went.

Alice's bedroom door was open. She lay face down on the bed, her forehead resting on one bent-up forearm, her blond hair hanging over the edge of the bed. She was wearing only a black, lace-trimmed waist slip. On the radio beside the bed Lana del Ray's dark voice sang *Once Upon a Dream*. Scattered over the bed were several small pill bottles.

Rhea rushed round to the other side of the bed. On the floor more bottles lay scattered. 'Oh, Alice.' She switched off the radio and bent to feel Alice's forehead. It was warm. She lifted the wrist of her free arm and felt for a pulse. It was there, but hardly discernible.

'Toby ...she's alive ...' She ran to the door and yelled for him again.

'Coming. I'm coming.' In a moment he was there. He felt Alice's neck. 'Ambulance. Quick.' He felt in his pocket and handed her his mobile. '999.'

Rhea's fingers were shaking so much she could hardly work the keys. She spoke and rang off. 'They'll be here as quick as they can. I'll ring Martin. He'll know what to do.'

'His number's probably on her phone. She's lying on it.' He eased it out from under her.

'It'll be locked. I've got it on mine.'

Martin picked up almost on the first ring. He cut in on Rhea's incoherent babblings with urgency but no surprise. 'Turn her on her side. Tilt her head back so she keeps breathing and keep her warm. I'm nearby, I'll be with you inside ten minutes. If she stops breathing – can you do CPR? Well, do it. Find any bottles you can so we know what she's taken. If she regains consciousness don't give her anything to drink.'

The small sofa under the window was covered by a leopard print throw. Rhea seized it and put it over Alice. 'We have to keep her warm. We have to turn her onto her side.'

'Recovery position.'

'Yes. And make sure she can breathe. Oh Toby, how could she?'

'We'll worry about that later. Now we've just got to see that she – stays alive. See what I mean?' he muttered as they turned her over and her face was revealed. 'Look at her face. Who'd believe she did that to herself? She did, I swear.'

Rhea winced at the sight of the scratches and the bruising on Alice's face. 'You don't have to say that, Toby. As if you'd ever have hurt her ... you couldn't.' She tucked the blanket gently in around her. 'I'll go down and open the door for Martin. Look at all these bottles ... what's this? Deprancol. Never heard of it.'

'They aren't all the same. This one is Extraveral. It's a barbiturate. And this one's an anti-depressant. My God, she really meant to do it.'

'She stinks of alcohol.' Rhea flew to the door. 'Back in a jiff. I'll leave the front door open for Martin.' Inside a minute she was back.

Toby was standing looking down at her. 'Perhaps she didn't really know what—'. He shook his head. 'No. She did know. She must have been planning this for ever. Look at all the bottles.'

'Should we try and work out how many she's taken?'

'No way of telling. God, this is awful. Poor silly girl.'

'I feel terrible. I didn't realise things were as bad as this.'

'How d'you think I feel? Come on. This isn't about us.'

'No. Toby – can you pray? Please pray.'

'Wait a minute.' Toby leaned down. 'She's stopped breathing.'

'Oh God. She hasn't.'

'Help me turn her onto her back. Come on, Alice, don't do this. Come on.'

Watching Toby, his mouth cupped over Alice's, the forefinger and thumb of his right hand pinching her nose, Rhea prayed, please, please don't let her die. Toby moved from breathing into her mouth to chest compressions then back to mouth to mouth. He seemed to know exactly what to do. Rhea watched Alice's damaged, mask-like face, willing her to breathe, to move, to live. Sweat gathered on Toby's forehead and dropped onto Alice's face. Breath after breath, pump after pump and no response. Nothing.

Then Martin Wood was there, taking over, pummelling

Alice's ribs, breathing into her, Toby sitting on the floor by the bed, exhausted, his face flushed and bathed in sweat.

'They'll bring a defibrillator,' Martin said. 'No. It's all right, here she comes,' and then Alice was heaving, coughing, her hands fluttering up like little white birds and Rhea remembered Alice sitting on the garden table that afternoon in the spring swinging her legs and admiring her own hands weaving this way and that – my mother, she said, my mother had very white hands.

Her eyes filled, tears were falling down her face and Toby was crying too, she could see a snail's trail glistening on his cheek before he turned his head away and slowly climbed to his feet.

You died, Rhea thought. *You died.*

'Alice,' she said. 'Oh Alice.'

Chapter Eighteen

THEY TOLD HER AT THE HOSPITAL THAT THE ANEURYSM that caused Laurie's death could have happened at any time and it could not have been avoided. Laurie would not have had time to be afraid or even to realise that he was hurt.

Rhea sat at her desk in front of the French windows, her hands resting on the unopened folder, her eyes fixed on the sunlit lawn beyond the tiny strip of terrace. How much worse it must be for those mothers in Afghanistan. In Ukraine ... in Libya, Ethiopia, Congo. There, amid the bloodshed, there must be panic, noise, confusion, fear. Here, in the quietness of the garden there had not been an instant's foreknowledge to bring dread. One moment Laurie was playing in the snowy sand pit while Rhea inspected the blackened flower beds close by, the next, he had stumbled, given a little, whimpering cry and fallen over. He was already picking himself up when Rhea looked up, only mildly alarmed, imagining the usual small bump or at the worst some snow or grains of sodden sand in his eye. 'All right, sweetie?' she'd said.

Again and again since that moment she had asked

herself, Did he hear me? Did he hear those last words of love and reassurance, or had he already gone?

He fell down again and this time she came running, picked him up in her arms and saw with an immediate icy detachment that was like a knife flashing down, cutting her off for ever from normality, his head loll back and the emptying of his still open eyes. She knew at once, with absolute certainty, that he was dead. It was as if she had been expecting it all along. She was not even surprised.

She pressed him close to her and held him, kissing the damp, sweet-smelling hair escaping from under his woolly hat and curling round his temples. Under his blue snowsuit his body was so very limp. She pressed him tightly against her breast and walked back up the garden, along the side passage and through the open gate into the street. At some point, she had no idea when or how, she lost her wellington boots, then her sodden socks. She walked for perhaps a half mile through the quiet suburb where they lived before the stranger, the man standing with his mates round a hole in the pavement, a mug of tea in his hand, approached her.

Rhea blinked, took a deep breath and arched her aching back to ease it. She'd been sitting without moving for so long that her body felt stiff and cold. She opened the folder in front of her and took out the pages inside. They were covered with writing, writing that had been done in that other life, the life before Laurie had died. The crossings out and additions, the circles and arrows connecting errant pieces of prose, all were evidence of an involved, captivated mind doing what it liked best.

She began to read, but the story she was reading seemed to have nothing to do with her. After ten minutes she lifted her head and looked out of the window again. It was happening again. Every time she tried to involve herself in the unfolding drama she was pulled back by the cadences of the prose to the winter evenings when she had begun the book: she heard the hissing, popping fire of apple wood and smelt the apple smoke; she saw the curtains drawn against the cold and remembered – although she couldn't feel it – the excitement and tension she must have felt. And underneath it all, woven into the fabric of the narrative, was the comfortable awareness that upstairs Laurie lay sleeping.

Night after night while he slept she had stayed up to write. The evenings grew longer, the weather warmer. Spring came. Still she wrote, oblivious to the change in the weather, the first snowdrops, the yellow crocuses by the front door ... the child sleeping upstairs.

Pursued by demons she scrambled out of her chair and made for the French windows. How could she have done that, ignored him and turned back to her writing again? She fumbled with the handles and flung the long glass doors open, gulped in the fragrant air and let the warm sunlight wash over her. She strode up and down the garden paths, arguing with herself: this was nonsense, of course she hadn't ignored him.

Just because she'd begun to find delight in her writing again, that didn't mean that she'd loved Laurie any less. His good came first always. So why did she feel this terrible guilt? Was she grieving over the hours she had given to her work when she might have been thinking of him exclusively and loving him?

She stopped by a flowering bush and breathed in the scent of oranges coming from its masses of white flowers. Perhaps it wasn't guilt she was feeling so much as regret. There were fewer moments with Laurie to remember now than there might have been ... she might forget him more quickly than she might have otherwise.

She was terrified of this forgetting. Her heart was beating too fast again. Panic mounted, a lump choking her like a hand gripping her throat.

This was no good. What she had to do was something practical, something grounding, not sit around feeling sorry for herself. She would clean the sitting room.

She tore at her wet face with one of Tom's hankies which she'd found in the pocket of her jacket and stepped back into the house. The sitting room was cool and dim after the heat of the garden. In the corner by the sofa was the turntable and the carved Chinese box which held Tom's vintage record collection, untouched since he had left. On top of the box was the smaller pile of children's records that had belonged to her grandmother.

She stood still. In her imagination the turntable started spinning; voices jumbled in the air, deep, jolly voices with gay American accents:

'I've got my feather duster! And I've got my broom! And Mister Moose and Bunny Rabbit are all fixed up to get the Treasure House ready for the boys and girls...Tumti-tum, tumpti-tum, tumpti-tiddly tum!'

Laurie was jumping methodically round the room, hopping from one foot to the other.

'Winnie the Pooh,' sang the gramophone now, *'Winnie the* Pooh! *Funny little tubby all stuffed with fluff, I'm Winnie the* Pooh, *Winnie the* Pooh, *funny little tubby old bear...'*

Dance, pleaded Laurie's soft little voice ... dance! His fingers plucked urgently at her jeans. She clapped her hands over her ears but now Laurie was watching CBeebies, sitting astride the blue velvet rocking stool, rocking backwards and forwards, his face absorbed. Backwards and forwards, backwards and forwards. She ran out onto the terrace, the blood pounding in her ears, deafening her, beating behind her eyes so that they throbbed. Was there nowhere she could hide, nowhere she could escape to?

She was pierced through by the agonising pang that had knifed through her once before while she knelt by the peonies. She doubled up and sank onto her knees on the terrace, gasping. That's better, she thought, winded and shocked, ramming her fists into her stomach ... I can cope with this, I understand this ... slowly it melted away, dissolving like a shaft of ice.

She stood up, calmer now. She was trembling and her legs felt weak but she was in control of herself again; the fever in her brain had gone. She walked slowly up the lawn to the sundial, planted around with rose bushes.

A pink Avalanche rose had bloomed in the night and she stopped in front of it and looked at it. Powder pink and perfectly formed it swayed in the light wind, vibrant with life. Look, how beautiful I am, it seemed to say. How warm the sun is, how sweet the air!

She stared into its centre for a long time, feeling that an answer lay somewhere within those furled petals, struggling to understand how it was possible for such beauty to co-exist with such pain.

You're so beautiful, she told the rose at last, inside her head. But Laurie – he is being denied all this loveliness. Where he is, it's dark and cold. He can't feel the sunshine or the rain – and I can't reach him.

It's not dark or cold where he is, the rose said. He's surrounded by light and beautiful colours. He is surrounded by life. He is with the angels. Why do you keep on and on about his body? He is made of light and full of grace ... he is blissful. Why must you keep pulling him back to earth?

Because I have to. I can't give him up – I can't. She was crying at last, the tears pouring down her face.

Your child isn't crying, the rose said. Death is ecstasy. It's bliss, even for your little boy who loved you.

'But I *hurt*,' she said passionately, out loud. 'I hurt and I can't give him up.' And she turned her back on the rose. But even as she said the words the pain inside her shifted and lessened a fraction, and she knew that she was at the beginning of understanding something so extraordinary that she couldn't completely grasp it. That there existed some great, mysterious and wonderful Truth compared with which her will was as one drop of water compared to the whole ocean; and that what she was being told to do was to trust, to surrender her will and to let Laurie go.

And just as she understood this she heard with a clarity and definition that was like a vision of sound, Laurie laughing; and – she couldn't help it – she laughed too.

SHE SAT on the edge of Alice's hospital bed. 'Are you feeling better? Really better?'

Alice shrugged. She lay propped up against the pillows, her face white and exhausted looking, the hollows under her eyes smudged with purple. She was looking towards the window. Hardly any light came in from a sky overladen with layers of cloud; it was so dark in the small private room that it might have been evening rather than morning. Alice watched the clouds being blown swiftly across the sky and the tops of the pine trees bending, their branches see-sawing in the sporadic gusts of wind.

'Your face is much better, the bruising has gone and the scratches have almost healed.'

Still staring out of the window Alice lifted her hand and

touched her face. 'Did I really do this?' She touched her neck cautiously, wincing. 'Dick won't even notice.' She turned to look at Rhea. 'I'm going out to Spain. I've decided, I've got to see Danny and Rose.' She closed her eyes and leaned back.

Rhea said with a feeling of thankfulness, 'I'm sure you're right to go. And it will be a break for you. But you mustn't think of going till you're ready.'

Tears trickled from under the closed eyelids.

'Oh Alice, *don't.*' Rhea reached out her hand and touched Alice's arm. 'It will all come right, you'll see.'

'I don't know why I'm so weepy.' She wiped her eyes with the hanky she was clutching. Rhea recognised it as one of Toby's. 'I'm sorry, Rhea.'

'You're weak still. You're bound to feel like crying.'

'I don't mean about that. I made such a fool of myself.' She struggled into a sitting position. 'I suppose he told you.'

'Hardly anything. He was terribly worried about you, and when he thought we were too late—'

'He's so kind. He was kind then, even when – I did the most dreadful things. I shan't ever be able to face him again – ever.'

'Of course you will.'

'I'd had too much to drink, I suppose. I just don't know what came over me.' She went on wiping away her tears which as quickly fell.

'Alice, was that why ... because of Toby?' Rhea saw in her mind's eye her own bathroom, the white pills scattered over the green tiled floor, and in another place Alice lying face down on a bed, empty bottles scattered over the duvet.

'It was Dick too.' Alice spoke languidly as if too exhausted to care. She pulled a tissue from a box on the bedside table and blew her nose. She said flatly, 'It was everything. I'm going to leave him; I've made up my mind. I can't go on like this.'

Rhea nodded.

'Anyway, now this has happened he won't want me anywhere near him. He can't stand that kind of thing – excesses of emotion, eccentric behaviour. He wouldn't let me stay even if I wanted to. He hasn't even bothered to visit me; he could easily have flown home. He's ashamed of me, I know he is.'

'The hospital had to tell him, you know.'

'Oh, I know. I don't mind, it doesn't make any difference, I don't care what he thinks. The thing is – I can't go on with my marriage if there isn't Toby. I just wanted to be able to feel – he was there, or something. I don't know. It was stupid. I can't explain.'

'You don't have to. I really do understand.'

'At least I've got the children. I do love them, you know. I do. I need them. It was them I thought about – then – when everything was going away, and I felt sorry – I wished I hadn't – but it was too late, I hadn't the strength to – it was too late.' She paused, her lips quivering. 'Was it – did he—'

'Toby saved your life, Alice. He went on and on and he wouldn't give up even when it looked hopeless.'

'And Martin? Him too?'

'Yes. But he said without Toby it would have been too late by the time he managed to get there.'

'Do you think he'll tell anyone? Martin I mean? I don't want people to know.'

'He won't.'

'The neighbours—'

'Nobody saw anything. It was late, everyone was asleep.'

'I can just see Isobel Boxer lapping it up.'

'She won't get the chance, Alice. Don't worry. It was all over so quickly.'

'I hate that house, Rhea.'

'Do you? Where will you go when you leave Dick?'

'God knows. I haven't dared think about it. In the country somewhere. I grew up in Dorset, I can't remember if I told you.'

'Are your parents there?' Rhea moved off the bed to an easy chair close to the bed.

'Only my dad. My mum died when I was fifteen. We don't really get on. He'll only say I told you so; he never could stand Dick. Perhaps Dorset isn't such a good idea.'

'He is the children's grandfather ... I suppose he'll have to know.'

'He's never seen them. He wouldn't have anything to do with us after I married Dick. He doesn't even know about the children.'

'But that's terrible!'

'It happens to lots of people. Parents can be awfully stupid and controlling. I don't want to be like that. I want to start being a proper mother to them. They won't like it a bit, they've been so spoiled, but I'm going to make it work. If Dick isn't there undermining me all the time it will probably be all right.'

'What about money? Do you think Dick can be persuaded to fork out for the children? I wonder if it makes a difference who divorces who. Whom. Perhaps he'll have to help till Rose and Danny are a certain age. I'm afraid I don't know anything about these situations. When Tom went, he just vanished and that was that, I had to fend for myself. Luckily my job doesn't involve going to the office.'

'I don't want Minna, she despises me. I want to make a fresh start.' She looked agitatedly at Rhea.

'Don't worry about all that now. You just need to rest and get strong again. You can go to a solicitor for advice; it will all work out. The important thing is to get better.'

They might say she wasn't stable, if they heard about this. They might say she wasn't fit to have charge of the children. What if she wasn't? Dick might insist on custody. Martin wouldn't tell anyone but the hospital might have to report it.

She remembered Martin after Alice had started breathing again, hauling her over onto her side, pulling her right leg up at the knee, stretching one arm down by her side and tucking her other hand under her cheek. He had exuded a calm efficiency that she couldn't help being impressed by. His face had been calm and composed, his presence infinitely reassuring.

Straightening up at last, standing looking down at Alice lying with her eyes closed and her face as white as death, he had said over his shoulder to Rhea, 'She'll do for now, till the ambulance comes. She's on her own here, you said?'

Toby put his head round the door. 'Here's the ambulance now, I'll bring them up.'

'Ah good.' Martin looked at his watch. 'Might be able to salvage what's left of the night.'

Rhea, exhausted herself from emotion and shock, felt suddenly infuriated by his brusque and unsympathetic manner. 'Aren't you glad you saved her?' she demanded rather dramatically.

He turned and looked at her in surprise. 'Alice's messes are none of my business. If I got emotionally involved with all my patients I wouldn't be able to do my job. I was with another patient, a girl of seventeen who has inoperable cancer and is dying by inches at home, until half an hour before you phoned. It's the middle of the night. What do

263

you expect me to do, leap up and down and shout for joy? And in case you haven't noticed, your arm is bleeding rather badly.' His face, she noticed, was hollowed out with exhaustion. She felt ashamed. He looked at her then with a different expression. 'Why don't you ever answer your phone?' He turned away.

Alice sighed and leaned back as if suddenly exhausted. 'It was nice of Martin to ring.'

'He's concerned about you. We all are.'

'I expect he wanted an excuse to talk to you again. I suppose Toby hasn't—'

'He's phoned, lots of times. He didn't think it would be a good idea to come but he will if you want him to. I think he's afraid it might upset you to see him.'

Alice turned her head and looked out at the sky again. 'I suppose he loathes me now.'

'Of course he doesn't, Alice, all he wants is for you to be happy, to sort yourself out. I think he blames himself for not realising how tough things were for you, for saying all the wrong things and making matters worse.'

'He's lovely. Ask him to forgive me, will you?' She leaned back and closed her eyes. Tears began to spill down her face.

Rhea leaned forward and put her hand on Alice's arm. 'He has forgiven you, of course he has. It wasn't anything so terrible anyway, he knows you'd been drinking. You must cheer up.'

'I can't seem to stop crying.' Alice opened her eyes, grabbed another tissue and wiped her eyes.

Rhea sat back again. 'Everything will be okay.'

'It will if I can just get away from Dick. It isn't that he hits me or anything like that, it's the dreadful coldness, the disapproval. It's like a dead place, that house.' She laid her head back again on the heaped up pillows and her glance moved again to the window, to the clouds, the dancing trees and the windy sky. 'I suppose it's just that we don't need each other anymore. He was infatuated for a bit, in the office, and I was so much younger than him I suppose he felt flattered, but that's all gone now. I'm always cold in that house and the cold upsets the children ... there's no love there.'

MARTIN RANG AGAIN, a few days after Alice had flown to Spain to join Dick and the children, to ask Rhea to have dinner with him that evening.

'It's evening already.' Outside it was raining heavily. She lay on the bed with the receiver pressed close to her ear. She frowned a little. He might have rung earlier.

'Well – now, then. An hour? Look, I apologise if I was a bit short the other night. I was tired   you know how it is – I was upset about the girl.'

'How is she?'

'She died a couple of days later.'

'I'm so sorry.'

'One of those things. She was on my mind; it was hard to be sympathetic about Alice. And I'd been trying to get you on the phone for so long.'

'I don't always answer my phone.' Rhea stared up at the white canopy over her head. The rain pattered on the roof and streamed from the gutters.

'That's honest, anyway. If a bit smug.'

'Is it smug?'

'It implies that you think you don't need other people.'

'It could just mean that I'm working.'

'Get an ansaphone. Gigaset do a good one.'

'I have been thinking of doing just that.'

She could sense him, slightly baffled by her detached attitude, the corners of his mouth drawn down, fingering the edge of his desk or leaning back on his chair in his surgery, kneading his tired forehead with thumb and forefinger, swinging slightly, left and right, in a leather swivel chair.

'Are you in the surgery?' she asked, carried away by this image.

'I'm at home in my study.'

'Oh. Books?'

'A great many books.' He hesitated. 'I have my feet up on the desk.'

She giggled. 'I didn't know people really did that.'

'You haven't said if you'll come.'

She was silent for so long that he said again, 'Rhea? Mrs Henderson? Are you still there?'

'I was wondering what to say.' The forgotten hunger opened in her again like a gaping wound. She said flatly, 'I don't know you very well.'

It couldn't be as simple as this, surely. This couldn't be how it happened, all at once, just like that. Still, he was only asking her out to dinner, not to get into his bed. A bubble of laughter broke inside her.

'That's why I want to see you again. It's all right, I'm not a murderer or a rapist, I'm perfectly respectable. I should simply like to see you again.' His tone was matter of fact, his voice attractive and deep. She sensed his mild indignation, his feeling that he wasn't accustomed to having to beg, with his looks and his manner – it was on the tip of his tongue to say – take it or leave it.

She smiled faintly. 'I'll take a rain check, if you don't mind. No pun intended. Thanks, but I was planning to have an early night. I have an appointment very early tomorrow morning. A breakfast engagement. Perhaps another evening. A bit more notice next time?'

She put the phone down. At least she hadn't told him the engagement was with a hilltop and the appointment with a tree. But that wasn't the reason she didn't want to see him tonight. She felt vulnerable. She was attracted to him, and if she said yes, she had a pretty good idea where the evening would end. And she wasn't sure she was ready. She held her palms against her flushed cheeks. Her body shook with the rhythmic beat of her heart. She was regretting her decision already.

She had known this would happen; she had seen it in his face the moment she met him; she had felt the attraction then. And she wanted it to happen. She wanted to feel again ... she wanted to live. Tears started in her eyes and she sat up and swung her feet to the floor. She began to stride around the room. It was more than three years since Tom had left and she had slipped into a way of celibacy without thinking. It had just seemed right; she had still felt married to him.

She still found it almost impossible to believe that he'd walked out just like that. She was certain he had loved her, and she'd always secretly believed that he would reappear one day. But now with Laurie gone she felt that she'd been living in a pipe dream; she hadn't faced up to the reality of the situation which was that she had no grounds whatever for believing that he would return. She was going to have to face up to this and organise her life accordingly.

She stopped by the window and stood looking out at the teeming rain, remembering the day she had told Tom she was pregnant. She recalled with a shiver of dismay the horror on his face.

'But you're on the pill,' he'd said, looking at her with

stupefaction and then with increasing aversion as though she was turning into an alien before his eyes. 'How can you possibly be pregnant?'

She'd smiled. 'Mistakes do happen.' What appalling trust, she had realised since, quaking at her own naiveté.

He'd said slowly, swallowing spasmodically, his eyes dropping to her stomach with an expression she'd interpreted at the time as one of pity and dismay but in retrospect she saw was of sheer cowardice, 'How appalling. What an appalling thing. What on earth are you going to do?'

'What do you mean, what am I going to do? Have it, of course.' She'd laughed at his slow bewilderment which she'd thought rather sweet.

'I didn't know you wanted a child. I never thought in terms of a child. What about your writing? How will you manage?'

'It'll be okay, Tom. I'll have to take time off sometimes, that's all. It won't be for long. Babies do grow, you know! And we've got plenty of time to get used to the idea, it isn't due for seven months or so. Oh Tom, our own child! You don't really mind, do you?'

But he had indeed minded. Her heart sank as she remembered the gradual breaking down of communication between them, the slow falling off into long silences as the months went by and he watched in silence her waist thicken and her white breasts become enlarged and tender. And she remembered his protests that first day, at the very beginning, his cry of dismay: 'But I'm not cut out to be a father! I'd be a hopeless kind of father. And what about my work? Would it cry? How can I work with a crying child in the house? And what will it do to you, having a child? I'm only just getting to know you. I don't want this. I don't want this.'

She had been angered by his selfishness. Instead of reassuring him she had turned away from him, waves of bitterness washing away her joy. Having hugged her secret to herself for several days she was by now quite used to the idea of the baby and already possessed by an unreasoning love for it. A strange protectiveness grew in her, hardening her heart.

She thought now – of course he left. He never wanted Laurie and he would have loathed it, the nappies, the wakeful nights, her preoccupation with her child. He wouldn't be coming back. He neither knew nor cared about Laurie's birth or his death. She wouldn't wait for him any longer, he didn't deserve it. He didn't care about her. She bit her lip, feeling real regret for the emptiness and the waste of it, a relationship she felt now had been so fragile it had disintegrated at the first knock, the first sign of trouble.

But although she could see why he might have left, she couldn't understand his never having attempted to get in touch. Not once. The complete silence following his departure seemed to show a degree of thoughtlessness that was not characteristic of the Tom she thought she had known. That Tom was a big-hearted man, a joyous, loving hedonist but never mean-spirited. Was it jealousy because she'd wanted the baby so much? Because she knew that had been one reason for his resentment. Tom, himself demanding as a child, wasn't stable or unselfish enough to cope with having to share her. And she was honest enough to admit that she hadn't helped.

She wandered back and sat down on the edge of the bed. If only she knew. It felt like unfinished business. If she could only talk to him, ask why he never got in touch …

perhaps he'd been scared she might start asking him for money.

She lay down with her hands linked behind her head, listening to the rain. She thought about sex – thoughts that had been banished for so long it was like moving into territory practically unknown. She hadn't believed she would ever feel like this again.

The rain drummed on the roof but still it was sultry; her dress clung to her back. She got off the bed again and stretched her arms above her head and stood looking out at the ceaselessly falling rain.

Chapter Nineteen

THREE WEEKS LATER SHE STOOD LOOKING OUT OF another window, in the sitting room this time. It was after midnight and she stood with her hand holding the edge of one of the curtains, trying to decide whether to leave it open or pull it across, shutting out the night and the darkness but also the hypnotic sound of the interminable rain.

'You'll have a job getting home. I hope there won't be flooding; it hasn't let up the whole evening.' Gusts of rain blew like hail against the glass and thunder rumbled in the distance like great doors being pulled back.

'Don't touch the glass.' Martin had moved to stand so close behind her that she could feel the warmth from his legs where her dress brushed against them, a hairsbreadth away. He was half sitting, half leaning on the desk behind her. She felt suddenly afraid to move.

She felt cornered. If she turned around there would be nowhere to go, she would be trapped between the window and the man. The desire she felt for him had been building and building over the days and weeks and had been swelling all evening so that now she felt heavy with it, swollen and vulnerable and wanting.

He stretched out his arm and put his glass down on the desk. She watched his hand, his wrist, the sleeve of his dark jacket. Dark hairs grew where his shirt cuff pulled back from his wrist. His hand was squarish and strong, the nails short and clean. A doctor's hand. Her lips trembled. The immediacy of her desire humiliated and surprised her.

She felt his arm gently encircle her waist. The other came to join it and he pulled her back gently to lean against him. She closed her eyes and let her head fall back against his shoulder. He turned her to him and kissed her fiercely.

After a time he lifted his head from hers but her lips, her darting tongue clung to his like a soft limpet; she put up her arms and joined her hands behind his head with a little moan of dismay and deprivation. She opened her eyes at last and saw the longing, the tenderness and triumph in his eyes, and closed her own again.

AFTERWARDS THEY LAY TOGETHER in her bed, their bodies damp, their senses dazed, exhausted by astonishment and delight.

'You are so beautiful.' Martin raised himself up on one elbow and traced with his finger the line of her body from shoulder to ankle as she lay on her side with her back to him.

She shivered with delight at the sound of his voice; her skin contracted with pleasure when he touched it. Her heart was still pounding; the pillow was damp under her cheek. She felt like a naughty schoolgirl.

What had she been missing all these years? She had not dreamed she would be capable of such sensuality, such abandon. She had cried, with joy, with relief, from the intense pleasure she had felt because she wanted him so much; and from an inexplicable melancholy that struck her as she lay there in his arms ... typical woman, never satisfied, she thought with an inward, slightly rueful chuckle.

She turned onto her back and looked at him, her face still flushed.

'Your eyes are huge. Liquid. Tranquil. I've been longing to see that look on your face.'

'What look?' But she knew.

He bent to kiss her round, white breasts, exploring them with his eyes like some wondrous new possession.

'Did I shock you, wanting you so much?'

'Why should I be shocked? Touched ... roused ... more roused,' – he kissed her again – 'than ever in my life, you little witch.'

She gazed at him thoughtfully. He said, 'What are you thinking? Do you always think? Don't you ever just relax?'

'You should know.' She laughed and closed her eyes, trying to shut out the thoughts which would come. He twisted his head round and nuzzled playfully at her stomach. She stroked his hair and he rested his head between her hips and closed his eyes.

He said drowsily, 'I misjudged you badly that evening. You looked far too frightened to go in for this sort of thing.'

She twisted a strand of his hair round her fingers and pulled it hard. 'I don't go in for this sort of thing. Apologise at once.'

'I'm glad to hear it. Stop that, it hurts. Okay, I apologise. Leave my hair alone, I want to sleep.'

And he did fall almost immediately asleep with one hand on her left breast, the other resting on her thigh and his head cradled on her stomach. Watching his face and listening as his breathing became increasingly deep and regular, she felt a tender protectiveness rise up in her. He looked young and exhausted, his mouth drooping, his eyes shadowed with blue. There was a look of stubborn satisfaction on his face.

He slept for perhaps twenty minutes then woke and said as though their conversation had not been interrupted, 'Anyway, that night I thought you were ill.'

'Don't let's talk about that evening.' Cold pimpled her skin. She stretched her arm down over the side of the bed and swished her arm about, looking for the sheet, trying not to disturb him too much.

'Are you cold, darling?' He raised his head and looked at her with concern, his forehead crinkling along the hairline like a bloodhound's.

'A bit.' Darling. He had called her darling. She felt unreasonably pleased. He lifted himself off her, letting in a draught of air over the damp, warm place where his body had rested so that for an instant her teeth chattered with cold. He pulled the sheet up from the bottom of the bed and tucked it round her shoulders.

'I'll make some tea. How's that for service? You keep warm.' He climbed into his underpants which were sexy black hipsters. He caught sight of her watching him. 'Normally I wear boxers, for health reasons. These were for your benefit.' He struck a pose, Atlas rampant.

Rhea laughed. 'You were sure of yourself.'

'Well. Just in case.'

'The rain's stopped.' Rhea turned onto her side again.

'So it has.' He paused for a moment to listen, his shirt pulled half on over his head. 'I told you they'd laid it on just for us.'

'Don't you ever undo the buttons?'

'Oh, I'm used to dressing and undressing in a hurry.'

She snorted with laughter.

'Night calls, you idiot.' He grinned and stepped into his trousers. 'Now I can't think why I bothered wearing this suit tonight. If I'd known, I'd have come in my pyjamas and saved all that bother. Never mind – next time—'

She turned over and buried her face in the pillow, muttering something indistinguishable. He leaned across the bed and pulled gently at her shoulder. 'Hey – hey. Joke. You're supposed to laugh. Come on, look at me – no, madam, not like that or I'll have to get undressed again ... oh, you devil ... okay, one more ...'

SHE KEPT Laurie locked in her heart. She told herself that her affair with Martin made no difference to her relationship with him but after a while she admitted to herself that this was not true; she was so much more content than she had been. Her thoughts often occupied by Martin, stimulated and physically more relaxed, she spent less time dwelling morbidly on her loss; sometimes she forgot her sadness for quite long spells.

Sometimes the realisation of what was happening stabbed her to the heart. But every now and again she would be reassured by a sudden, bracing awareness of Laurie that felt as real as an actual meeting would have been. And she knew, in these her sanest moments, that nothing that happened to her, neither the passage of time nor any event, could affect her relationship with him.

Now she had gone beyond fear; how, when, she didn't know. Perhaps the slow change had started when she had first felt him come to her and she'd realised that he was still himself, a personality existing independently of her, not simply a picture inside her head, a memory. Somehow, at last, through patience and love, they had set each other free.

She found herself thinking one day as she watched the rain falling on the apple trees and running down the steep arms of the climbing frame to melt into the long, thick grass – how would I describe that? How should I describe the slow shifting of the apple boughs under the weight of water, the particular drumming sound the rain makes on the water butt and on the upturned wheelbarrow? The way the air seems to shake with the rain? Words began to string themselves into groups and patterns to be memorised and stored away.

She watched a long-tailed tit feeding from the nut holder and asked herself how she would describe the exact shade of the pink smudge on its tiny chest. Or the shape of the magnolia boughs, angled like elbows? Like candelabra? Or the peculiar texture of orange pips, slimy between her fingers? The cold feel of an apple as smooth as bone ... the air after the rain has stopped, glass-fragile, woven of water and brilliance, the sun gleaming through, rimming the puddles with brightness. Diamonds sparkled in the long grass and rainbows lay in the crooks of railings. And she noticed them.

She asked herself how her bare feet felt as she waded through the cobweb-spangled grass, her fingers as she brushed them along the wet railings, gathering drops of water as they went. How would she describe the smell of rich earth steaming after rain? Words began to stream through her mind, gathering momentum as the days passed. She made notes and left pencils and notebooks lying about. A few ideas occurred to her, a theme began to develop.

Sometimes she felt exhausted and resentful. Why couldn't she leave it alone? Was she condemned forever to see everything in terms of the moods they provoked and the patterns they made? Was there nothing that could escape this obsession to analyse all her impressions and emotions? Is that all her life was for, to be grist to the writer's mill?

She had promised herself that she wouldn't see Martin too often; she wouldn't let it get serious; it was just an affair, just for fun. She didn't love him, not the least little bit. All the same she thought about him far more than was sensible and met him more often than she had told herself she would. She grew more and more fond of him, and as for him, he was in grave danger of falling hopelessly in love.

One day she bumped into Alice in the market and invited her home to tea. It was a warm day for late September and they sat in the long chairs in the garden making the most of the mellow sun.

Alice looked older and calmer. 'The divorce is going through,' she told Rhea, turning her face up to the sun. 'I'm almost beginning to believe it was a good thing it happened, all that. Sometimes I find it difficult to believe it did: I must have been in one hell of a state. I suppose it's a good thing Toby's going – you know he's going, don't you – next week? Well, of course you do.

'I'm glad he got that Cambridge job; he'll be brilliant with all those students. He came over a little while ago, to clear the air, he said, and he told me about it. I was devastated of course, even though I never see him now. Just the thought of him not being around ... it brought everything back for a while but I've been having counselling, you know. Martin suggested it and I talked to her about Toby and it really helped. It's all about taking responsibility and not kidding yourself about things. I really was kidding myself big time about Toby. When he said he was leaving I thought it was because of me but I don't think it can be, at least I do hope not. I hope he doesn't think I'm the kind of person who'd turn into a stalker like that *Fatal Attraction* woman. Surely he can't think that?

'I know I made an absolute fool of myself over him. I misjudged him – you were right about that, he was so shocked that evening when I threw myself at him, that's what I couldn't stand – his reaction – he looked so horrified, when I'd been under the impression that he quite liked me ...

'I honestly didn't realise there were men like that left – men you can't seduce, I mean. All the men me and Dick know are so sleazy, you wouldn't believe what it's like up there in the Crescent; wife swapping is where it starts. They've all got too much money; all they think about is sex and money and how they're going to make even more money next time. And shoving coke up their noses. I could write a book about the things that go on up there. Perhaps I should.

'I wish I hadn't, though, thrown myself at him like that I mean. We could still have been friends if only I'd been a bit cleverer about it. I never see him now except that one time recently. I never go to church ... well, let's face it, I only went because of him ... I expect he thinks I'm a useless, shallow kind of person. But if you see him you will tell him I'm trying, won't you? I really am trying to be a better person, be a bit more use.

'Minna's leaving in October. The children don't seem to mind at all; it's most odd, I thought they'd be devastated but when I said they'd have to put up with me they actually seemed quite pleased! I was gobsmacked. I think it's up to me to be confident with them and tell myself I'm good enough and that they don't need anybody else. Since Dick's agreed to the divorce I've started standing up to him a bit more and he's beginning to treat me with a bit more respect. I've got a brilliant solicitor. She says Dick has to give me something whether he likes it or not, so things may not be as bad as I thought. Maybe I'll be able to work part time and not start till Danny's in primary all day, something like that. Anyway, you were right, things are sort of working out for me.

'If you see Toby you will tell him what's happening, won't you? I can't forget I owe him my life, but he got horribly embarrassed when I tried to thank him. I just want him to know how grateful I am and that I'm trying. I know if you tell him he'll listen, Rhea, he'll know I mean it.'

Toby rang and to her surprise suggested they meet up for tea at *Annie's*, a café in town. She guessed he didn't want to come to the house and he didn't suggest her going round to his cottage.

When she walked into the café he was already there, seated at one of the small, pink- covered tables. The café, beamed and low ceilinged, was in a sixteenth century building in the centre of town. Although it was only half past four the pink-shaded lamps were lit, giving the room a cosy, old fashioned feeling. Rhea felt that Toby had chosen the right place to meet. Comfort, that was what they needed; comfort and hot tea. She stepped in and closed the door behind her.

Toby looked up from his mobile and stood up as she approached the table. 'I've ordered tea. This is on me. Would you like something to eat? Teacake? I know you love them.'

Rhea shook her head. She had been nervous, wondering if he might have heard some gossip about her and Martin, and fearful of how she herself would feel, seeing him again. But the moment she saw him the old familiar warmth and affection welled up inside her and she couldn't stop smiling as she sat down and tucked in her chair. 'It's lovely to see you. I'm so pleased about the job, Toby, Alice told me. You must be so pleased. I've got a message from her, by the way.'

Toby sat down and put down his phone. 'I've got something to tell you too. I don't know how you're going to feel about it. It's got nothing to do with the other thing ... the me and you thing. I've forgotten all about that.'

'What is it?'

'I decided to do some research. I should have done it a long time ago but time sort of rushed by and I never got around to it; then after we had that talk I started thinking how difficult it must be for you, not knowing ... about Tom.' He looked at her steadily. 'This is about Tom, Rhea.'

Rhea sat very still. Her heart began to beat very fast. Oh God, she thought, Oh God.

Their tea arrived in a pretty rose-patterned teapot with a matching milk jug and china cups. Rhea thanked the young waitress and they waited in a tense silence for her to leave. She probably thought they were having a row.

When she'd gone Toby fished inside his jacket pocket and pulled out a photocopy of a newspaper cutting. He pushed it across the table and Rhea looked warily down at it. There was a long column of print and at the bottom a photograph.

Tom! Her heart started to pound. She snatched up the cutting and looked at the headline: *Briton Drowned in Devastating Floods*. The article was dated December 2020.

'What? My God ... what happened? He'd only been gone a few weeks. So that's why he never got in touch ... that's why ... Oh, Tom.' She looked up, tears stinging her eyes. 'He wasn't angry with me. He didn't hate me. He was dead ... oh, poor Tom.' She began to read.

Toby poured the tea and pushed a cup towards her, but Rhea was engrossed.

'Kashmir. What on earth made him go to Kashmir?' She finished scanning the article and looked up again. 'Toby. Thank you so much for doing this for me. I'll read it properly later.' She sat for a few minutes trying to compose herself. She had come to see Toby; she couldn't spend all their time together crying over Tom. But the shock had been huge and her feelings of sadness and pity almost overwhelming.

Toby looked mortified. 'I should have prepared you for this. Sorry. It was thoughtless of me. This was supposed to be a happy occasion.'

'How can it be happy when you're going away?'

'Now that's the kind of remark that's open to misinterpretation.'

Rhea felt the edge of criticism behind the jocular tone. She sipped her tea. 'Aren't I allowed to still be fond of you? Especially now that we understand each other. You always think I'm flirting when I'm not. I just want you to know.'

'Agape rather than Eros.'

'Exactly.'

'I suppose it's better than nothing.'

'A whole lot better.'

'What's this about Alice?'

Rhea relayed Alice's message. It felt weird to be sitting with Toby in this intimate environment drinking tea as though they were two old acquaintances to whom nothing unusual had happened, when they had been through so much together, maybe as much as some people go through in a whole lifetime. Looking across the table at his dear, familiar face which brought Laurie so much to mind she wondered if perhaps that had been the problem, if that was why she couldn't love him, because he had gone through all that grief with her, and because looking at his face reminded her of all the pain.

'Hello?'

Rhea jumped. 'Sorry. I was just thinking about something.'

'You were miles away. Listen – will you come and visit me in Cambridge?'

'Try and keep me away! Can we go punting?'

'Of course! Seriously, will you come and visit sometimes, Rhea? I'd like us not to lose touch.'

Rhea put her hand across the table and took his. 'Toby, you are the most important person in my life.' As she said it she realised that it was true. 'I never want us to lose touch. I want us to be able to tell each other things. Will you write? Or phone? Something? Do you need any help with the move?'

'You know what the parish is like. Armies of volunteers, I'll be fine. But thanks.'

'Everybody will be sorry to see you go. Oh Toby, I forgot to tell you. Nurse Paul phoned to say that Mavis died, in her sleep at the weekend.'

'I'm sorry.'

'She went downhill quickly after the move. I've been to see her every week and recently she hardly knew where she was; she didn't always know me. It's terribly sad. I can't help feeling it's better for her, though. She had nothing left to live for.'

Outside the café they stood opposite each other and held each other's hands. Rhea thought how much she would have loved to be able to confide in him about Martin but of course that was impossible. If it ever turned into anything serious then she would have to, but not now. She felt so deeply glad that somehow, by some miracle, they were friends again. Perhaps what they had went too deep for an ordinary falling out. 'Write soon,' she said.

'Goodbye, Rhea. God bless you.'

TOBY WATCHED her walk away with her familiar graceful, swinging stride. Goodbye, my love, he thought. Along with his sadness at seeing her walk away with so much unsaid and unresolved, he felt a new sense of purpose. He would always be there for her, and maybe when she'd really got through all this and spread her wings a bit – who knew?

Rhea was like a wild creature, instinctive and easily scared. Toby smiled to himself, he couldn't help it, he loved her and always would. He stood and watched as her tall figure grew smaller and smaller, as she rounded the corner of the bank at the end of the High Street without looking back and was lost to his sight.

RHEA SAT down at her desk and pulled towards her the new refill pad she had bought that morning from Smiths. She picked up her biro. It was one of those chunky ones with a square top, black, that you got at the newsagents for a couple of pounds. She always wrote with those.

She could hardly breathe from excitement. It was beginning again, the familiar, wonderful obsession which she should never have believed would desert her completely. Writers are sick people, she acknowledged with a rueful little smile. They can't help it any more than you can help knock knees or a squint or arthritis. She ought to have had more faith. On her desk were three folders, pink, yellow and green. She picked up the green one, pulled out sheaves of notes and began to read.

Outside the window a blue tit flew down and attacked the fat balls hanging from the apple tree. A woodpecker alighted on the squirrel-proof bird feeder, setting it swinging, and in the angle of the climbing frame a spider's web flashed and glittered in the rays of the descending sun. But Rhea was oblivious, she saw and heard nothing. Not the young fox, running across the garden on its way to raid next door's dustbin, nor the sound of the Jack Russell three doors down showing his objection by barking his head off, nor the distant sound of the 5.54 pulling in at the station a mile away.

She picked up her biro and began to write.

The End

Have your say

Did you enjoy **The Bird and the Rose**?

If you did, please leave a rating or a short review.

Your feedback is much appreciated.

Also by Bonar Ash

Now I Can See the Moon

Shadows on the Wall

Florabella

The Bird and the Rose

Show Me Your Darkness

My Heart in Hiding

Please visit **Bonarash.com** to learn more about me, my writing life, and my forthcoming novels.

Printed in Great Britain
by Amazon